Once Over Lightly

"The human body can only take so much," the dog chided, "and you have been overloading yours the last couple of years. How many Italian hot dogs smothered with potatoes, onions, and grease did you think you could consume? You were getting old, you know."

"Old? I'm only seventy."

"Were. You were seventy."

"I still don't understand." Lincoln was puzzled. "How could I die from eating Limburger cheese?"

"You had a heart attack. Face it, Lincoln. You have been overloading your body with junk for years. The cheese was the last straw. Your pump broke down. At least you went peacefully, in your sleep."

Lincoln looked down at his pale, quiet face, and his chest that no longer rose and fell with each breath. So it was true. He knelt down to hug his dog, but his transparent light body blended with Gershwin's body, like a double exposure photograph.

Gershwin sneezed. "That tickles."

"I'm sorry, old boy. What is going to happen to you now, without me to take care of you?"

"Oh, don't worry about me." Gershwin attempted to lick Lincoln's new face. When his tongue touched only air, the dog struggled to maintain his balance. "Your daughter will take good care of me. I'll be like a part of you left behind for Jeanette. I am getting rather old myself, Lincoln. It won't be long before I join you. I'll probably just pine away for you like the faithful dog I am." Gershwin looked at Lincoln with his irresistible puppy face. He had a wistful expression in his big brown eyes.

"Do they let dogs into heaven?" Lincoln wondered.

"Who says you will go to heaven?" Gershwin teased. The old dog's ears perked up. He sniffed in the direction of the wall next to the bed. "Here he comes," he barked.

A doorway appeared where before was only wall. The darkness beyond filled with a bright light. The brilliance was very seductive. Lincoln longed to cross the threshold and immerse himself in its rays.

From out of the glow stepped a man made of shadows. The light fol-
lowed the shadowy man, infusing his darkness with liquid gold.
Magnificent rosy wings unfurled, and an angel stood in full glory before
Lincoln. The angel smiled radiantly. "Hello, Lincoln," Mario Lanza said.

Lincoln just stood there with his mouth gaping.

Gershwin thumped his tail on the floor. Mario patted the dog's head.
"How are you doing, old buddy?"

"As well as can be expected, considering my grief," Gershwin sighed.
"I suppose you will take him away now?"

Mario Lanza nodded. A balmy breeze filled the room when he opened
and closed his rose-colored wings. "You have taken good care of Lincoln
all these years. You are a good dog." The angel scratched Gershwin
behind the ears. Gershwin grinned as he nuzzled the angel's knee.

Lincoln shook Mario's outstretched hand. This produced a curious
giddy sensation. Lincoln wanted to giggle. He felt like a little boy. "Are
you my guardian angel?"

"Yes." The creature laughed. A sound like tiny tinkling bells filled the
room. "Just call me Mario."

"My guardian angel is Mario Lanza?"

"Well, that is who you see me as, Lincoln. I am not actually that
person."

"Can you sing like him?"

Lincoln's question amused Mario. Tiny bells rang again. "*Because you
come to me with naught save love,*" he crooned.

Lincoln could hardly believe his ears. "You **are** Mario Lanza!"

The angel beamed. "No. Shall we simply say that your favorite singer
channeled the music of the angels, and leave it at that?"

"This is so unexpected," Lincoln said.

"What? Death, or guardian angels?"

"Both."

Stirring up a breeze with his wings, the angel pointed toward the
portal of light. Lincoln saw a long dark tunnel slanting upwards beyond

the doorway. At the top of the tunnel, a familiar silhouette stood in the distant glow. She waved to him, and he heard her voice calling to him from that far off place. "Lizzy!" Lincoln gasped. "Is that my Lizzy?"

Mario nodded. "She is there, and Lizzy is not alone. You have quite a welcoming committee waiting for you."

Lincoln stepped toward the opening. "Lizzy," he breathed. His light body filled with butterflies, like the awakening thrill of first love. All the years of missing her and longing for her had finally come to an end.

"Wait." Mario reached for his hand. "Let me lead the way. You could get lost in the darkness without my help."

The dog lay down with his head on his paws, looking very sorrowful.

"Goodbye, old friend," Lincoln said. He knelt down beside Gershwin.

The dog tried once more to lick him. "Goodbye, Lincoln. I'll see you soon." The fur around Gershwin's eyes was moist.

Lincoln turned to Mario. "When his time comes, will they let my dog into heaven?"

Mario smiled, sending rays of light shooting around the room. "Of course they will. There are a couple of dogs waiting there for you already, and a cat."

"Pushkin? Pushkin's in heaven?"

The angel nodded. "Come, Lincoln, it is time to go."

"See you soon," Gershwin sniffed.

"Soon," Lincoln said. He took hold of Mario's shimmering hand and stepped into the darkness.

Strange sounds borne on a peculiar wind blew through the tunnel. The wind carried tiny multi-colored lights toward the earth. Lincoln reached out to touch them, but the lights passed through his hand like a transparent rainbow.

The angel explained, "Those are the souls who are on their way to be born."

Lincoln heard the echoes of many voices calling. Plaintive melodies drifted through the air. Someone was crying. Several times he had the bizarre sensation that a shadow passed through him, and he shivered. Dark hands reached out for him from the tunnel walls. Illuminated by the light of Mario's presence, faces pressed out of the walls into the tunnel. The macabre countenances were disturbing, their mouths agape with silent screams. Lincoln shrank away from the walls, gripping the angel's hand as they proceeded steadily on an upward incline toward the light.

"Some souls get lost in here," Mario explained. "Some, who do not believe they are dead, spend eons trying to find their way back."

"Lost souls? Is this hell?"

"It is not the hell you envisioned, Lincoln, although it becomes hell for some."

Lincoln shuddered as another shadow passed through him. "I don't understand. If these souls are stuck here, why don't their guardian angels guide them through the tunnel, like you are guiding me?" Lincoln drew back from a clutching disembodied hand in the darkness.

Mario shrugged. "Maybe they let go of their angels' hands. Some souls refuse to go toward the light. Not all souls have as much faith as you. Lots of things can trap a spirit in darkness."

"Why don't their angels make them go the right way?"

"Oh, we never interfere, Lincoln, you should know that. God gives all souls the gift of free will. It is their responsibility to use that gift wisely."

"But to let a soul wander in this purgatorial state for inestimable periods of time is so tragic." Lincoln shook his head sadly.

"Time has no meaning here. Eventually all the lost souls will find their way to the light, each in his own way, each in his own time. All are loved. None are denied. We angels wait patiently for the lost souls to be ready. Sometimes we wait many lifetimes. But when the beloved ones reach out for us of their own free will, the winged ones are always ready to lead them to the light."

Lincoln looked up the tunnel. The light ahead was so bright. A small figure emerged from the brilliance and stepped into the darkness. She shone with a light that was only slightly dimmer than Mario's. Lincoln watched the beautiful little girl approach. She appeared to be about five years old, with dark curly hair, and a sweet bright smile. The child skipped down the tunnel toward them.

"Is that an angel?"

"Not exactly," Mario replied. The angel laughed when the child threw herself into his arms and hugged him tightly. Sparks of light danced through the darkness like lightning bugs on a warm summer night.

The child smiled at Lincoln. "Hello," she said.

"Hello, little girl." Lincoln let go of Mario Lanza's hand and knelt down so he was level with her face. "Why are you going the other way?" he asked. "Don't tell me an innocent child like you is a lost soul."

"Oh, no, I am not lost. I am trying to get born. Don't you know that?"

"How would I? I have never been in this strange place before."

A group of multi-colored lights sped by. "Goodbye!" Isabelle called. "Good luck!" She giggled as she waved to them. "I have been trying to get born for so long," the child sighed. "Now I am almost out of time."

"I don't understand," Lincoln said.

Mario interrupted. "I am just going to sit over there for a bit. I think you two should talk." The angel sat down tailor fashion a few feet away. A circle of golden light radiated from the tips of his rosy wings to surround Lincoln and the child. The angel hummed "*Be My Love*" softly.

"What is your name?" Lincoln asked.

"Isabelle."

"And why can't you get born?"

"My parents won't get together to make me."

"Why not?"

"It is a long story," she said, "but if they don't get together soon, it will be too late, and I will never be able to fulfill my destiny."

"And what is your destiny?"

"I am going to be the first woman President of the United States," the child said. She raised her chin proudly.

Isabelle reminded Lincoln so much of someone. "My goodness," he said, "that is an important life, isn't it?"

"Yes. I am destined to do great things. I will appeal to the mothers of the world in the name of their children, and there will be peace. Many people back there are counting on me," she pointed toward the light at the end of the tunnel, "especially my great-great-grandfather."

She was such a serious, intense child. "And who is your great-great-grandfather?"

"He was the last living Civil War veteran in Bloomfield, New Jersey."

Lincoln scratched his head. "How can that be? My grandfather was the last living Civil War veteran in Bloomfield. When I was a little boy, I used to ride in an open horse-drawn carriage in the Memorial Day parades with him. Everyone cheered when we went by. That was very, very long ago, when I was as small as you."

The child nodded. "That was my great-great grandfather, all right. He came to America from Alsace-Lorraine when he was just my age. His name was Joseph Stoeckel."

Of course! That little turned up nose was so like Lizzy's. Her deep blue eyes were just like his. "What did you say your name was?" Lincoln asked.

"Isabelle Fortune." The child giggled. "If I can just get born, I will be your granddaughter."

CHAPTER TWO

Sunday, October 1, 1973

Eddie Lightly lay in Olivia Delvecchio's arms, his head resting on her shoulder. He tried to calm himself by focusing on the rhythm of her breathing. Olivia's long black hair framed her face against the white pillow. Eddie ran his hand over her ripe, ample breast, absent-mindedly kneading it like dough. His mouth tasted of stale beer, cigarettes, and Olivia.

Eddie reached across her body to pull a Marlboro from the pack lying next to the mattress on the floor that served as their bed. He rolled over onto his back beside Olivia and lit the cigarette, blowing smoke toward the crack in the ceiling. He wished the crack did not look so much like the fucking Ho Chi Minh Trail.

White embryonic shapes floated in the blue lava lamp on top of the wooden milk carton against the wall. He thought of the big white bubbles that popped up from the ocean every week to chase Patrick McGoohan across the sand in his favorite television show, "The Prisoner". Each week Patrick cried, "I am not a number! I am a man!" Eddie knew how the Prisoner felt, because he often had the sensation that big, invisible, glopping things out of lava lamps were chasing him.

The sound of traffic in the street below, and the light beating against the yellowed window shades told him it was mid-morning. The odor of

9

cooking tomatoes and cheese drifted in the open window from the pizzeria downstairs. Olivia sighed in her sleep. Eddie wanted to scream. He wanted to shut out the light that meant he would have to endure another day. He would have to act like life was normal. He would have to pretend his life had not been torn asunder in the rice paddies of Vietnam.

While Eddie was in Nam, life back home had been going on as usual. The traffic ran up and down Bloomfield Avenue the same as always. Mom made sausage and eggs for breakfast every Saturday just like always. Dad ran errands and spent Saturday afternoons at the bar just like always.

Eddie looked at the yards of white satin and lace draped over Olivia's sewing machine. Olivia was making her wedding dress. In two more weeks she would be his bride, just as they had planned, just as if nothing had happened. He had come home from Nam, and they had all acted like none of it ever happened. They expected him to act the same way.

The war was over, but it would never be over for Eddie. His life had been irreparably altered by what he had been through. He felt disoriented. He couldn't talk about it, and it seemed to him nobody wanted to listen anyway. They were all playing "let's pretend". "Let's pretend we never heard of Vietnam," the war that should never have happened. Hell, they even called it a conflict instead of a war, as if that softened the reality. There had been no softening of Eddie's reality. He thought he would never be able to erase from his mind the countless horrors he had seen. He wished he could forget. He wished for oblivion. Most of all, he wished he could die.

Back in Nam, Tommy Lawton had taken the bullet meant for him. Sometimes Eddie hated Lawton for cheating him out of death. If the bullet had hit its intended mark, he wouldn't have to remember the tunnel, and the bodies they had left there. He wouldn't have to remember the moment Lawton died in his arms.

*   *   *

Six men went into the tunnel. Only four came out. Eddie and the others spent eight endless days and nights in the stinking darkness with the Viet Cong camped over their heads. For eight days, they silently fought off the rats and other vermin that infested their hiding place. For eight interminable days and nights they were buried alive.

On the third day, Witkowski, who had lost most of his right leg, succumbed to his wounds. On the fourth day Lawton died. Witkowski and Lawton were the lucky ones.

It rained, and the tunnel became a world of mud, and rot, and excrement. The tunnel became a world of putrefying darkness filled with the horrible smells of blood, death, and fear. And Lawton, the big fucking hero, saved Eddie from the bullet, and left him with the memory of sitting next to his rotting corpse forever.

In the dark tunnel, Eddie held Lawton in his arms while the kid convulsed and slowly bled to death. Tommy must have been all of nineteen years old. He begged Eddie to take the Saint Christopher medal that hung around his neck and give it to his mother.

"Tell her I'm sorry," Lawton gasped. "Tell her I love her."

Day and night were all one in the tunnel. The other guys were there, but to Eddie, who held Tommy Lawton in his arms the whole time, it seemed it was just the two of them, bound together in some rotten cavity in time.

"Tell me about Olivia," Lawton pleaded, and Eddie told him. "Picture Sophia Loren," he whispered.

"Oh, yeah." Lawton sighed, and Eddie knew he was smiling, even though he couldn't see his face in the darkness.

"Olivia's got spirit and energy. She don't take shit from nobody. Olivia's got long, shiny black hair, and big, deep eyes you can get lost in. And she's proud. She's got a mouth like ripe plums, and a tongue like…"

"Go on," Lawton begged, "tell me about her tongue."

"Christ, kid, she can tie cherry stems in knots with it. She can do things with her tongue you can't believe, like you died and went to heaven. And she tastes like warm honey right out of the comb."

"Sweeter than wine?" Lawton whispered.

"Yeah, just like that. Just like the song."

"When you get home, kiss Olivia for me, will you, Lightly?"

"Sure, kid. Hell, when we get home, I may just let you kiss her yourself."

Then Lawton started to cough and gurgle blood.

$$\ast \qquad \qquad \ast \qquad \qquad \ast$$

Sometimes now when Eddie made love to Olivia, her orgasms made him flash back to the spasms of Lawton's death throes, and he screamed and pushed her aside, leaving her confused, frightened, and tearful. It didn't happen all the time, but it happened without warning. All he could do was get alone in the bathroom, where he sat naked on the cold tile floor, arms hugging his knees to his chest, sobbing uncontrollably.

$$\ast \qquad \qquad \ast \qquad \qquad \ast$$

Eddie made good on his promise to the dying soldier. He took the Saint Christopher medal to Lawton's mother. She did not cry. She just stared at him with eyes as dead as Lawton's, too dead to show grief or anger, eyes bereft of emotion. Eddie guessed Lawton's mother had no tears left. It was more horrible than if she had gone hysterical. Hysteria he would have understood. His mother cried all the time. That was familiar. That he could deal with.

"Thank you," Mrs. Lawton said, and her voice was cold, and flat, and terrible.

Tommy had been her only child. She set his medal on the mantle in front of his military picture. He looked like a little kid playing soldier for Halloween. A small vigil light stood in front of Lawton's picture, and a holy picture of Saint Sebastian. The saint was tied to a tree, eyes toward heaven, his body full of arrows, blood dripping from the wounds. The holy picture was old and wrinkled, with crayon marks scribbled on it by some little kid. It must have been Tommy, Eddie realized. His heart lurched when Lawton's mother asked him how her son had died.

"Did he have a peaceful death?" she asked, just as if she was asking if he would like a cup of tea.

"Yes," Eddie lied. "H-he never knew what hit him."

"He died instantly, then?"

Eddie nodded. Well, that wasn't completely a lie, was it? Wasn't the actual moment of death an instant thing, no matter how long it took to get there? After all his agony, Tommy Lawton had finally just sighed and been gone.

"Yeah," Eddie told her, "he died instantly."

Eddie figured this mother, who had made the greatest sacrifice a woman can make in the service of her country, didn't need to know about the tunnel or how Lawton's last days on earth had been spent in unspeakable agony. How could you describe to anyone back here what it was like over there? How you could you tell what you saw? How could you tell a mother that her child had died full of holes, just like that picture of Saint Sebastian?

Outside Mrs. Lawton's house the forsythia bloomed. It was spring, and it was like every other spring. Her laundry hung on the clothesline in the backyard, crisp sheets that would smell fresh and clean from the May wind blowing through them. Everything smelled like lilacs. There was no mud. There was no blood. There was no death, not like over there.

When Eddie said his goodbyes on her cleanly swept porch, Mrs. Lawton gripped his arm with a strength he would not have expected in such a small, feminine hand. She hissed, "Why?"

Eddie had no answer to give her.

       *   *   *

Eddie told himself the drugs helped, so he took them in any form he could get, alcohol, pot, uppers, downers, LSD. He figured since he was crazy anyway, it didn't matter. His world revolved around loud music, sex, his motorcycle, and where his next stash of drugs would come from. He ignored his mother's pleas to find a job. It was easier to live off unemployment, and the money Olivia made working as a bank teller.

Faye prayed endless rosaries for her son. Eddie wanted to tell her she was wasting her time. If there even was a God, He wasn't listening. There had been no God in the tunnel. He never told Faye that, though, because she would only start crying again. That was all she ever did these days.

Eddie thought it was better to avoid his mother. Then he felt guilty about that. He felt guilty because avoiding Mom meant avoiding the twins, too. Mary and Terry were seniors in high school. They idolized their big brother. Sometimes he would head over to the house on a Sunday afternoon and take the kids for a walk in the woods. They loved that, and Eddie loved their company. The twins were giggling pretty Barbie dolls. Eddie had forgotten such girls existed. He was twenty-eight years old. High school was lifetimes ago.

It had been six months since Eddie got back from Vietnam, six months since he was discharged from the army. By now, he didn't recognize himself in the mirror anymore. His hair was almost as long as Olivia's, his full beard scraggly and unkempt.

Eddie got up and padded across the wooden floor to the kitchen. He got himself a beer, popped it open, and lit another cigarette. He opened the cupboard. "Shit," he muttered. The happy face cookie jar where he kept his stash was empty. He and Olivia had smoked up the last of his doobies last night.

Olivia would be working on her wedding dress today. Eddie decided he would go down to Spike's Tavern and get drunk with Dad. Since he got back from Nam, drinking was their favorite bonding ritual. Eddie used to hate it when Dad drank, because it made his mother cry. But ever since Eddie realized that everything made his mother cry, he didn't hate his father so much. Maybe there was bad some stuff Dad was trying to forget, too.

He could always go pay Uncle Lincoln a visit. He was the one person Eddie could confide in about the tunnel. Uncle Lincoln wasn't a priest, but he almost had been. Eddie always felt like could tell his father's brother anything. He could even tell him how he thought God was dead, and Uncle Lincoln would understand. Nah, he wasn't ready for that yet. He didn't want to think about Nam and Lawton today. He didn't want to talk about it yet. Hell, Uncle Lincoln would always be there for him. There would be plenty of time to talk later.

If he went down to Spike's, Eddie thought, he could challenge Dad to a game of pool, and they could get drunk together. Yeah, that would be cool. He would put on his fatigue pants, his Grateful Dead tee shirt, and his combat boots, and go get drunk with Dad. Maybe Dirty John would be down at Spike's, and he could score some mind-altering substances. Dirty John was always holding.

Eddie heard the toilet flush, then Carole King's voice assailed his ears from the stereo, "*I'm gonna follow where you le-e-ad...*"

Olivia came into the kitchen, stretching her naked body and yawning. Her olive skin glowed from their night of lovemaking. "God," Eddie thought, "she's beautiful. She has the most perfect tits I have ever seen." Olivia rubbed the sleep out of her big dark eyes. Eddie took a swig of beer and another drag from his cigarette. He was getting hard again.

"Any plans for today?" Olivia asked.

"Thought I'd do a little muff diving."

"You're incorrigible," she laughed. When she laughed like that, her tits jiggled.

"C'mere," he said huskily. Olivia walked across the kitchen, swaying her perfect hips seductively, a mischievous grin on her face. Her eyes shone when she saw his hard on. She licked her lips. Shit, the woman could take as much as he could dish out. She was as insatiable as he was.

Olivia took the beer from Eddie's hands, raised it to her lips, but suddenly poured it on his cock instead.

"Jesus!" Eddie shrieked from the sudden shock, but before he went soft, she had him in her luscious mouth, licking the beer off him. Eddie leaned his head back, and moaned with pleasure.

"*If you need, you need me to be with you...*" Carole King sang. Nothing could make him forget as good as Olivia. He grabbed her perfect ass in his hands, and she ground her hips into him. Eddie took her right there on the kitchen floor.

CHAPTER THREE

Sunday, October 1, 1973

Lincoln Lightly caught his granddaughter up in his arms like a newly discovered treasure. He swung her high in the air. He danced in circles. Isabelle Fortune giggled and squealed.

"Saints be praised!" Lincoln cried, "but I thought you would never be born."

He set her down and sat on the floor of the tunnel tailor-fashion. The child imitated her potential grandfather.

"I never shall be born," she sighed, "if my mother does not get back together with my father so they can make me."

"Can't you pick another set of parents?" Lincoln wondered.

Isabelle shook her head. Lincoln observed that she did not seem five years old when she spoke. Her appearance was that of a child, but she spoke from a soul that was much older. "I need the precise combination of their genes. If I have to pick other parents, it will be a different life, a different destiny, a different me. A great deal will be lost. A noble potential will be wasted. No, Grandfather, to fulfill the destiny of the life I have chosen, I must be the child of Jeanette and Christopher Fortune. If they do not conceive me by Halloween, it will be too late, and I will have to choose another path."

"But Jeanette is divorcing Christopher Fortune. She will never have his child now, especially since…"

"I know, Grandfather especially since my brother died." Isabelle's beautiful blue eyes spilled over with tears. "It is no use," she sobbed. "I will never get born. I will never be able to do the great things I planned to do down there."

Lincoln turned to the angel. "Mario!" He crawled over to the seraph and knelt in front of him. "Please, there must be something we can do for the poor little thing. She could be my granddaughter. Can't we help her?"

Mario shrugged his shoulders and continued humming a Puccini aria.

"Mario," Lincoln pleaded, "Is there nothing I can do?"

Mario Lanza shook his wings, sending tiny sparks shooting through the dark tunnel. He smiled, and the light grew brighter. "Why do you want to help Isabelle be conceived?" he asked casually.

"Why? Just look at her! Look at how beautiful she is. Have you no compassion for her tears? She is my flesh and blood!"

"Not quite," the angel pointed out. "She does not have an earth body, so she can hardly be 'flesh and blood'. Actually, Isabelle has taken the form you see for the sake of communicating with you. She really looks more like a ball of light. Your life is done, Lincoln. Why should you care if one child gets born?"

"But, Mario, look at the fire in her eyes. Can't you see how intelligent she is? Must she be denied her destiny when it might be for the good of the country? Why it might even be the good of the world. And the child is so like…"

Mario leaned closer to Lincoln with eyes full of compassion. "So like you?" The angel laughed, filling the dark tunnel with fireflies and tiny bells.

"She is like the best of me," Lincoln murmured. "But it is not just that Isabelle is like me. Why, she comes from the heart and soul of the working class, the people who built America, defended it in battle, and made it great. As my guardian angel, you must know how many times my grandfather sat me on his lap and told me the story of that day at Gettysburg when he saw Abraham Lincoln. I remember how his eyes filled with tears, and how proud he was."

Mario nodded. "I know. I was there with you, just behind your left shoulder. Your grandfather served his adopted country well in more than one war. He was a brave soldier, many times decorated. He saved many lives. Your grandfather served his God well, too, Lincoln. Joseph Stoeckel helped many soldiers cross the threshold between life and death. His empathy transcended whichever side he happened to be fighting on. Because he embraced all humanity, he has always been held in high regard on my side of the veil."

"So what is wrong with helping Isabelle, who would honor my grandfather's memory and his ideals?"

A rosy glow, reflecting off the angel's wings, infused the air around them. "You speak of the child's destiny, but people create their own destinies, Lincoln. You know that. They are not subjected to some arbitrary fate carved in stone."

"I do not want to argue semantics with you now, Angel. I only want to help her. Think of it as my dying wish."

"My beloved Lincoln, you are very precious to me." Mario rose and spread his magnificent wings. His voice reverberated through the darkness. "Isabelle Fortune has until the moment at midnight when All Hallows Eve ends and the Feast of All Saints begins. If she is not conceived by then, she must choose another life. In appreciation for the way in which you, in your lifetime as Lincoln Lightly, shared your compassion and gifts with all who crossed your path, I grant you this grace. Until midnight, All Hallows Eve, you may return as a ghost and do what you can to reunite your daughter with her estranged husband. But be warned, you cannot interfere with their free will. You cannot trick them in any way. They must come together of their own accord. If you fail, Isabelle must choose another path."

"Oh, thank you," Lincoln breathed, shaking the angel's hand enthusiastically. He jumped effortlessly to his feet and looked back down the tunnel toward the dim light of earth. He shivered as a dark shadow passed through him and hurtled down the passage. "Come on, Mario, let's go."

The angel shook his head. "I cannot go back through the tunnel with you. Lincoln, you must understand. If you choose to go back, you will be between life and death, and you will not have an angel to guide you. You will be moving through the realms of the dead. When your time is up, whether you are successful in helping Isabelle become your granddaughter or not, you must make your way through this tunnel alone. It is a very big risk to take. You could become one of the lost souls and wander in darkness for eternities of earthly time."

Lincoln looked up the tunnel and saw his beautiful Lizzy standing in the bright light. She waved. Behind her appeared another figure that looked like Tom Burke. Oh, how Lincoln wanted to see his old friend Tom again. He looked down the tunnel toward the narrow opening that led back to earth, and it looked most unappealing.

Yet, in the darkness of the tunnel sat the lovely child, who could become his granddaughter, Isabelle. Lincoln saw something in her eyes that reminded him of the people he had loved most in his life, an ageless and beautiful flame that shone there. Her eyes were filled with strength and hope.

"Do you want me to help you?" he asked Isabelle.

"Yes!" she cried, and he took her in his arms and rocked her, drying her tears with his kisses the way he had dried his daughter's tears when she was a little girl with skinned knees.

"There now, darling," he said. "I am going back. And if I have anything to say about it, you will get born."

Lincoln turned to the angel. "Will you take care of her for me until I get back?" he begged.

Mario smiled and nodded. The angel patted his knees, and Isabelle climbed up on his lap, resting her head against the soft fleece robe that covered his chest. The angel wrapped his wings around her.

Lincoln Lightly turned and made his way back down the dark tunnel, avoiding the grasping hands, ignoring the frightening faces that pressed out of the walls.

"He will help me!" Isabelle cried, hugging the angel.

"I told you he would." Mario smiled.

The child looked into the angel's bright face. "Will you sing me a lullaby?"

The last thing Lincoln heard before he stepped back into the cold, clammy air of his bedroom was Mario Lanza singing, "*Deep in my heart, dear, I have a dream of you.*"

*   *   *

Gershwin lay next to the bed, head on his paws, feeling very forlorn and lonely. Suddenly the dog looked up and growled, sniffing the air. The specter stepped into the room. Gershwin recognized his master. His heart did a flip-flop. The dog jumped up, excited as a puppy, leaving a puppy-like puddle on the floor next to the bed. Gershwin ran around Lincoln Lightly's feet, leaping up and barking happily. Lincoln looked different. He was transparent.

"What are you doing here?" the dog woofed. "You look like a ghost!"

Lincoln bent down and scratched his old friend behind the ears. "I guess I **am** a ghost."

Gershwin saw the puddle. "Uh oh," he whined, "I am going to get in a lot of trouble for that."

Lincoln smiled. "Pull the rug over it, and maybe they won't find it."

Gershwin grinned, took the end of the small throw rug in his mouth and dragged it over the puddle. "Brilliant!" he barked. "What would I do without you?"

Twilight filled the room. Lincoln's bed was neatly made. "Where is my body?" he asked.

"They have already taken you away," the dog explained. "Teresa came down this morning to bring you tea and toast. She found you. Naturally, she handled everything with her usual efficiency. I watched her make all the phone calls and arrangements. Your body was at the funeral home being prepared for the wake by early afternoon, even before they found Jeanette and told her you were dead."

"What about Jeanette? Is she all right?"

"None of them are really all right, Lincoln," the dog remarked. "Your death came as a shock to your loved ones."

Lincoln looked stricken, and the old dog nuzzled the palm of his hand until he petted him. The dog rolled over, encouraging Lincoln to pet his stomach.

"Can you feel me petting you?" Lincoln asked. He still wasn't used to this light body.

"Yes," the dog woofed. "I couldn't when you first died, but now that you are a ghost, I can feel you just fine. It does not feel the same as a meat hand. I would say your touch feels more like a breeze. It tickles, but it makes me feel good. It makes the hurt of losing you go away."

"I am worried about Jeanette," Lincoln sighed. "She has had more than her share of loss."

"Jeanette is strong and resilient," the dog observed. "She'll be fine. I'll take care of her."

Lincoln leaned down and kissed the dog's fuzzy snout. "You're such a good dog."

Gershwin sneezed. "So tell me, Lincoln, how come you came back? Gonna haunt the place?"

"Gershwin," Lincoln Lightly declared, "we have work to do."

CHAPTER FOUR

Sunday, October 1, 1973

"Really, Jeanette, you are too young to give up like this."

"Who says I'm giving up?" Lincoln Lightly's daughter splashed a handful of water in her friend Lamont's face.

"Look out for my hair," he whined.

As Lamont rowed under the old stone bridge, Jeanette's laughter echoed off its cool walls. Lamont's golden mane was his pride and joy. He fussed with it more than any woman she knew, refusing to be seen in public if his hair did not look perfect. Jeanette often protested that mussed hair would not detract from his handsome classic features, and his beautiful gray eyes. Still, Lamont remained as obsessed about his crowning glory as he was with the rest of his body, which he exercised compulsively every morning.

"What are you going to do," he persisted, "crawl back into the safe womb of Daddy's house, and try to be his little girl again?"

"Lamont, that is not fair. Do not assume that because I am my father's daughter, I am his 'little girl.' Temporarily staying in my old room does not mean I have regressed back to childhood. Just because you had a miserable relationship with your parents doesn't mean we all do."

"I know you and your father are close, Baby Cakes. And you're right; there is no love lost between me and my old man, so it is hard for me to understand."

"Dad was always my mentor, and now he is my friend, Lamont. In some ways, the tables are turned, and he depends on me now. Thank God I had somewhere to go when I needed it. I'm sorry if you can't understand that."

"Touchy, touchy," Lamont pouted. "Aren't we a bit defensive? Excuse me for worrying about you, Jeanette. I think it's time you get back to life, that's all."

"Will you just not rush me? I haven't even filed for divorce yet, and you're pressuring me to 'get back to life.' I didn't think I left life, Lamont. I just left Chris."

Lamont sulked.

"Oh, now don't get into a snit," Jeanette chided.

Lamont rowed toward the boathouse in silence.

Jeanette watched an elegant pair of swans glide gracefully under the white stone bridge. The lake was so beautiful this time of year, with the trees changing and the migrating Canadian geese touching down to rest in the water. The weeping willow trees had stood as sentinels for more than two centuries. They lined the shore, their graceful branches teasing the water with leafy kisses. Ducks floated in their shade on hot summer days, and lovers rested their oars to steal kisses beneath the green curtain of their boughs.

Jeanette had been coming to Verona Lake for as long as she could remember. It had been her father's favorite spot for a Sunday picnic when she was a little girl. They would hurry home from church, pack a bag full of bologna sandwiches, apples, and potato chips, and spend a lazy day reading and daydreaming in the park.

The air was starting to chill now. Soon the snow would come, and people would ice skate on the lake's frozen face. Most of the ducks would be gone until spring.

"Will you look at that?" Lamont exclaimed, pointing toward the south shore. A big white duck waddled up the path toward the parking lot, following an old man in a blue plaid shirt. Every few seconds the man turned around and yelled something at the duck, which stopped and cocked its head as if listening, only to chase after him as soon as he turned his back. The laughter of the witnesses to this amusing scene carried across the water to Jeanette and Lamont.

"Oh, that's Smitty and Quacks. Hi, Smitty!" Jeanette called to the old man. Smitty grinned and waved.

Lamont raised a quizzical eyebrow. "Mr. Smith lives down the street from my Dad," Jeanette explained. "He raised Quacks from a duckling. The neighbors complained because Quacks attacked everyone that came near Smitty's yard."

"A watch duck? I don't believe it."

Jeanette nodded. "I know, but Quacks can get vicious. Smitty said that duck was better than his useless dog, which would only lick you to death. But the neighbors gave him such a hard time, that Smitty decided to bring the duck here to set it free. He drives up every weekend to feed and visit his old pet. The poor old guy has had a hard time getting Quacks to stay in the lake, because the duck keeps trying to follow him home."

They watched as Smitty repeatedly picked Quacks up and threw him in the water. No sooner would the old man start back up the path toward the parking lot, than the duck would hop out of the lake and waddle after him, quacking loudly.

"*Born free...*" Lamont sang.

"It was even worse the time Smitty turned the homing pigeons loose."

"Homing pigeons?" Lamont's left eyebrow tilted at a rakish angle.

Jeanette laughed. "Smitty raised a whole bunch of them. He decided the pigeons were too much trouble to care for, so one day he put their cages in his car and drove down to Cape May, all the way to the end of the Jersey peninsula, where he set them free. When Smitty pulled into his driveway after the three-hour drive home, he found every one of the pigeons waiting for him in the backyard."

Splash! Quacks hit the water again. Smitty waved his fist and shouted at the duck. He turned and ran for his car. The cranky duck scrambled up the bank and waddled frantically, and noisily, after Smitty.

"That duck has the same problem you have," Lamont observed wryly.

"Which is?"

"He needs a mate." Lamont responded to Jeanette's icy expression with a shiver. "Brrr, there's a chill in the air."

"I'm hungry," Jeanette said. Lamont swung the boat around toward shore. He maneuvered the boat next to the old wooden dock, nimbly climbed out, and offered his hand to Jeanette.

She took a deep breath, relishing the musty smell of the damp wood. The air was redolent with the delicious aroma of a fire that was burning in the massive flagstone fireplace inside the boathouse. It was autumn again, the time of year when Jeanette felt the air tingle with magic and possibilities. It had been a long time since she had felt so carefree. "Maybe I'm finally over it," she thought.

They walked across the white stone bridge and sat down under a weeping willow tree where Lamont had set up his old plaid blanket and picnic basket. Lamont opened the basket. He handed Jeanette a red-and-white checked napkin. He popped the cork on a bottle of chilled champagne and filled up two wine glasses. Then he unwrapped and arranged a tantalizing assortment of finger sandwiches on blue willow plates along with generous dollops of homemade potato salad.

Jeanette took a sip of champagne. She sighed. "Lamont, you even make a picnic seem luxurious."

Lamont flashed her a brilliant smile. "Look up 'luxurious' in the dictionary," he teased, "and you will see it defined as 'Lamont Feather.'"

"You are bad." Jeanette laughed.

"And that's good."

"I love that you picnic all year 'round," she observed, gobbling her sandwiches appreciatively. "That picnic we had in the snow last year on my birthday was so great."

"The day we had the sushi and plum wine?"

"Oh, yeah. That was such a wonderful day, taking the train out to the country and hiking along the banks of the river. And when it started to snow we found the cave by the waterfall, remember? We sat in the cave, ate your sushi, drank the rich wine, and bared our souls, while the world around us turned into fairyland."

"I remember we froze our butts off," Lamont complained.

"Yeah. That was really a great picnic."

"Speak for yourself, girlfriend. But seriously, I do appreciate your sense of adventure, Jeanette. You're like the baby sister I always wanted and never had, you know." He poured them some more champagne. "I don't know anyone else who would picnic with me in the snow. I wish I could find a lover like you."

"You're like a sister to me, too," Jeanette teased, clinking glasses.

Lamont put his hand on his hip and pursed his lips. "Will you be serious for one minute? You're only thirty-three years old. Are you planning to stay celibate and lonely for the rest of your life? It's against the laws of nature. Look at you. You look like Audrey Hepburn in 'Love in the Afternoon'. You should be having this picnic with Gary Cooper, while violins play 'Fascination' in the background."

"Yeah, thirty-three," she said dryly. "I'm the same age Jesus was when they crucified Him. And what about you, Mr. Romantic? You have only got two years on me, so cut the fatherly advice. I don't care about violins playing 'Fascination', Lamont. I don't need Gary Cooper. Anyway, he was way too old for Audrey. And alone does not equate with lonely. I have my dad, and my family and friends. I'm not the least bit lonely. I don't seem to have very good luck with relationships, anyway. I think I'm meant for a life of solitude. Maybe Sister Vincent Marie was right. Maybe my true destiny was to be a nun, and I blew it."

Lamont closed his eyes and rocked his head back and forth. "*Very superstitious,*" he sang.

"You do a lousy Stevie Wonder," Jeanette teased. "Keep your day job."

"And you, my dear, would be a lousy nun, no matter what Sister Mary Elephant said. Life without sex?" He wrinkled his nose. "I'd rather die. Baby Cakes, you are not old enough or experienced enough to give up on sex. What a waste."

Jeanette sighed. "Well, Anne Landers, it seems to me you have a few relationship glitches in your closet too."

"I have been out of the closet for years, darling, and don't bring my ex no-mind loser into this. At least I didn't crawl into an emotional fetal position when he turned out to be a rat. I dusted myself off and found a new lover."

Jeanette raised her eyebrows over the rim of her champagne glass. "So now you're lovers? I thought you and Glitter Man were just friends."

"Don't mock true love. I'm very happy with Glitter. I think he might be the one. At least he's monogamous." He added as an afterthought, "So is Chris. He still loves you, you know."

Jeanette frowned. She picked up a loose rock and tossed it into the lake, startling a nearby group of ducks that fled, squawking and splashing downstream.

"Could we not talk about Chris?"

"Still carrying a torch for him, aren't you?"

"Could we not talk about my love life?"

"What love life?"

"Exactly."

"Try one of these," he coaxed, unwrapping a plate of neatly sliced pickles. "They're to die for. The trouble with you, Baby Cakes, is you don't get enough…pickles."

"Pickles and champagne," Jeanette sighed, ignoring him. She leaned back on her elbows and cherished the moment. "You do know how to live."

Lamont studied Jeanette's profile. Her head was tilted back, making her long neck look swan-like. The sun shone on her long dark curls. Her green eyes reflected the willow trees. Her flawless skin was as white as alabaster, sculptured around high cheekbones and a perfect nose.

"If I were straight, I would find you irresistible," he said. "The way you eat that pickle is very sexy."

Jeanette took a vicious bite of the vegetable.

"Ooh," Lamont bit his lower lip. "You are such a tease. So why weren't you?"

"Why wasn't I what?"

"A nun. Why didn't you become one?"

Jeanette drained her glass and held it out for him to refill. "I discovered sex."

"I rest my case," Lamont sighed.

*   *   *

Jeanette decided to walk home from Verona Lake. Lamont had asked her to come over and watch old movies on television with him, but she preferred to be alone. The afternoon shadows were lengthening. The champagne had made her feel giddy and philosophical, and she wanted to walk in the fresh air to clear her head.

She cut down the hill along the railroad tracks through Montclair toward Bloomfield. She lingered for a few minutes at the small waterfall behind the Glen Ridge train station, watching it empty into the brook that ran behind her father's house and down through Watsessing Park. When she was little, Dad used to bring her to this spot. They would set leaf boats afloat to ride the cascade, hoping the boats would float downstream past their house.

Jeanette had not seen Dad before she left this morning. On Sundays, he usually liked to get to the first mass at dawn, but he must have been tired, because he had slept late today. Maybe, like Lamont, Dad would like to curl up and watch old movies on T.V., while the lazy Sunday afternoon drifted into evening. Jeanette decided she would make him his favorite spaghetti dinner later. He would like that. So would she.

She walked down to Bloomfield through the streets of Glen Ridge. Along the way, she filled her eyes with the riot of color in the trees. Fat gray squirrels gathered nuts for winter. She savored the pungent aroma of the piles of leaves being raked and burned in the gutters. After the humid dog days of summer, Jeanette wanted to believe this autumn was a beginning, instead of an ending. Life and abundance filled the world, while Mother Nature put on the show she had rehearsed for all spring and summer long. This year's award-winning performance had produced spectacular trees.

Jeanette waved to Mr. Montrose. He stood leaning on his rake, two neat piles of leaves at each end of his front yard. "How are you, Jeanette?" he called.

"Fine, just fine. You?"

"Can't complain. It wasn't that long ago, you would have jumped in my leaves, young lady." He wagged his finger.

"Don't tempt me, Mr. Montrose. They look very inviting."

"Looks like rain," he said, examining the sky. "You'd best hurry if you want to beat the storm home."

"Say hi to Mrs. Montrose for me."

"My best to your father." He bent to the task of raking his yard clean.

Jeanette continued down the street, kicking leaves as she went. She was resolved to think in terms of beginnings, not endings. Life was presenting her with a chance to start over, not to dwell on the past or its losses. She had had enough loss. She didn't want any more. She reached down and picked up a handful of fallen leaves. They would make a lovely bouquet for the table. Jeanette had always brought Dad a bouquet of autumn leaves when she was little, and he pretended it was the most beautiful thing he had ever seen.

Jeanette crossed Washington Street, the boundary line between Glen Ridge and Bloomfield. The Bloomfield side of Thomas Street was quiet. There were no neighbors in sight. Smoke from fireplaces filled the air, mingling with the smell of approaching rain. The sun disappeared behind a dark cloud. She shivered with a sudden chill.

The Harrington's black cat ran across the street and sprang up a tree effortlessly. Pookie was an adept tree climber. Unfortunately, he could not always get himself down. The cat sat on a low branch and meowed at her. "Hi, Pookie," she called.

As Jeanette approached the big yellow two-family house where she had been born, a strange feeling gripped the pit of her stomach. Something wasn't right. Was it the porch? What was different? Maybe it was the electricity in the air from the approaching storm.

Uncle Bill's car was parked out front. Dad had company. Jeanette tried to ignore her feeling of foreboding. She would make dinner for Dad and the company, she told herself. She mentally ran over the night's menu, wondering if she had enough ingredients for extra sauce, and enough garlic bread.

Jeanette ran up the steps. Before she fit her key in the lock, Aunt Faye opened the door. Her dyed blonde hair shot out from its dark roots like a fright wig. Her eyes were red. She threw her plump arms around Jeanette and sobbed.

"What's wrong?" Jeanette cried. She gently pushed her aunt aside and ran into the front hall without waiting for an answer.

"Dad?" Jeanette called. Lincoln's brother, Bill, came into the living room. The hand that held his lit cigarette was shaking. Bill was a younger, shorter version of his brother, Lincoln. Only a hint of gray had begun to creep into his temples, and unlike Lincoln, he was smooth-shaven. Uncle Bill's gaunt face was so pale and drawn it looked skull-like in the fading light that poured through the living room windows.

"Jeanette...your father..."

"Has something happened to Dad? Is he all right?" She heard Aunt Teresa, who lived upstairs, coming in the kitchen door.

"Faye?" Teresa called, "I finally reached Lamont, and he said Jeanette is on her way home. He's coming right over." Teresa entered the living room. She gasped when she saw Jeanette.

Jeanette unconsciously crushed the leaves she clutched in her fist. She felt like she was moving full-speed. The others were in slow motion. In some black hole inside her, she knew what had happened.

Bill Lightly reached out and rested a hand on her shoulder. "Your father is gone, dear. He couldn't have suffered. He went peacefully, in his sleep. We have been trying to find you all day." Bill's voice broke, and he sat down on the old easy chair, rested his forehead in his hands, and wept.

"No! No! Dad!" Jeanette ran into her father's bedroom. It was empty. The bed was newly made. The windows were open, filling the room with cold air, making the lace curtains billow like sails. The room seemed so empty. He was gone. She could feel that he was gone. Oh God, was he already dead when she left this morning? Why hadn't she looked in on him? She had left Dad to die alone. This was all her fault.

Rain blew in through the screen of the open window. Her head spinning, Jeanette thought they had better put up the storm windows soon.

Gershwin sat next to the bed. He looked up at her with his soulful brown eyes like he wanted to tell her something. Jeanette knelt down on one knee and put her arms around Gershwin. Whining, he rested his paw on her knee.

"Oh, Gershwin," she moaned. "Where is he? Where's Dad?" The dog licked her hand and nuzzled his nose against her knee. Jeanette felt the black hole inside her expand and swallow her up, leaving only a white hot feeling with no place for tears.

Uncle Bill and Aunt Teresa had followed her into her father's room. Jeanette watched from outside herself as Aunt Teresa crossed the room, closed the windows, and mopped up the wet windowsill with a rag she took out of her apron pocket. She wondered why her mother's sister moved in slow motion.

Teresa leaned over and turned the handle on the radiator, which sputtered and hissed as the heat came on. Teresa straightened up and smoothed a hair back into place in the impeccably neat salt-and-pepper bun at the nape of her neck. Aunt Teresa's eyes were ice blue steel. She didn't speak. She just nodded, tight jawed, at Uncle Bill.

"Where is my father?" Jeanette asked in a voice that did not sound like her own.

"We have taken care of everything, dear. His body is at the funeral home," Teresa replied efficiently. "We have been looking for you all afternoon. We didn't know where to find you."

Jeanette buried her head in the dog's fur. There would be no new beginning after all. Once again, she was being devoured by a nightmare of devastating loss.

CHAPTER FIVE

Monday, October 2, 1973

The African plain rolled lazily in deep orange and scarlet waves toward the rim of the world. Eddie, also known as Tarzan, stood in the shade of a baobab tree. Sultry heat embraced his muscular body like a woman's hands. He stood naked except for the leopard skin loincloth he wore.

The elephant herd grazed along the edge of the horizon. Suddenly, the massive bull elephant looked up and sniffed the air with his trunk. Eddie/Tarzan felt the beast's eyes on him even as the elephant trumpeted a challenge.

"Tantor!" he called. But the bull elephant was not Tarzan's faithful friend, Tantor, and now the whole herd turned to face him. The enormous animals thundered across the plain in a blinding dust cloud toward Eddie.

Eddie/Tarzan ran toward the line of trees that marked the beginning of the great forest. The ground shook as the trumpeting herd gained ground on him. He felt the great bull's hot breath on his neck.

*   *   *

Eddie's feet were like lead. His boots were thick with mud, and the mud slowed him down, making him run in slow motion. He fell to his knees and was instantly covered in whining, biting mosquitoes. He knew it was a waste of time to try to kill the insects, because he knew where he was. Nam again.

Eddie tried to wipe sweat and grime from his eyes. He squinted in the darkness toward the light at the end of the tunnel. Oh, God, how did he get in the tunnel? He looked behind him. Witkowski and Lawton were crawling toward him, grinning at him out of their dead rotted faces. Witkowski reached a skeletal hand toward Eddie's foot, like he was trying to grab him and make him stay forever in the tunnel with them.

Someone knelt in the light, reaching a hand toward him. Eddie could barely make out the silhouette of the old soldier. "Come on boy!" the old soldier cried. "Come on, man, you can do it. Take my hand. Let me help you!"

The tunnel was smaller than Eddie. He struggled to crawl on his stomach through the tight space. Eddie reached for the old soldier's hand. "I was there the day the generals died," the old man said. Witkowski's claw grabbed his ankle and dragged him back.

*   *   *

Eddie stood in front of the altar at Sacred Heart Church. He was dressed in a tuxedo. His hair was tied back in a ponytail. He faced the church filled with wedding guests. Mom was crying on Dad's shoulder. Uncle Lincoln sat next to Dad. Eddie waved to Lincoln. Lincoln's death had only been a dream after all. What a relief.

The organist played the wedding march, and Olivia glided up the aisle on her father's arm. She looked like an angel. If only he could see her face through her veil. His eyes felt so tired and grainy it was hard to see.

Olivia's father placed her hand in Eddie's. Eddie turned to raise the bridal veil. His heart swelled with love and pride. At last he would look into her amazing eyes, and he could become a part of her. Maybe then the wounds would heal. Her love was the only thing that had kept him going all these months.

Eddie lifted Olivia's veil. Lawton's putrefying face grinned back at him. The priest intoned, "I now pronounce you man and wife." Eddie screamed.

Lawton reached out his rotting arms to embrace Eddie, and when he did, his guts spilled out and stained the white wedding runner red with his blood.

Eddie ran from the church into the middle of Broad Street, dodging cars and buses. If he could only get a good running start, he could fly away. He spread his arms and rose fitfully into the air, but the mud on his combat boots was so heavy it pulled him down. Eddie could not get any altitude. Frantically, he tried to fly higher.

A helicopter buzzed overhead. Eddie called up to the bat, "Wait! Wait for me!" He tried to fly up to the huey that would take him to safety, but he got tangled up in the telephone wires. As he watched the chopper disappear, hundreds of volts of electricity coursed through his body.

         *   *   *

His mouth was full of stinking mud. Eddie lay on his back in some kind of dark, tight space. What was this? He reached out his hand and touched Uncle Lincoln's body. He was in his uncle's coffin. They had buried him alive. Hysterically, Eddie pushed up on the lid, but it would not open, because they were buried under tons of dirt.

He heard the rat before he felt it crawl up his body. The rat sat on his head and began to eat. Eddie screamed, but no sound came out. The rat bit into his head and spit out a mouthful of hair and skin. It was eating its way into his brain.

Eddie's screams made no sound, because the rat had already eaten that part of his brain.

         *   *   *

Eddie tried to run up the hill into Olivia's open arms. She called to him, "Eddie, Eddie!" But when he took a step he sank into a pit of quicksand. He tried to call for help, but his mouth would not work.

A hazy figure appeared at the edge of the quicksand. It was the old soldier again, dressed in a First World War uniform. The soldier held the butt of an old rifle toward Eddie. Eddie grabbed it, and felt the quicksand loosen its grip as the old soldier pulled him to safety.

Eddie lay on his face in the grass and sobbed. He heard Olivia calling his name. He heard the rat scrabbling toward him.

*   *   *

Eddie woke up screaming in Olivia's arms. He was covered with sweat. "Oh God!" he gulped. "Oh fuck!" He clung to Olivia.

"Eddie! Eddie! It's okay!" Olivia cried. "You were dreaming. It was just a dream, Baby." She rocked him in her arms like he was a child until his heaving sobs calmed down. He held onto to her like a drowning man clings to driftwood.

"I'm sorry, Olivia. Oh, God, I'm so sorry."

"Shh, it's okay, Baby; it was just a dream, just a bad dream. I'm here. Everything is fine. Go back to sleep now."

Eddie lay with his head on Olivia's breast listening to her heartbeat. Lately he had come to hate the fucking night, when lethal shadows lurked in corners and everything was exaggerated. In the day you could drink and take dope and fuck and numb your mind. At night your mind was loose, dancing with demons in the shadows. And all you could do was lie helpless, while rats ate your brains. In the day you could find ways to forget. At night there were only memories and monsters in the dark. Night was the tunnel.

He heard the clock ticking, and the rain outside, and the refrigerator turning itself on and off. Olivia's breathing was calm and regular. She slept easily and innocently, like a child. She never remembered dreaming. Eddie wished he could be like Olivia.

Quietly, he crept out of bed, pulled on a pair of jeans, and grabbed his leather jacket. He tiptoed out of the apartment, carefully closing the squeaky door behind him. He hurried up the stairs and pushed open the heavy metal door that led to the roof.

The tar roof was wet and cold under his bare feet. That was okay. That meant he wasn't dreaming. Eddie hated dreams. He sat down on the edge of the roof. The New York skyline lit the horizon with mystic light. It would be morning soon, and it looked like it was going to be a gloomy, wet day.

Eddie lit a cigarette. By the third drag, his breath came less ragged. He fumbled through the pockets of his jacket and was rewarded with half a joint. He lit the joint and gulped in a hit that made him choke. He leaned his head back and let the cold rain wash the tear trails from his face.

How long could he go on like this? How could he do this to Olivia night after night? How long could a man live without sleep, and how could he rest when sleep brought only nightmares?

They had all begged him to get counseling. Olivia, his always-tearful mom, even his bleary-eyed father. Fuck that. What could a shrink do? Take away the tunnel? Eddie laughed. Not bloody likely. Every morning on his way to work Dad dropped off the newspaper with jobs Mom had circled in red. They were all on his ass to make something of himself. "For what?" he argued. "Why bother when you're just gonna die sooner or later anyway?"

"You need to make a contribution to society," Dad would say.

Eddie would reply, "I made my fucking contribution. What has society ever done for me? Why should I contribute to an establishment I don't believe in? Society is nothing but a big fat lie."

That always made his mother cry harder. "But that's just life," she said.

If that was life, then life sucked. Shit. Only Olivia seemed to understand that for him it was easier to drop out and turn on. And even she didn't know how often he thought, "Why not end it? Why go on? What's the fucking point?"

Only Eddie knew that he had pretty much decided to end his life. The only question, since he was a coward, was when? When would be the best time to do it? Not tonight, he decided. He couldn't do that to his father. Not while Dad was so grief-stricken over Uncle Lincoln's death. It would be too cruel.

And what about Olivia? He wanted to make sure Olivia was taken care of somehow. Shit, she was the one who took care of his useless fucking ass, not the other way around. But if he died, and she was his legal wife, Eddie reasoned, and if he made his death look like an accident...yes, it had to be that way. Then Olivia would get the life insurance his parents carried on him.

Not that his waste of space ass was worth insuring, but that was how his parents were. They still lived in an orderly little "*Leave it to Beaver*" world. Hell, Mom had never recovered when they stopped delivering milk and bread to your door in the morning. She had no clue about real life. How could you explain to Mom that nuclear weapons were stockpiled all over the planet, just waiting for some fucking idiot to push a little red button and treat everyone to world annihilation? "You're worried about there being no more milkman?" Eddie wanted to say. "Our water is poison, Mom! Our food is full of poison!"

The best time to end it all would be in a couple weeks, he thought. After the wedding, the trauma of Uncle Lincoln's death would be softened. That would be a better time. Eddie decided he would do it right here. He would come up to the roof one night just like this. And in the highest, cleanest spot he could find, as far away from the fucking tunnel as he could get, he would end his life.

"Poor guy," they would say. "He was so depressed. Hasn't been the same since he got back from Vietnam. Musta had too much to drink and lost his balance."

Olivia would get over it. His parents would get over it. It would be no loss, really. He was just a waste of space in a life that sucked, in a world that sucked...

        *   *   *

Tuesday, October 3, 1973

"What is this crap?" Joseph Mustachio shoved his plate toward his wife.

"Joseph, you know I didn't have time to cook a gourmet meal tonight. We have to go to the funeral parlor," Anne Marie said.

"You don't have the brains you were born with," he snapped. "Since when do I eat leftovers? I don't eat leftovers. And I'm not going to any funeral parlor. I work hard all day to keep your ass in designer clothes. I don't need to see dead bodies on my personal time."

"Marone! Joseph, it's my Uncle Lincoln. He practically raised me. Mother is picking us up, so you don't have to drive."

"Damn straight I don't have to drive, because I will not be going. Nice way you treat your husband. You can't even put a decent meal on the table. Real nice. Just shows how selfish you are. What the hell do you do all day, anyway? I'm killing myself at work so you can sit on your fat ass. What, were you too busy gassing on the phone to make a decent meal?"

"I'm sorry, Joseph."

"So I suppose you and the old lady are going to the stupid wake tonight?" He laughed. "Like the dead guy gives a shit. And just when did you plan to pack for my trip to the motorcycle races this weekend?"

"I'll do it tomorrow. I promise."

"Fine. Just make sure you clean up this mess before you leave. Place looks like a fucking pigpen."

"Well, if you really want me to stay home with you…"

Joseph laughed. "Yeah, right." He tossed his fork across the table. "I wouldn't feed this slop to a pig. You can eat it yourself. At least get me a fucking beer."

Anne Marie jumped up and hurried to the refrigerator. "Ba fongool," she whispered to herself. She popped open a beer and took it to her husband. Annie thought that just this once, given the wake and all, he could have been a little understanding about dinner. Sometimes it felt like she just couldn't win with Joseph. The last time she threw out leftovers, Joseph was livid, and he screamed at her for wasting food.

"Joseph," she said, "do you love me?"

"Don't start that crap again. I live with you don't I?"

"Yes, but a woman likes to hear those three little words."

"Bite my ass. There's three little words for you. I don't have to tell you anything. You should know. Don't I pay all the bills around here? Nobody else would put up with you. What the hell is that you're wearing?"

"Do you like it?" Anne Marie turned in circles so her Indian print skirt billowed out around her. "I got it on sale. I saved you so much money."

"I can see right through that thing. You are not leaving the house looking like that. Go upstairs and change."

"Marone, Joseph, it's perfectly modest! The skirt goes all the way to the floor."

"No wife of mine is going out in public looking like a whore. You will change it before you leave here or you won't leave here, dead uncle or not."

"But, Honey," she whined, "everything is too tight on me. This is the only thing I have that fits right now."

"And it's my fault that you are a fat pig?"

Anne Marie sighed. "Look, I'm really sorry about the dinner. You want me to bring home a pizza from D'Agostino's?"

"Forget it. I'll just go hungry."

"And I am not obtuse. I weigh perfect for my age and height. I didn't exactly sit on my ass today either. I went to the doctor."

"You're a hypochondriac, you know that, right?"

"I didn't want to say anything to you until I was sure, but you know how I was feeling so sick the last couple of weeks? And I thought I had the influenza?"

Joseph sneered and slammed his beer on the table. Anne Marie jumped up and wiped up the spill with her apron before it could leave a ring. "I'll get you another one," she said. She waited until he drank a few gulps.

"You're always sick. Don't expect me to wait on your lazy ass hand and foot. You're problem is you go to the wrong kind of doctors. You're sick in the head. If that asshole rips me off with a big bill, it will come out of your allowance."

"Yes, I know, Joseph. But I had to go, okay? I have wonderful news, Honey."

"You're leaving me?"

Anne Marie giggled. "Oh, Joseph, you're so sargastic."

"Yeah, I'm a riot. So since I won't get any peace until you tell me, what's the big news?"

"We're gonna have a blessed event. So there."

He frowned. When he frowned, his thick eyebrows met in the middle of his forehead. "A what?"

"I'm expecting. You're gonna be a Daddy. We're gonna have a little bambino. Isn't it wonderful?"

When his eyes went black like that he scared her. His handsome face turned ugly. "You stupid bitch!" he yelled. "How did this happen?"

"Don't yell at me," Anne Marie begged. She sat across from him, her hot tears splashing in the mashed potatoes.

"I said how the hell did this happen?"

"Well, honestly, if you don't know how babies are made…"

"Don't you smart mouth me or I'll give you something to cry about. How far along are you?"

"Maybe two months. Joseph, I was so happy when I found out. Please don't ruin this, please!"

"You bring these things on yourself. How many times did I tell you no kids? How many times did I tell you not to get pregnant?"

"But…"

"Now, you explain to me how this happened. Whose baby is this?"

"That's not fair!" Anne Marie cried. "You know you are the only man in my life. I don't know how it happened. Marone! I must have forgotten to take a pill or something."

"Forgot? You stupid bitch, you must think I'm as stupid as you are. Do you have any idea how much this is going to cost me? Do you ever think of anyone but yourself?"

"I'll cut back, Joseph, I promise. I'll cut back, and you won't even know the baby is in the house. When you see the baby, I know you'll love it. Just, please…"

"Damn straight I won't know the baby is in the house, because there isn't going to be any baby."

"Oh, no, you can't mean that!"

"You will take care of this immediately, and the cost will come out of your household money."

"Joseph, it's murder! I'll be excommunicado from the Catholic Church! Joseph, it's a moral sin! I'll go to hell! Abortion is illegal! You can't ask me to do this!"

"The mortal sin was deceiving your husband. I know you did this on purpose. You don't fool me. I told you we would have a baby when I say the time is right, and the time is not right. I will not let you jeopardize my career advancement by tying me down to a screaming brat and making me lose sleep. I'm not asking you. I'm telling you. It's me or the baby. Make up your mind."

"No! You can't do this!"

"I am the captain of this ship. I am the man in this house, not you. Don't you dare start acting like a fucking feminist in my house. I'll tell you one thing, if you decide to have the brat, don't think you'll get a penny from me. I'll divorce you so fast your head will spin. And since I can afford the best lawyer and you can't, see if your pea brain can fathom who will win. You and your mother can raise the kid together, because that's where you'll be living. I'll leave you without nothing."

"God, no, Joseph! Please!"

"And if you weren't so fucking stupid, you would know that abortion was made legal in January of this year. A little thing called 'Roe versus

Wade.' God forbid you should watch the news. You wouldn't know how to handle the real world if it bit you in your fat ass."

They heard a car horn outside. Joseph got up and pushed aside the curtain. "Your mother's here. I suppose you already told her?"

"No," Anne Marie sobbed. "I didn't tell nobody. I told you first."

"We'll talk about this later," he said grimly. "Go wash your face, and don't you dare let anyone know about this, do you hear me?"

Anne Marie nodded.

"Do you understand me?"

"Y-yes, Joseph." She ran into the bathroom and ran the cold water, splashing it on her face and frantically trying to repair her makeup.

Joseph Mustachio opened the front door with a charming smile on his face. Teresa Tempesta sat in her big blue Impala with the motor running. He waved and called, "Annie will be right out, Mom!"

CHAPTER SIX

Tuesday, October 3, 1973

"He looks so natural, just like he's sleeping."

Jeanette smiled weakly as she accepted the condolences of her mother's sisters, Irene and Rose.

Lamont leaned over and whispered, "Funny, he looks kinda dead to me."

Jeanette was grateful that Lamont was staying close to her through this. She detested wakes. She had not allowed one for the baby. She was only going through with this for the sake of her father's brother, and her mother's sisters. Jeanette understood how important a traditional wake was to them. Besides, she was too numb to argue.

In the case of Jeanette's maiden aunts, Irene and Rose Callahan, who picnicked in cemeteries, viewings of the dead were a hobby. They were the most eccentric of Elizabeth Lightly's three sisters. Irene and Rose seldom showed up for birthday parties or weddings, but they never missed a funeral. The sisters faithfully scanned the obituaries in the newspaper every day.

Aunt Rose leaned over the open casket. "Tsk, tsk," she said. Jeanette watched, horrified, as her aunt removed Lincoln's glasses and replaced them with her own blue cats-eye frames with the diamond studs in the corners. Rose placed Lincoln's wire-rimmed spectacles on the end table next to the couch where Jeanette and Lamont sat.

"I hope you don't mind," Rose whispered. "My glasses look better with his blue suit, dear." Rose dabbed at her eyes with a delicate lace handkerchief. She patted Jeanette's shoulder with her free hand. Her sister beckoned, and Rose scurried to Irene's side. Soon she was caught up in a spirited conversation with Lincoln's neighbors.

"Such a good man," Vinny Vizzone sighed. "Such a shock. He was so young."

Irene nodded. "Yes, Lincoln was only seventy-one."

"No, he was seventy," Rose corrected.

"Oh, you are wrong," Irene insisted. "I distinctly remember that Lincoln was born in 1902."

"No, he was exactly seven years older than Lizzy. That's how I always remember. That would make it 1903."

"I believe you are wrong, Rose. But at any rate, it is a blessing our dear Lincoln did not suffer. He is with our sister now, in heaven."

"I know just how poor Jeanette feels," Rose sighed. "I felt the same way when my dog died last year. Sparky had cancer, you know."

"Lincoln was a good man," Vinny Vizzone said.

"A good man," Mrs. Vizzone echoed.

Teresa Tempesta approached the casket, running her finger along it to check for dust. She was dressed in her formal widow's weeds, which she had first worn at her husband Tony's funeral. Teresa clutched her mother-of-pearl rosary beads in her hand. Jeanette reflected that her mother's older sister must have been beautiful when she was young. Teresa was still striking, in spite of the hard line her mouth had developed, and the perpetual martyr's furrows time had carved into her pale forehead. Her blazing Irish eyes reminded Jeanette of a smoldering volcano. The ice inside Teresa must be the only thing keeping the magma from erupting.

Teresa read the cards on the floral arrangements surrounding the coffin. She fluffed up the white carnations, sending their cloying fragrance creeping through the room. She straightened out the souvenir holy cards on the table next to the body. The front of each card portrayed Leonardo's *"Last Supper"* in miniature. On the back was Lincoln's name in bold print under a little black cross, the date of his death, and a prayer for the dead.

Teresa peered into the coffin. Jeanette wondered if she planned to dust off the corpse. "What is this!" her aunt exclaimed. Teresa snatched the glasses from Lincoln's face. She stormed over to Jeanette. "Who changed Lincoln's glasses?" she demanded.

Lamont pointed to Rose. "She thought the blue ones went better with his suit."

Teresa harrumphed, set Rose's glasses on the table, retrieved Lincoln's glasses, and replaced them.

Lamont whispered, "Shall I get him a book to read?"

*   *   *

This was the scene Lincoln Lightly encountered when he appeared at his own wake. It was a strange experience observing his old body, embalmed and laid out in his best blue suit.

"Is that what I looked like?" He frowned as he examined the waxy face with its stitched smile and cotton-stuffed puffy cheeks. The mouth stretched frog-like from ear to ear.

The funeral parlor was full of people. Lincoln moved around the room full of mourners who had come to pay him their last respects.

"Everyone loved Lincoln," they said.

"We'll miss him."

"He was such a good man."

"I was loved." Lincoln thought. Maybe his old friend Tom Burke had been right. Tom had always said, "The value of a man is not measured by his success in life, but by how much love he leaves behind."

"I'll have to tell Tom about this," Lincoln resolved, "as soon as I see him."

Lincoln discovered that when he focused on the different faces of the mourners, he knew what they were thinking and feeling. His nieces and nephew were keeping to themselves, in the shadows of the farthest corner from the coffin.

Teresa's daughter, Anne Marie, was talking to Bill's son, Eddie. Lincoln didn't see Anne Marie's husband, Joseph Mustachio, in the room. "Joe probably wouldn't come with her," he thought.

There were his twin nieces, Mary and Terry, hovering shyly behind Eddie. Lincoln knew they were here to appease their parents. It was obvious they could not wait to escape the uncomfortable atmosphere of the Quinn Funeral Home. Well, he couldn't blame the girls. The young people would rather remember him as he had lived, not as the strange empty shell of a frog man that lay surrounded by the odious perfume of carnations. Why would someone so young and vital want to be around death? The kids still thought they were immortal, and it was not normal for immortals to be morbid.

Eddie did not seem to be paying attention to what Anne Marie was saying. He was gazing at the stained glass window in the alcove. Eddie was so stoned, his eyes looked glassier than the window. Lincoln tuned in on Eddie's thoughts, which were surprising. He had misjudged his nephew. It seemed Eddie was well acquainted with mortality. Lincoln had had no idea his nephew was in so much emotional pain. There was something Eddie had wanted to tell Lincoln, and now the opportunity was gone forever.

Lincoln put his ghostly hand on Eddie's shoulder. "Poor Eddie," he said. "I am so sorry. I had no idea."

There was old man Reinhart from next door. Lincoln was touched that Fritz felt sincere grief at his passing. Vito Ferlato, on the other hand, had a very sorrowful look on his face, but Lincoln discerned that the barber was feeling only regret at having lost one of his best customers.

Also, Vito was hungry. His mind was filled with visions of lasagna and garlic bread. Lincoln found that very amusing. He laughed. "Vito is only here because the missus is in the Rosary Society, and she dragged him along. All he wants is to get this over with so he can eat." Vito stared at Eddie Lightly and sighed. Apparently, he would also like to get his scissors into that head of hair.

Lincoln spied Phil Folse sitting in the corner by himself. Who would walk to the park with Phil and his dog, Tippy, now? Who would sit with him on the bench under the trees, and watch the old men play bocchi ball on a lazy summer afternoon? Lincoln's death had blown a hole wide open in Phil's heart. They had both buried their wives, and now Phil had lost the one friend who understood him.

"I hope Jeanette takes Gershwin over to play with Tippy," Lincoln thought. "It would mean a lot to Phil."

Benny Bernstein from the delicatessen had come to pay his respects. Benny sold the best gefilte fish in the western hemisphere. Lincoln glided over to him. "Thanks for coming, Benny," he said, although Benny could not hear him. Their friendship had spanned many years. Who would debate theology and philosophy with Benny now that Lincoln was gone? Who would argue that the Old Testament was better than the New Testament?

"You've had that guy hanging on the cross for 2,000 years," Benny used to say. "When are you gonna give the poor schmuck a break, and take him down?"

The Swedish ladies, who lived in the green house across the street, approached the coffin. In spite of all the years they had lived there, most of the residents of Thomas Street could not tell you their names. Those who knew their names could not pronounce them.

The old sisters were recluses, but they knew Lincoln. The Swedish ladies knew it was Mr. Lightly who left the baskets of food on their doorstep every Thanksgiving, Christmas Eve, and Good Friday. Lincoln always waited until the dark of night to deliver those baskets, because the Swedish ladies would never accept charity openly. Lincoln understood what it meant to be poor, but proud.

"How kind of them to come here tonight," Lincoln thought, "when they are so uncomfortable around people."

"He looks wonderful," the younger one said.

"But that doesn't look like Mr. Lightly," her sister replied. "His mouth looks so odd."

Lincoln agreed. He felt completely detached from that empty shell which used to be his body. The slight tingling sensation in his navel where the silver cord had dissolved was beginning to fade. This new light body was much better. It had no aches and pains.

Lincoln hovered next to his daughter. "My death was such a terrible blow to her," he thought. Lincoln could feel Jeanette struggling to summon the courage to get through this ordeal. She was using humor as a tool, laughing with her friend, making silly small talk with Eddie and her cousin, Anne Marie.

No doubt Jeanette's behavior shocked and horrified the three weird sisters, as he called them. Lizzy's clan would brand Jeanette irreverent and disrespectful when they talked among themselves. Lincoln had already tuned in on Teresa's thoughts that Jeanette's "fairy" friend had no business at this wake. But he had also tuned in on Lamont's love and concern for his daughter. Lincoln was grateful that Lamont Feather was there for her.

Jeanette looked beautiful in her black suit with her shining curls piled carelessly on top of her head. Her mother used to wear her hair that way. Jeanette was wearing the pearl and diamond earrings Lincoln had given Lizzy on their wedding day. He had passed them down to his daughter on her twenty-first birthday, as he had promised Lizzy.

Lincoln knelt down and rested his hand on Jeanette's shoulder. She was so pale. "I'm here with you," he whispered. A strange expression crossed Jeanette's face. She reached up and touched her shoulder. "Can she actually hear me?" he wondered.

"Can you hear me?" Lincoln asked. "Do you know I'm here?"

"Is everything okay?" Lamont whispered.

Jeanette nodded.

"For a minute there, you looked like you were going to flake out on me. Listen, Baby Cakes, I've got a flask in my pocket. Do you want to step outside?"

"I'm fine, Lamont. It's just that for a second I thought I felt my father close by."

"I'm sure he is," Lamont said matter-of-factly. "The Lincoln Lightly I knew would never miss an opportunity to go to his own wake."

"How right you are, Lamont," Lincoln laughed. "Lamont Feather knew me better than I thought. So, Jeanette can sense my presence. This is going to be a cinch. I'll be in heaven with Lizzy before the week is out, now that I know I can get through to Jeanette. It will be a piece of cake."

"Come on, let's step outside," Lamont urged. "They'll never miss you. Not with the Twilight Zone twins over there." He pointed to Irene and Rose, who were holding court at the other end of the room. They had the ears of the Swedish ladies and Mr. and Mrs. Vizzone. Irene and Rose waved their hands in the air as they reminisced about how Lincoln had left the seminary all those years ago to marry their beautiful young sister.

The way they told the story, it sounded like Lincoln loved Lizzy more than God. Although Lincoln had indeed given up his plans for the priesthood to marry Lizzy, she had never been in competition with God. However, in their vicarious rendition of their sister's romance, Irene and Rose did not correct any misconceptions that might diminish the drama. Irene even suggested that Lizzy's death, shortly after Jeanette was born, had been God's vengeance.

The Swedish ladies smiled and nodded. They did not understand English very well. The Vizzones looked at their watches. They really must leave. If there was anything they could do…so sorry they couldn't stay for the rosary.

When Jeanette and Lamont reached the door in the outer lobby, Teresa Tempesta appeared out of nowhere to block their exit. "Where are you going?" she demanded.

"Lamont and I are just going outside for some air, Aunt Teresa."

"The Monsignor will be arriving any minute, and my whole Rosary Society has come tonight. We are doing the five sorrowful mysteries. You know it is your duty to be here, dear."

Lamont rolled his eyes behind Teresa's back.

"Aunt Teresa is the President of the Rosary Society," Jeanette explained.

"How nice," Lamont remarked.

Teresa puffed up like a proud hen. She looked at her watch. "The rosary is scheduled for 8:00. It is 7:45 now. As Lincoln's only child, you must not think that because you are a fallen away Catholic you can let your family down now. I hope you are not planning to embarrass us with the Monsignor here."

"Don't worry, Aunt Teresa. We won't be long."

"See that you are back in time for the rosary, dear." Teresa smoothed the bodice of her black dress like a nun patting down her wimple. She went back in to check for dust on the coffin.

"I marvel at your composure," Lamont whispered to Jeanette. "That woman is like a big black bat. Why do you put yourself through this? I'm sorry, Baby Cakes, but your Aunt Teresa is a real witch."

"Funny you should say that, Lamont. Dad used to call my aunts 'the three weird sisters', after the witches in 'Macbeth,'" Jeanette said.

"I'll buy that."

"To be fair, Lamont, Teresa is my mother's oldest sister. She always had to be strong, and that makes her seem cold sometimes, but in her own way, I believe my aunt is mourning too. Teresa would die if she didn't feel in control. And if she revealed her emotions, she would probably disintegrate."

"Well, get ready, girlfriend." Lamont pointed to the coffin. Rose was switching the glasses on the corpse again.

CHAPTER SEVEN

Tuesday, October 3, 1973

Monsignor Donovan walked through the door of the funeral home as Jeanette and Lamont were leaving. He wore his long cassock with the purple sash and buttons, and his hat with the fuzzy purple ball on top. Jeanette's heart skipped a beat, like she was still in grammar school. She felt as if she should stand at attention and say, "Good morning, Monsignor." She was embarrassed that she reacted to the priest's presence like a schoolgirl. "You're a grown woman," she reminded herself, "and Monsignor Donovan is one of Dad's closest friends."

Jeanette said, "Good evening, Monsignor." She curtseyed.

Jack Donovan, never one to stand on formalities, hugged her warmly. "And how would ye' be now, me darlin' girl? It's shocked and sad I am for your loss. Sure and Lincoln Lightly's passin' is all our loss. May he be through heaven's doors before the devil knows he's dead."

"What a lovely thought." Lamont reached out and shook the Monsignor's hand. "I'm Jeanette's friend, Lamont Feather."

"It's glad to be meetin you I am, and gladder still you're here for the dear girl."

Jeanette thought that the more the Monsignor aged, the more he looked like a leprechaun. She loved his humor, and his ready smile, and the laugh lines that accentuated his dark eyes.

"You can tell Jack Donovan anything in the world and feel safe with him," Dad always said. "He's a leprechaun whose pot of gold is hidden deep in his heart."

"Thank you so much for coming, Monsignor," Jeanette said.

"And where else would I be wantin' to be? Sure and I'd never miss paying my last respects to himself. You'll be lettin' me know if you'll be needin' anything, won't ye, Mavourneen?"

"I will," she promised, smiling at his use of the ancient Celtic endearment.

The Monsignor entered the funeral parlor and was swallowed up by the weird sisters, and the women of the Rosary Society. They bobbed their heads and cackled around him like a brood of black hens.

Jeanette and Lamont stepped outside. The night was clear and cold. Jeanette noticed that the big dipper had moved aside so Orion could take its place as the prominent constellation in the night sky. Her father had taught her to watch the changing seasons in the stars. A blast of chill air struck a dull chord inside her, reminding Jeanette he was gone, and that he left a void that would never be filled.

Uncle Bill and Aunt Faye came up the walk from the parking lot. Bill Lightly reached out and squeezed Jeanette's hand. Bill's grief over the loss of his only brother was evident in his face. Jeanette swallowed the lump in her throat. She wanted to be strong for her uncle's sake.

"I'm here for you, sweetheart," Bill said huskily. His breath smelled of booze and cigarettes.

Jeanette kissed his cheek. "Me too, Uncle Bill."

Faye sobbed into her soggy handkerchief. As usual, Bill's wife looked like she had been struck by lightning. Her hair resembled a sheaf of harvested wheat sitting atop her pumpkin face. Jeanette hugged her warmly. Faye blubbered something incoherent.

"I know," Jeanette said quietly, patting Faye's ample back. "I know."

*   *   *

The ghost of Lincoln Lightly watched his only brother, Bill, stagger into the funeral home. William Lightly was an incorrigible drunk, but Lincoln loved him dearly. Bill had obviously stopped to fortify himself at Spike's Tavern before facing the corpse. He looked like he had a few highballs too many. Well, who could blame him? Lincoln sensed his younger brother's heartbreak. Bill was in his late sixties now. He looked more like Groucho Marx every day. It could not be an easy thing to bury your only brother.

Lincoln whispered in his ear, "We had some great laughs over the years, didn't we, Billy?"

Bill shivered.

Faye was still crying. In all the years he had known her, Lincoln had hardly ever seen his sister-in-law when she was not in tears. The three weird sisters hurried to Faye's side to comfort her with their maudlin clucking.

Monsignor Donovan moved gracefully through the room, greeting his parishioners. He blushed at the adulation of the women in Teresa's Rosary Society. To Lincoln's amusement, the old leprechaun obviously loved the attention.

The Monsignor knelt by the coffin for a private prayer. Lincoln was moved when he perceived Jack Donovan's sincere grief and love for him. He moved closer to his former teacher and friend. Jack Donovan had been his spiritual advisor since he was a young seminarian. The priest had married Lincoln and Lizzy, baptized Jeanette, and buried Lizzy, as well as Jeanette's poor little baby. Now Jack Donovan would bury him.

"Thanks for everything, Jack," Lincoln whispered. He felt sure the Monsignor heard and was comforted. Jack heaved a ragged sigh, crossed himself, and rose stiffly. He turned and smiled benevolently at the women who waited to pounce on him. Rose took his arm and led him back into the room, chattering away.

Bill Lightly approached the bier. Lincoln's brother's hands shook as he lit a cigarette. Faye knelt down, and Bill stood by her side. She blew her nose loudly. The candles in the vigil lights sputtered.

"What the hell is this?" Bill cried. "What did they do with his feet?"

Teresa Tempesta hurried to her brother-in-law's side. "Bill," she whispered, "you are making a scene." She grabbed the cigarette out of his hand and stubbed it out in a plant. "It is disgraceful to smoke in the presence of the dearly departed."

"Oh, pardon me," Bill muttered. Taking two cigarettes out of the pack, he placed one between the corpse's dead fingers and lit the other one. "How thoughtless of me not to offer a cigarette to the dearly departed."

Faye burbled into her soaked hanky. Mascara rivulets ran down her face, making her look even more like a pumpkin. Bill helped his wife to her feet. He handed her a dry handkerchief. She honked into it like a goose.

Teresa looked into the coffin. She gasped as she retrieved the offensive cigarette. She snatched Rose's glasses off the corpse and placed them on the table next to the holy pictures. "You are a crude man, William Lightly, and it is very rude of you to make a scene at your brother's wake. Have you no respect for the dead?"

"Make a scene? Damn straight, I'm making a scene," Bill Lightly blustered. "My brother was six feet four inches tall. This coffin is no longer than six feet long. Speaking of respect for the dead, what the hell did they do with his damn feet?"

Teresa pulled Bill aside into a curtained-off alcove. "Pull yourself together, Bill. They didn't do anything with his feet."

"Then how the hell did they get him into a coffin that's four inches too short? When I told you to take care of the arrangements I didn't mean to cut off my brother's damn feet!"

"Bill, I don't know what you are talking about. My sisters and I did our best with the budget you gave us. We saved a lot of money on this casket. If you don't like it, next time do it yourself."

"Next time, I'll be the damn corpse. Do me a favor, Teresa, and don't take a hand in burying me. What did you do, poison my brother with some of your witch's brew? Maybe he died so he wouldn't have to look at your ugly thick Irish mug anymore."

"You should be ashamed of yourself, William Lightly. Have you forgotten that you are half Irish?"

"Fuck you."

"I shall thank you not to use profanity in my presence. If you don't stop your drunken raving, I will have to ask you to leave. The Monsignor is getting ready to lead the rosary, and I will not have you making a scene at Lincoln's wake. I will not have you upsetting everyone."

Faye sobbed into Bill's handkerchief.

"Profanity is taking the Lord's name in vain," Bill retorted. "Pointing out your fucking ignorance doesn't qualify as profanity. And if anyone leaves this funeral parlor, it will be you."

"Nazi," Teresa sniped.

"I am Alsatian," he seethed. "Alsace Lorraine is in France."

"This week it's in France," she said. "Next week, who knows? It is a fine thing when a whole country is so confused it doesn't even know what nationality it is. It doesn't matter to me. German or French, you are equally offensive."

"And you are a thick Irish witch. So, tell me, Teresa Tempestuous, you know-it-all-nothing hag, did they at least stick my brother's feet in the coffin when they cut them off?"

"Well, I never!" Teresa turned icily, leaving Bill and Faye standing alone in the alcove.

"Yeah, that's your problem, you old biddy. You probably never did." Bill lit another cigarette from the butt of the one he was still smoking.

"Oh, Bill," Faye sobbed, "let's just go home."

"And miss the rosary? No, dear. Lincoln is my brother, not hers." Bill took a silver flask from his pocket, unscrewed the top, and guzzled the contents.

Lincoln put his ghostly arm around Bill's shoulder. "It's okay, buddy," he said, "I don't need those feet anymore."

*   *   *

"The five sorrowful mysteries. The first mystery, 'The Agony in the Garden.' Our Father, Who art in heaven…" Monsignor Donovan's mellow brogue resounded through the funeral parlor. The mourners droned their responses to the prayers of the rosary.

Jeanette knelt next to Lamont, fingering her crystal rosary beads. She could see rainbows inside them when the light was right. She remembered her Confirmation day, when Dad gave her these beads. He bought her the prettiest sky blue dress he could afford. He pinned the white lace chapel veil on top of her shining black curls. He handed her the crystal rosary and told her, "Now you are a soldier in Christ's army."

"Now, and at the hour of our death, Amen."

The cloying scent of carnations was overpowering. Jeanette never wanted to see another carnation. She closed her eyes and let her mind wander. They were making love in the Inn in the Highlands of Scotland. She could feel the warmth of the fire in the hearth, and hear the rain kissing the diamond-shaped windowpanes. The air was alive with the scent of the roses and heather which filled a vase beside the canopy bed. The memory came through so vividly, that Jeanette could feel the heat of his kisses, and the passion that had consumed them.

The movie in her mind played back the morning she and Chris had made love in the mist on a heather-filled hillside, next to a low stone wall. "Forever," he had whispered, just before the ecstasy took her out of her body and filled her with shooting stars. Christopher's eyes were filled with an expression of such tenderness that she had thought their love would fill her up enough to last forever. She started to cry.

"Glory be to the Father and to the Son and to the Holy Ghost," the Monsignor intoned.

"As it was in the beginning…" Jeanette felt the cold air that flooded the room when the door opened. She knew he was there before she saw him.

"Is now and ever shall be…" She felt him behind her. Her face flushed hot. She turned, and there he was, standing in the doorway. His eyes burned into hers, melting the ice. Had she conjured him up like some wild Celtic witch?

"Chris," she breathed.

"World without end, Amen."

CHAPTER EIGHT

Wednesday, October 4, 1973

Gershwin's deep sleep was shattered by the sound of Teresa Tempesta walking around upstairs. He heard Jeanette begin to stir in the next room. The dog lifted his paw off his nose to sniff the cold morning air. He raised his head, shook it, blinked, and yawned. Judging from the pale light in the room, it was too early for the humans to be up.

"Be quiet so I can go back to sleep," he shouted at the ceiling, although all Teresa would hear was "Bark, bark, bark." Too bad humans had that handicap. Teresa thumped down the hall to the bathroom. Gershwin heard the water running. The dog felt a tickle behind his ears. He reached up a hind leg for a good scratch.

"Morning, fella."

Gershwin rolled over and looked up into Lincoln's face, sleepily thinking for a moment that his master was alive and he had only dreamed otherwise. Lincoln smiled. Tiny white lights sparkled in his beard. Gershwin could see the flowered wallpaper right through Lincoln's transparent face. "You're still a ghost," he woofed.

"Still a ghost." Lincoln nodded.

Somebody dropped something on the floor overhead. Gershwin looked up and growled.

"Today is my funeral," Lincoln said matter-of-factly.

"No kidding? I guess that's a special occasion, huh?"

"It is the last special occasion for Lincoln Lightly," the ghost replied.

"You talk about yourself like you're someone else."

"In a way I am. I mean I am Lincoln, but he is only a part of who I am. I can't explain it because I don't understand it. I am between people, yet all these people I have been and will be are still me."

"That's as clear as mud," the dog observed, licking his paw. Gershwin always liked to take time to groom himself. Lincoln used to tease him that he was like a cat that way. He dug his teeth into his fur. Had to get that flea.

"Maybe it will make more sense on the other side of the tunnel," Lincoln sighed.

"What wouldn't?" the dog agreed.

Lincoln glided over to the window and looked out at Fritz' garden. His neighbor's late-blooming flowers were opening to the morning light. Fritz Reinhart's pumpkins were growing fat on their vines, along with rich yellow squash and big green zucchini. Life was going on. "Fritz is a genius gardener," Lincoln remarked.

"Uh huh." Gershwin was working on his other paw. "I like his wife better."

"Hilda is a fine woman," Lincoln agreed, "but why do you like her better than Fritz?"

"Are you kidding? Have you ever smelled Hilda's kitchen? Fritz grows the stuff, but what she does with it is magic. What a cook!"

Lincoln laughed. He rubbed Gershwin behind the ears. "For a dog, you're a real one-way-street. I do admire Fritz' garden, though, Gershwin. Look how he grows flowers and vegetables side by side, so he can eat out of his yard nearly all year 'round, yet he has this beautiful haven that is always filled with bird song and fat squirrels. I took it all for granted before. I never realized what a sanctuary from the gloom of the world Fritz has created."

"Squirrels?" Gershwin jumped off the bed and stood on his hind legs with his paws on the windowsill. "Where are the squirrels? Are they out there now?"

Lincoln laughed. "I'm sure you'll be the first to know."

"Because I'm primarily olfactory?"

"Yes, Gershwin, you will smell them before I see them."

The dog sat back on his haunches and looked up at Lincoln. "So are you going?" he asked.

"Going?"

"To your funeral."

"I wouldn't miss it for the world."

Jeanette came into the room. Her grief certainly did not detract from her beauty at all, Gershwin observed. She was lovely, even in mourning clothes. Maybe it was the unconscious grace with which she carried herself, or her subtle dignity.

"So here you are!" she exclaimed.

Gershwin ran over and sat looking up at her, tongue hanging out, tail wagging, irresistible puppy face, until she knelt down and gave him a hug.

"I should have known you would be sleeping in Dad's room. You miss him, don't you, boy?"

"Not yet," Gershwin barked, "he hasn't gone anywhere yet."

"I know, puppy. It's just you and me now." Gershwin loved it when she called him "puppy." He licked her knee.

"I've got to go, Gershwin. Be a good dog till I get back, okay?"

Gershwin looked over his shoulder at Lincoln, who was hovering around the radiator watching his daughter. "Have a good funeral," the dog barked.

"Thanks." Lincoln smiled as he drifted out the door following Jeanette.

Gershwin sat on the rug and watched the dust motes settle. He heard the front door open and close. He ran to the living room window and watched Teresa and Jeanette drive away.

The ghost sat on top of Teresa Tempesta's blue Chevy Impala with the big fins. Lincoln waved to Gershwin. He pretended to fall off the car when it turned the corner at Washington Street. After a pickup truck and a motorcycle ran over him, the ghost jumped to his feet and executed an Irish jig. He grinned at the dog. Then the ghost shrugged his shoulders and ran after the car until he was out of sight. Gershwin chuckled. As far back as he could remember Lincoln loved to clown around for him. Even when he was a puppy, Lincoln pulled stunts to trick him. His beloved master was such a tease.

Gershwin experienced a brief moment of dog panic. He suffered from the problem most dogs have when they find themselves left alone. Gershwin hated dog panic, the never knowing if you have been abandoned, never being sure if your human will come back to you or not. It was awful. It made some dogs bark and howl. Gershwin preferred to keep busy. He preferred to keep his mind off dog panic and focused on something more productive.

He was hungry. He padded out to the kitchen, hoping Jeanette had remembered to feed him. She had. He gobbled up the fresh meal in his bowl, washing it down with lots of fresh water. Then he did his morning run around the house. He had to make sure the mice were staying inside the walls where they belonged. He sniffed at the mouse holes in the baseboards, even though he had not seen or smelled any mice in a long time. Teresa's mean cat, Igor, must be doing his job. Still, Gershwin had to be sure. Such an important duty could not be trusted to a cat. Cats, except for mousing, were useless animals in his opinion. He never could understand why humans liked the nasty things. They were not the least bit loveable like dogs, although some of them were pretty good actors.

Gershwin knew Lincoln depended on him to protect the place. Now Jeanette would depend on him too. The dog sniffed every windowsill. Nothing unusual. Everything checked out around the doors, too. No scent of any intruder threatened his sanctuary.

Satisfied that all was well in his master's house, Gershwin let himself out by the dog door in the kitchen. Knowing Teresa was not upstairs, he ran up the back hall steps and sniffed the bottom of her door. He only did this because he knew it would drive Igor nuts.

He barked. Sure enough, a probing cat paw shot out from under the door. Gershwin sat back and laughed as he watched the paw sweep back and forth along the floor. Igor's paw faced up; which meant the cat was on its back, stretching to its limit. Gershwin reached out his own paw and anchored the cat's paw down. Igor let loose a low howl. He yanked his paw back inside. Gershwin listened to the claws scratching the door from the other side. This was great. Igor would get in trouble when Teresa saw the claw marks.

"Woof," he teased.

Igor hissed. That soft thumping sound must be the cat batting its head against the door. Perfect. Satisfied that he had made Igor miserable, Gershwin ran back downstairs and nosed the screen door open. He jumped off the stoop and ran for the back of the garage to take care of his morning toilet. That out of the way, he sniffed his way around the garage. Nothing new there. He circled the trees, marking his usual places.

A rustle in the leaves behind Fritz' garden caught his attention. Gershwin perked up his ears. If only his eyes were as good as his nose. He smelled it before he saw the fat gray tail. Oh, boy, a squirrel! Gershwin bounded into Fritz' yard. He chased the squirrel through the corn and tomatoes into the empty field behind the houses, the place Lincoln called "the lots". He had a good run chasing the squirrel until it ran up the monkey tree. The coward. Squirrels were so schizophrenic.

The monkey tree had gotten its name when Jeanette and her cousins, Anne Marie Tempesta and Eddie Lightly, were kids. They had built a tree house in the upper branches, where they held secret club meetings and played Tarzan. Eddie was a wiry, athletic kid, who used to swing through the branches like a real monkey. That's how the tree got its name. All that was left of the tree house now was its weather-beaten floor.

Gershwin stood on his hind legs, forepaws on the monkey tree, and barked up at the squirrel. The rodent sat on the remnants of the tree house, chattering angrily until Gershwin trotted away.

Most of the bugs were gone this time of year. The field was not the buzzing summer place it had been just a few weeks ago. Gershwin rolled in the high grass. He jumped over rocks as he sniffed his way to Jim Dougherty's yard. It was time to wake up the neighborhood.

Jim Dougherty had chickens. There were six of them in a makeshift wire coop by the old shed. They made a real racket when you crawled up on your stomach and suddenly popped your head up into their field of vision. You could really freak the chickens out if you barked, but that wasn't always necessary. It was best to set the chickens off and run away. That way nobody could pin anything on you. Gershwin crawled up on his belly, then jumped up, paws on the fence, tongue hanging out, grinning. The chickens screamed. This was fun.

Gershwin left the screeching chickens behind. He walked along the top of the man-made wall bordering the brook that flowed down from Verona Lake to Watsessing Park. There were a lot of leaves in the water today. One time he had seen a dead rat float down the stream. He did not like the way the dead rat smelled. He did not like the way live rats smelled either.

Gershwin trotted out of the lots through the alley that led to Washington Street. Two cats ran the other way when they saw him coming. That was okay. He was getting too old to chase cats. He was already panting. He got out of breath so fast lately. Gershwin was glad he had a reputation, though, or he would have had to chase them, and then he would have run out of energy before he finished his walk. It was better the cats didn't know that about him.

Gershwin sniffed around the windows of Rossi's candy store. He sat down in front of the door, one ear folded down, assuming the irresistible puppy face. He planned to thump his tail heartily on the sidewalk when Rossi came out. Rossi usually had a morning cigarette around this time.

Where was he? Gershwin looked in the windows, but Rossi was not inside the store. His daughter was behind the ice cream counter, though. She had on a long granny dress. Daisies were woven into her long red braids.

Gershwin barked until Ruth Rossi saw him. She smiled. To his delight, he watched her put some vanilla ice cream in a cone. By the time Ruth opened the door and knelt down, patting his head, the dog was salivating.

"Here you go, Gershwin. Poor little fella, you need something to cheer you up don't you?" Ruth Rossi sat cross-legged on the front steps of her father's candy store and petted the dog while he ate the ice cream. "My father is at Mr. Lightly's funeral," she said.

"So is Lincoln," Gershwin woofed. He munched the cone. Delicious. He gave her a big grin and licked her hand when he was done.

"'Bye, Gershwin." She smiled, and the dog continued on his way.

He zigzagged down Washington Street between the curb and the buildings, sniffing out who had been there before him. Butch the bull-dog had left his mark at the foot of the tree in front of the apartment house, but it wasn't fresh. Butch had not been here this morning. Good. The first dog always got the best treats. By afternoon the shopkeepers were annoyed and chased the dogs away. Gershwin left his own signature next to Butch's.

An angry squirrel chattered at him from a high branch. Somebody had chased the nut case up there. Gershwin nosed around the tree. Must have been Laddie, Dr. Montero's collie. Laddie didn't get out alone very often. He must have jimmied the gate to his pen open again. Laddie would be bragging to the whole neighborhood all week. Gershwin made a note to avoid his pen for a few days.

Laddie had such a superior attitude, just because he was pure bred. You would think nobody else ever chased a squirrel up a tree. On the other hand, Laddie was too dumb to make the rounds of the shops. The collie was so sheltered, he didn't know enough to keep away from the two Dobermans on Maolis Avenue. Those dogs were so vicious, that no one even wanted to smell their butts. Except, of course, Laddie. That was how dumb he was. Didn't say much for good breeding in Gershwin's opinion. He followed the collie's scent. Sure enough, Laddie had turned off at the train tracks and headed in the other direction. The coast was clear. Next stop the German butcher.

By the time Gershwin got to the Green, he was tired. He took a break under his Sunday bench. Everyone had been overly generous with him today. The German butcher gave him a whole bratwurst, instead of the couple of slices of bologna he usually got. Mrs. Bernstein at the Jewish delicatessen gave him a whole heel of salami, instead of chasing him away like she usually did. Mrs. Bernstein stood over him wiping her eyes with her apron while he ate it. The poor woman was sobbing and speaking in Yiddish. The only word he understood was "Lincoln". Something about Lincoln, followed by "oy, such a poor dog." She followed up the salami with a generous helping of Bernstein's incredible gefilte fish.

Gershwin picked up the stomachache at the French bakery. It got worse as he made his way down Broad Street through Bloomfield Center, sniffing the boring clothing stores, the five and tens, and the drug store.

Gershwin did not see any other dogs this morning, although their markings told him some had passed this way. He left his mark on all the hydrants and trees, after checking who had been there before him.

The crumb bun from the French bakery finally got to him. He threw up in the alley behind the Royal Theater. As if that wasn't bad enough, the pigeons that nested in the air conditioning unit that protruded from the theater's roof dropped their splattering white bombs on his head. Gershwin didn't like pigeons. He barked at them, but the filthy birds just laughed. He had to run out of the alley dodging another of their dive bomb attacks. It was definitely time for a short nap.

The Green was like a town square, except it was a long rectangle of grass. Dozens of park benches sat in the shade of leafy trees. Most of the town's churches were built around the Green, as well as the library and the civic center. At one end was the small campus of Bloomfield College with its old colonial buildings.

The Green was beautiful today, with the trees in their full fall splendor. Gershwin's Sunday bench faced Sacred Heart Church. He had waited there for Lincoln every Sunday since he was a puppy. He always watched the people go into the church and come out. He wondered what they did in there. The dog tried to get in once, but they shooed him away. No dogs allowed. Bigots.

The church doors opened, and Lincoln's ghost came out, saw him, and waved. Gershwin watched the pallbearers carry the coffin down the church steps, followed by the mourners. All the cars in the cortege assembled with their lights on. They followed the big square car up Broad Street toward Mount Olive Cemetery.

Gershwin knew the way. He had walked there with Lincoln every Sunday after church for years. He trotted off down the Green following the funeral procession. He ignored the blue jays that screeched stridently at him, and the startled chattering squirrels that bolted through the leaves when they saw him coming.

"Hey, Lincoln!" Gershwin panted, "Wait for me!"

CHAPTER NINE

Wednesday, October 4, 1973

Lincoln Lightly enjoyed his funeral. Monsignor Donovan pulled out all the stops with a solemn high mass, like in the old days. He read the mass in Latin. Lincoln liked that. Jack Donovan made Lincoln's funeral a celebration of his life.

The usual nasal soprano had not been called in to sing depressing dirges. Instead, in honor of the man who had served as head of the Saint Vincent De Paul Society, the Monsignor asked the nuns from Sacred Heart School to sing Lincoln's favorite Gregorian Chants. Jack fondly remembered their days in the seminary, when they had stood side-by-side in the chapel at Darlington and sung the ancient Latin verses.

"*Patrem omnipotentem*," the nuns sang, "*Factorem coeli et terrae…*" Their sweet voices, singing a cappella, echoed through the church.

The spell woven by the combination of music, candles, incense, and the ancient language comforted the mourners who had come to say their final farewell to Lincoln.

"*Visibilium omnium*," the nuns sang.

"*Et invisibilium*," Lincoln joined in.

The ghost floated through the church where he had spent so many years of his life. He loved the stained glass windows, especially those in the corner that depicted the creation of the world, the flood, and the animals coming out of the ark. Lincoln had married Lizzy beneath the domed canopy of the intricately carved altar. In this sanctuary, he had said goodbye to his beloved wife, who had died too soon.

Jeanette had been baptized here. He remembered the spring morning so well. Still mourning Lizzy's loss, Lincoln had laid the little bundle that was his new daughter on the altar of the Virgin and consecrated her to the Blessed Mother. He had reasoned if he had to be both parents, he would need all the help he could get. The rays of the morning sun had shone through the windows and bathed his baby in rainbows.

This Church had been Lincoln's spiritual home for most of his life, ever since he left the seminary. Now he watched as his friend, Monsignor Donovan, circled his flower-draped coffin with a censor, filling the nave of the church with the evocative aroma of frankincense.

*   *   *

When the funeral cortege arrived at the cemetery, Lincoln stood next to the mourners at his grave. They buried him with Lizzy under the old maple tree. Jeanette was so pale. She stood stoic and dignified, putting on a brave front. His daughter would hold herself together and cry privately. When he tried to tune in to her thoughts, Lincoln felt only a dark, sad numbness. Jeanette was not letting herself think. She was not letting herself feel. She had locked up her heart and thrown away the key.

"Jeanette looks just like Jackie Kennedy," Irene whispered to her sister, Rose.

Rose dabbed at her streaming eyes. "She is so brave," she agreed.

"She is so fragile," Lincoln thought.

Christopher Fortune stood beside Jeanette through the service. Lincoln's daughter let down her guard enough to lean against her husband's broad shoulder. He put his arm around her protectively.

Lincoln focused on Chris's feelings. "Why, he still loves Jeanette!" he realized. "He's thinking he would lay down his life for her right here if he could. He's thinking he would throw himself in my grave if it would bring me back so she wouldn't have to bear another loss. The Saints be praised. I'll be with Lizzy soon. This is gonna be so easy."

Monsignor Donovan finished the prayers for the dead. He waved the censor over the grave.

"Thanks for the nice send off, Jack," Lincoln said.

Snow flurries filled the air, quickly turning into fat lacy snowflakes. Lincoln was delighted. There was something full-circle about being buried in the first snowfall of the season. It seemed clean and complete. He stuck out his tongue to taste the frozen treat, like when he was a boy.

"If I can still smell the incense," he reasoned, "maybe I can still taste the snow."

"It is not the real thing. These sensations are only memories of what was. They lack the sharp quality of life."

Startled, Lincoln spun around to find himself face to face with a sturdy old man dressed in a worn black overcoat, a black felt hat set jauntily on his head. White teeth flashed under a big moustache. The man leaned on a polished cane that had an elaborate silver handle carved in the shape of a wolf.

"Gockie!" Lincoln cried. "What are you doing here?"

"I have been given a special dispensation," Joseph Stoeckel replied. "I have a stake in this operation, too, son."

Lincoln embraced his grandfather. Their light bodies crackled and flashed like lightning in the snow. Lincoln was so excited he danced an enthusiastic jig around the gravestones.

"I see you inherited more of my Annie's Irish heritage than mine," Gockie chuckled.

"There is nothing wrong with the Irish, Gockie. Bill is not crazy about his Irish side, but I love being part of such an indomitable breed." Lincoln executed an intricate dance step.

"Morbid, too," Joseph Stoeckel observed as he pointed his cane toward Rose and Irene in the dispersing crowd. Irene was taking flowers from Lincoln's funeral arrangements and putting them on empty graves. Rose appeared to be having a conversation with a gravestone.

"Well, those are two of my wife's sisters. Rose and Irene are a bit eccentric."

Gockie laughed. "You think?"

"Still," Lincoln said, "you gotta love them. They always made me laugh. Rose and Irene are misunderstood. Their hearts and intentions are so sensitive and sincere."

The snow was starting to stick like powdered sugar sprinkled on chocolate cake.

"So what is your plan?" Joseph asked. "How are you going to reunite them?"

"Oh, that will be easy. Jeanette and Chris are so much in love. A gentle shove should do it. But tell me, Gockie, have you seen my Lizzy? Is she as beautiful as I remember? Does she know I'm on my way? Will it bother her that I am so much older?"

"Lincoln Lightly, pay attention to the job at hand," his grandfather scolded. "Yes, your wife is even more beautiful than you remember, and age is meaningless where there is no time. You have an eternity to enjoy with Lizzy. But you are wrong about your daughter and her husband." Gockie pointed with his wolf-headed cane toward the limousine where Jeanette and Chris stood, head to head, talking to each other. "It is not going to be that easy to get them back together," he observed.

"Oh, I'm wrong am I? Look at them. Have you ever seen a more handsome couple? Why he looks like Cary Grant. And you have to admit your great granddaughter is a beauty. Have you ever seen two people so much in love?"

"Come closer." Lincoln and Gockie suddenly stood at the couple's side.

"How did you do that?"

"I have more experience being dead than you," Gockie said. "Now be quiet and listen."

"I'm not going with you," Jeanette insisted. "I can't believe you have the lack of sensitivity to think that on this day…God, Chris, I just buried my father!"

"You can't keep running away from this forever, Jeanette," Chris argued, "When are you going to face what happened and stop destroying yourself?"

"I don't know. Maybe when you're dead."

Chris threw his hands in the air as his wife got into the limousine alone and slammed the door. He leaned down to knock on the window. She opened it half way.

"Jeanette, please."

"Are you coming back to the house?" she asked coldly.

He nodded.

"I'll see you there, then."

"If you would only listen…"

She closed the window in his face. The limo pulled away, leaving Chris standing alone in the snow.

"See?" Gockie said to his grandson, the ghost.

Lincoln shook his head. Maybe this was not going to be as easy as he thought.

Teresa approached Chris. "Do you need a ride back to the house?" she asked.

"Good old Teresa," Lincoln said, "making sure no one is left stranded in the cemetery."

"Yes, I guess I do," Chris sighed, "but first I wanted to…"

"I know, dear." Teresa patted his arm.

"I was hoping Jeanette would come with me," he said sadly.

"You go ahead, and take your time. I have to wait for my sisters anyway. They are always the last ones to leave the cemetery, you know."

Chris pointed to Irene, who was still going from grave to grave, putting Lincoln's flowers on the empty ones. "What is she doing?"

"Oh, she feels sorry for the neglected graves. She thinks the flowers will make the dead ones feel less lonely. You go on now, Christopher. We won't leave without you."

Chris pulled his collar up around his cold ears. He stuck his hands in his pockets. His footprints disturbed the fresh snow as he walked down the path.

"Where is he going?" Lincoln asked curiously.

"To his son's grave," Gockie answered.

Teresa walked slowly back to Lincoln's grave. She knelt down and removed a single red rose from the flowers that had been placed there. She raised it to her nose as she whispered a prayer. She kissed her gloved hand and touched the coffin with her fingers. "Goodbye, Lincoln," she whispered. Teresa placed the rose carefully inside the prayer book she carried, lowered her head, and burst into tears.

"You see, son," Gockie said quietly, "Teresa loved you like the brother she never had and always wanted. But she never let you know."

Lincoln knelt down next to Teresa. He placed his spectral hand on her shoulder. "Thank you for taking care of me all these years, Tee. We fought like alligators, but in my way I loved you too, old girl."

Teresa took a deep breath. She dabbed at her eyes, stood up, squared her shoulders, and set off down the rows of gravestones calling to her sisters

Rose stood over their Uncle Albert's grave, talking down to it. "If you run into Lincoln, Uncle Albert," Rose said, "take care of him. Maybe you could put in a good word for him so he doesn't burn in hell."

"Rose, dear" Teresa said softly, "the snow is sticking. We are needed back at the house. Jeanette should not receive the guests alone."

Lincoln sat down next to Gockie on a marble bench under the tree next to his grave. They watched the weird sisters pull away in the last car. No sooner had the fins of Teresa's big blue Impala disappeared around the bend of the road, then a truck pulled up. The gravediggers had arrived. The diggers lowered the coffin, hastily shoveled the dirt in, patted it down with their shovels, and piled the rest of the flowers on top of the fresh mound. Then they rattled away in the old truck.

Silence descended on the cemetery, so profound that Lincoln could hear the whisper of the snow falling. He stared at the new grave, now blanketed in white. "So I guess that's that," he sighed.

Gockie nodded. "When I was an old man and I could still walk, I used to come to this graveyard every day," he mused.

"I remember. Sometimes, when I was a boy, you took me with you."

"It was the time in my life when all I had left were memories. I sat on the bench in the veteran's section by all the small white crosses, just remembering. I knew so many men buried there, from the Civil War and the Spanish American War. I had friends who fought in the Great War, the one I could not fight in." The old ghost sighed and patted his leg with his cane. "We called it the 'War to End All Wars.'"

"It wasn't. There were more," Lincoln told him.

Gockie nodded.

"Well," Lincoln observed, "the wars got worse, if you can believe it. The weapons became deadlier; the enemy more insidious."

Gockie shook his head. "Will it never end?"

"I always felt conflicted," Lincoln confessed. "I was glad my bad knees kept me out of the military, yet at the same time I wanted to be able to fight like Bill and you had."

"On the battlefield at Gettysburg," Gockie said, "a man named Jack told me 'being a soldier ain't all glory.' He was right. I buried so many men in my lifetime. Some of them were my buddies. Many of them died in my arms." He shook his head. "War is a terrible thing, no matter how just the cause. That is why your mission is so important, Lincoln. Isabelle Fortune has the chance to put an end to war."

"Bill's son, Eddie, has not been the same since he came home from Vietnam," Lincoln sighed. "He is shell shocked, but there is something worse. He says he feels no sense of honor about what happened over there. Then he won't tell anyone what he experienced. He won't talk about it. His fiancé told me Eddie wakes up screaming."

"It used to be easier to go to war," Gockie said. "The reasons for it were dramatic and clear. The causes were just and unquestionable. Eddie is the real reason I am here."

Shadows moved through the graveyard, wispy at first, then taking shape.

"Who are all those people out in the snow?" Lincoln wondered.

A pale woman in a turn-of-the-century white ribbon dress sat on a gravestone. She waved.

"Look at her. She doesn't have a coat. She'll freeze."

"No. She is beyond cold, Lincoln. She is ghost. They are all ghosts," Gockie explained. "We are in the realm of the dead now. The shadows are like us, but without purpose. Some of them cling to life too long and do not make the transition easily. Some of them hang around here for centuries, loathe to admit they are dead."

"Like the lost souls in the tunnel?"

"They **are** the lost souls from the tunnel. Do not linger too long in the realm of the dead, son. They are a sad lot."

Lincoln shivered. "That's just what the angel Mario said." The cemetery was full of shadows now.

"I would love to sit here and philosophize, son, but we have work to do."

"How am I going to bring them together, Gockie? Jeanette and Chris are so much in love, and so torn apart."

"If love were the be-all and end-all, it would be much simpler," his grandfather said. "Unfortunately, people are more complicated than that. Grief is as powerful an emotion as love, and your daughter has had more than her share. Her walls must be even more impenetrable since your passing. Those we leave behind do not have the comfort of being able to see beyond the veil. Lord knows my life would have been easier if I could have known the men I buried were in such a good place, or if I could have been sure there was 'life after death', as they call it."

"I never doubted life after death," Lincoln observed.

"Well, son, I lacked your strong faith. I never studied theology and philosophy. I was a simple man, an immigrant, and a soldier. When I died and reviewed my life, as you will do when you get to the other side, I was ashamed, because I did not think I had been that good of a man. I could have been a better father, a better husband. When I summon the courage to live again, I have resolved to appreciate and honor my relationships."

"I know one relationship you did not fail at," Lincoln said gently, patting the hand Joseph Stoeckel rested on his cane. "You were a wonderful grandfather."

A small dark shadow moved toward them. Gershwin, sniffing his way down the road, saw the two ghosts on the bench and ran over to them. He tripped over his paws and somersaulted over to them. His snout was covered with snow.

"Gershwin!" Lincoln cried, "You good old dog."

"Hi, Lincoln," Gershwin panted.

Lincoln knelt down and hugged the dog. He scratched him behind his ears.

"That your dog?" Gockie asked.

"Gockie, this is Gershwin, probably the best dog alive. Gershwin, this is my grandfather's ghost."

Gershwin grinned. He held up his paw for Gockie to shake. "Nice to meet you, Mr. Gockie," he barked. "You guys go on with your conversation. Don't let me interrupt you. I'll just sit down here and catch my breath." The dog turned in circles and pawed a space for himself before curling up in the snow at Lincoln's feet.

"Gockie," Lincoln said softly, sitting back down next to his grandfather on the bench, "would you do something for me?"

"What, son? I will not refuse you on the day of your burial."

"Before we leave here, will you tell me one more time about Gettysburg?"

CHAPTER TEN

Wednesday, October 4, 1973

"Back in 1863," Gockie began, "my family lived in Bordentown, near the Pennsylvania border. It was seven years after my family came over from Alsace-Lorraine, the Civil War was raging, and I wanted to be soldier. I was only twelve years old, too young to be a soldier. I ran away to be a water boy for the Union Army. I was there at Gettysburg. Me and Captain Jack worked side-by-side burying the dead after the three-day battle that turned those peaceful fields into a hellish inferno. That July was so hot and humid you could hardly breathe. Hell, you could swim through the air. I saw men with their bodies so torn apart they hardly looked human. I saw men with no faces. So I was very young when I found out that war wasn't so glorious after all.

"Me and Jack, we didn't care what color their uniforms were. We buried the blue and the gray side-by-side, where they had fallen. I shoveled dirt on top of boys who were hardly much older than me. Kids were fighting and dying in the fields of Pennsylvania, kids who had mothers and fathers waiting for them back home, just like me. I can still remember how sticky and thick their blood was when it mixed with the dirt on my hands.

"And when those Rebel soldiers walked across that wide open field into the fires of hell…" Gockie put his head down and sighed. "I never saw anything so brave or so tragic. In all the wars I fought in, nothing was ever as bad as that. Nothing was ever as horrible as the hand-to-hand combat, with men looking in each other's eyes before they slaughtered each other."

"Tell me about Abraham Lincoln."

"Well, now that was later, in November of that same year. Me and Captain Jack, we went back to Gettysburg to see Lincoln. We was leaning against the tree that was the nearest to the open-air platform.

"A man got up and gave a speech. He had a deep voice that droned like the hum of bees. His name was Edward Everett, and he was a polished gentleman, handsome and graceful. Everett was just like a regular actor on the stage, the way he moved, and the way he talked. He addressed the multitude on the battlefield for almost two hours. Everett spoke about the war with a fire that was like a torch to men's passions. There was bitterness in his words when he called the opposing cause, for which honest Americans were giving their lives, a crime.

"Me and Jack, we didn't think the boys in the gray coats who we buried were criminals just because they were fighting for a way of life we believed was wrong. Hell, they were fighting for their land and their homes was all. Guess if the shoe was on the other foot, we would have done the same. Captain Jack, he was wounded. He was going home. But he harbored no bitterness toward the opposing side.

"The crowd was getting restless. Many of them had seen the men who were buried on this battlefield die. Some of them were wounded themselves; others must soon go into battle again. Some had brothers who were Rebels.

"And me, well, I had served the needs of the living and dying in the sweltering July heat during those three horrible days and nights at Gettysburg; so today I was making sure no one went thirsty. You see I understood thirst, especially the thirst for freedom. Yeah, I was just a kid, but people don't give kids credit for how much they can understand sometimes. And that war made us all grow up mighty fast."

Gockie leaned on his cane and looked up at the sky. The snow piled up on his hat. Some of the shadows had drawn in closer, like they were listening. Gershwin whined nervously, and Lincoln patted his back to quiet him.

"It was a crisp, cold November day. The last riot of color in the trees, and the smell of burning leaves filled my senses. Flocks of migrating geese flying in formation blazed a trail across a sky so blue it would make you dizzy. The Marine band was there, all the way from Washington D.C., the city I heard was built of shining white marble. My, but they were good.

"I watched the faces on the platform. There were the Judges of the Supreme Court, the General-in-Chief of the Army and his staff, and the members of the President's Cabinet. I searched for the one face I had come to see."

"The President?" Lincoln said. This was so great. He had not heard Gockie tell this story since he was a boy.

Gockie nodded. "The President of the United States had come to consecrate the National Cemetery at Gettysburg that day. I had heard the story of the self-educated President who was born in a log cabin. I wanted to see this man who had come from such humble beginnings to lead a whole country.

"Finally, Everett finished talking. He bowed to a storm of applause. 'They clappin' 'cause his speech was so good, or 'cause it's finally over?' Captain Jack said. He had such a good sense of humor, that Jack. I thought he was such a fine big man, but now that I think back, I bet he wasn't more than twenty or twenty-one years old.

"The Marine band played ruffles and flourishes. Then a tall, gaunt figure rose and approached the podium. Lincoln stood six feet four inches tall. He slouched awkwardly across the open space. His clothes didn't seem to fit him. He faced the multitude and felt around in his wrinkled pockets until he found what he was searching for. Pulling out what looked like a piece of brown wrapping paper, he unfolded it, adjusted his wire-rimmed spectacles, looked it over, and cleared his throat.

"'Four score and seven,' he began, but a sudden fit of coughing seized him. The crowd tittered, surprised by the President's strange appearance and his queer, squeaky voice. Struggling to regain control, Abraham Lincoln straightened up. I saw that his eyes were ringed with dark shadows that made his haggard face look like a skull. Lincoln cleared his throat again. He gazed into the crowd like he was looking into their souls. He looked down at the sleepy town at the foot of the big green hill that had run red with blood.

"'Four score,' he rasped in a strident falsetto, and the cough threatened to overpower him again."

"And that's when you jumped up," Lincoln interrupted.

"Yes, sir. That's when I sprang into action and ran up to the foot of the platform with my water bag. I realized too late I had left the tin cup under the tree with Captain Jack. I held the weathered bag up so Lincoln could lean over and grab it. The President reached down with his huge bony hands and took hold of the bloodstained bag. He raised it to his lips and drank deeply. He handed the bag back to me, smiled, and said, 'Thank you, young man.' He called me young man. It made me proud. I remember he had such a sad smile, and the most amazing eyes.

"I stood at the foot of the platform and listened as Abraham Lincoln began to speak again. After a dozen or so words, the President's tones gathered volume; he spoke with power and dignity. The crowd gathered on the battlefield was like they were hypnotized by his words.

"'Fourscore and seven years ago, our fathers brought forth on this continent a new nation, conceived in liberty and dedicated to the proposition that all men are created equal,' the President said. I will never forget his words."

Gockie's eyes misted over as he spoke. "'Now we are engaged in a great civil war, testing whether that nation, or any nation so conceived and so dedicated, can long endure. We are met on a great battlefield of that war. We have come to dedicate a portion of that field as a final resting-place for those who here gave their lives that that nation might live. It is altogether fitting and proper that we should do this.' The battlefield was so quiet you could hear the wind blowing the red and gold leaves out of the trees." Gockie relived the memory.

"'But in a larger sense,'" he continued, "'we cannot dedicate, we cannot consecrate, we cannot hallow this ground. The brave men, living and dead, who struggled here, have consecrated it far above our poor power to add or to detract. The world will little note nor long remember what we say here, but it can never forget what they did here. It is for us, the living, rather, to be dedicated here to the unfinished work which they who fought here have thus far so nobly advanced.'

"I watched a hawk soar over the rolling hills and fertile farmlands that surrounded Gettysburg. I heard the President's words with more than my ears. I understood them in my heart."

Gershwin rested his nose on Gockie's knee and looked up at him. "What happened next?" the dog woofed.

"Then Abraham Lincoln said, 'It is rather for us to be here dedicated to the great task remaining before us, that from these honored dead we take increased devotion to that cause for which they here gave the last full measure of devotion.'"

"And then, son," he said, as Lincoln remembered him saying so many times before, "Then Abraham Lincoln said the words that burned in my heart until the day I died, and burn in my soul still. 'That we here highly resolve,' he said, 'that these dead shall not have died in vain; that this nation, under God, shall have a new birth of freedom; and that government of the people, by the people, for the people shall not perish from the earth.'"

The silent snow fell around the ghosts and dog. Lincoln murmured, "But the people did not clap."

Gockie shook his head. "No. The thousands who heard those words were stunned and silent. The crowd was so deeply moved that no applause followed the President's speech. The President stared at them sadly, resignedly, and they stared back at him. He folded the brown paper and stuck it in his pocket. Then he turned, his shoulders bent by the heaviness of his burden.

"The Marine band broke the silence when they launched into '*The Battle Hymn of the Republic*'. The dignitaries on the platform rose and followed Lincoln down the steps. Some of the people stood in place singing as the majority of the crowd began to leave. Lincoln stopped to shake hands with a number of spectators, paying special attention to the soldiers and the wounded.

"'Damn!' Captain Jack said, 'I got somethin' in my eye. Hey, Joe, gimme some more water, will ya?' I refilled the tin cup, knowing that it was tears Jack had in his eye.

"'What're you gonna do now, Joe?' Jack asked. 'I want to be a soldier,' I told him proudly.

"Jack patted his bandaged leg, and I helped him to his feet. I set the crudely carved crutch under his arm to support him. He winced, and that's when he said, 'Bein' a soldier ain't all glory, son. Guess I'm out of it now.'

"I looked around me at the more than three thousand mounds that marked the graves of the dead. Me and Captain Jack had dug many of those graves together. Jack seemed to read my thoughts when he said, 'I think I got the dirt and blood from Gettysburg stuck in my fingernails forever.'

"We watched the stove pipe hat that towered over the crowd disappear into the distance. 'Government of the people, by the people, and for the people,' Captain Jack repeated. 'Guess old Lincoln summed it up pretty good. Guess it's worth fighting for.'

"We said our goodbyes, and Jack followed the crowd out of the field. Then I raised the water bag President Lincoln drank from to my lips and quenched my own thirst.

"Later, when I married my beautiful Annie Ryan, I longed for a son so I could name him after Lincoln. That was not to be. God gave us beautiful daughters, but no sons. I had to wait for your mother to have you. I convinced my daughter to name you Lincoln. And that's how you got your name."

Lincoln hugged his grandfather. "It was almost worth dying to hear you tell me that story one more time. I missed you so much, Gockie."

"I have always been nearby." Gockie smiled.

Gershwin shivered. "Hey, guys, it's freezing out here."

"Let's go," Lincoln said. "My dog is still in a solid body, and he's cold. He should go home."

The two ghosts and the dog walked out of the cemetery together. They left no footprints in the snow, only one set of paw prints.

CHAPTER ELEVEN

Saturday, October 7, 1973

"This was always my favorite," Jeanette said.

Jeanette and her cousin, Anne Marie Mustachio, stood in a narrow corridor of the Hall of North American Mammals in New York's American Museum of Natural History. The diorama they were looking at depicted a pair of massive timber wolves hunting on a snowy night. Blue lights dimly lit the cold dark scene. The lupine male and female were beautiful specimens. They were fierce and frightening as they ran toward the observer. The diorama looked so real, it was easy to imagine the wind blowing through the tall pine trees that blended imperceptibly into the skillful background painting. The wolves' swift silent passage was portrayed as vividly as the snowy night in which they remained forever frozen.

"Look how powerful they are," Jeanette remarked.

Anne Marie shivered. "Them wolves scared the hell out of me when I was little."

Jeanette smiled. "I remember. Uncle Tony used to say 'how would you like to meet **them** on a dark night?' and you would start screaming bloody murder. Your father always seemed to find that hilarious."

"Yeah, scare the crap out of the kid. Real funny. Daddy was a regular riot. They were bigger than me, and I didn't believe they were dead."

"Uncle Tony was always so much fun. Remember the time he had the monkey quarantined for possible rabies in his veterinary office, and he brought it home for us to play with?"

"Hey, I loved Bonzo. It broke my heart," Anne Marie pouted, "when he got a clean bill of health and Daddy had to give him back."

"I can't believe your mother allowed that monkey in the house at all."

"Oh, she was putty in Daddy's hands. Ma was so different when he was alive. She bitched about the filthy animal, but she basically worshipped the ground my father walked on. He always got his way. He would bat those huge dark eyes and say, 'Please, Tee?' in this little boy voice, and he had her every time. Put the kids' lives in danger? No problem!"

Jeanette and Anne Marie laughed as they turned the corner into the main hall. They stopped to admire the gigantic Grizzly. The bear stood on his hind legs, looking down at them like he wanted to crush them in his huge paws. His mate peered out from behind him. Her forepaw rested on a bloody fish.

"It didn't help to run away from the wolves only to come face to face with this towering monster." Anne Marie's laughter echoed through the high-ceilinged gallery.

"He does inspire awe," Jeanette agreed.

"I used to think if I screamed loud enough, Ma would hear me and come and save me. Obviously, Daddy was trying to kill me or he would not have brought me here."

Jeanette laughed. "I think I was in high school before I ever saw this whole gallery, because once you got to the bear your screams created such a racket that Uncle Tony had to carry you out. I'm surprised Aunt Teresa didn't hear you all the way in Bloomfield, because the noise was deafening."

"Yeah, these rooms have cool athletics."

"You mean acoustics?"

"Whatever. When I was little all I knew was they were dark and scary. It's all that old wood. These galleries are probably haunted. I'm not sure even now that I believe the animals in these cases can't hurt me. My biggest fear was being locked in this museum at night, because Eddie said that's when the animals in the dioramas come to life. Just look at the size of that damn moose over there!" She shuddered.

"You believed everything Eddie told you."

"I still do. So there." Anne Marie ran her fingers through her wispy bangs. Her frosted brown hair was pulled into a thick braid that hung down her back almost to her waist. Electric blue eye shadow and heavy black eyeliner and mascara highlighted her big brown eyes. Anne Marie had inherited her father's dramatic Italian features, but she had her mother's delicate Irish complexion. She wore no rouge on her pale cheeks. Glossy white lipstick polished her pouty lips.

Having just turned thirty, Jeanette's cousin was revising her long-held opinion that everyone over the age of twenty-nine was the enemy. She still favored clothes like the long Indian print dress she wore today, with earth shoes and love beads.

The cousins had grown up in the same house. The Tempestas lived upstairs from the Lightlys. When they were children, Jeanette and Anne Marie had played together. They walked to school together. Teresa mothered Jeanette, and when Tony Tempesta died Lincoln played father to Anne Marie. Their shared past had forged a strong bond between them.

The two women ascended the museum's marble staircase. They entered the Hall of African Mammals with its double-floored gallery. The ceiling was so high you could barely see it in the dim light. An entire herd of African elephants charged down the middle of the room toward them.

"I used to have nightmares about those elephants," Jeanette said. "And that gorilla over there gave me a few sleepless nights, too."

The huge bluish-black ape stood in the treetops of a beautiful green jungle, looking fierce and thumping his chest. "He looks like my husband, Joseph," Anne Marie observed.

Jeanette giggled. "He acts like him too," she thought. She checked her watch. "I promised Lamont we would meet them in the Hall of Dinosaurs at four o'clock. We better hurry."

On the way to the elevator, they passed the bronze bust of a Bantu woman, whose bare breasts were highly polished by the hundreds of people who rubbed them for good luck. Anne Marie laughed at the boy who glanced around to see if anyone was watching before reaching up to pat the shining protuberances. "I wish I could spend one day on that pedestal," she said.

"Come on," Jeanette replied, "the elevator is here."

In the crowded elevator, Lincoln Lightly stood just behind his daughter's right shoulder. His light body shared the same space as a middle-aged woman in a flowered dress. The woman appeared uncomfortable. She squirmed as the crowded car moved slowly upward. The elevator operator announced the exhibits on each floor in a slow, nasal whine.

Lincoln, perceiving the other ghosts around him, chuckled. The living people would have been surprised to know just how crowded the car really was. If everyone in the elevator had been alive, the weight would have far exceeded the safe maximum. He thought it was a good thing ghosts didn't weigh anything.

A specter with a handlebar moustache, wearing a turn-of-the-century seersucker suit, touched the tip of his finger to his straw hat. Lincoln smiled and nodded. In his new form, he saw ghosts everywhere. Sometimes the spirits appeared solid. Most of them looked fairly normal. Others had a look of decay about them. Still others were little more than shadows. Just like the living, the wraiths radiated negative or positive vibrations, depending on their thought patterns. The elevator of the Natural History Museum was full of ghosts. In fact, the streets of New York were teeming with phantoms.

Between the third and fourth floors, Lincoln heard Gockie call to him. By focusing on his grandfather's energy as Gockie had taught him, he moved through a timeless space and instantly stood at Joseph Stoeckel's side. He found his new ability to do this a bit disconcerting.

The few people in the Hall of Dinosaurs stood as still as the massive skeletons which were on exhibit. The spectators did not appear to be breathing. Lincoln found himself standing in a dinosaur footprint next to the Stegosaurus. The ghost of his grandfather sat perched on the skeletal tail. He leaned both hands on his cane.

At the other end of the hall loomed the mighty Tyrannosaurus Rex, set in an attack stance. Even without meat and skin, the monster's bony eye sockets and toothy jaws looked hungry for a kill. A man who was well over six feet tall stood dwarfed at the Tyrannosaurus' feet. The man did not move or blink.

Masterful murals painted by Charles R. Knight covered the walls above the glass exhibit cases. Dinosaur life in the Mesozoic era was depicted in muted, subtle colors. The sun's rays pouring through the high windows above the murals lit the polished brown bones of the once great creatures. But the dust motes in the sun's rays were motionless. Gockie tipped his hat to his grandson.

"What is this?" Lincoln asked pointing to the inert people. "Why aren't they moving?"

"It is just a slight suspension of time," Joseph Stoeckel explained. "It has more to do with us than them. Shortly, they will resume their lives exactly where they left off without a second lost. But first, I want to show you this."

Gockie pointed to a man who was leaning over peering into one of the exhibit cases. His pencil was poised over a small pad he held in his hand.

"Chris!" Lincoln exclaimed.

Christopher Fortune stood frozen in the act of sketching the model of a small, red, leaping dinosaur identified as Ornitholestes. Behind the model was a drawing by Knight of the dinosaur. Ornitholestes held an Archaeopteryx, which he had caught in mid-flight, in his talons. The grinning dinosaur appeared to be enjoying his short dance of life. The prototypical bird in his grasp looked terrified.

Lincoln peered over Chris' shoulder. Chris had copied the drawing precisely. A piece of sketch paper lay on the floor at Chris' feet. Lincoln bent down to pick up the fallen page. It was a picture of Jeanette. Using nothing more than a pencil, Christopher Fortune had captured his wife's beauty, especially her eyes. Lincoln was delighted. Chris had obviously been thinking of Jeanette. Maybe he had done this sketch on the train ride into the city.

"This is a perfect coincidence!" he exclaimed, "Jeanette is on her way up here right now to meet Lamont and his friend in this gallery. She is sure to run into Chris."

Gockie was using his cane to play a tune on the Stegosaurus' tailbones. "Do you like my ancient xylophone, Lincoln?"

"Look at this sketch, Gockie. Love simply oozes off the paper."

"Well, what are we waiting for?" Gockie said. "Let's resume the time continuum!" Gockie waved his cane. The Hall of Dinosaurs came back to life.

Lincoln focused on Jeanette, which placed him instantly behind her in the elevator. The squirming lady in the flowered dress straightened out her skirt. Lincoln tried to ignore the inquisitive stares of the other ghosts. Both the angel and his grandfather had warned him not to linger too long in the realm of the dead.

"Hurry," Lincoln whispered in his daughter's ear. "Chris is there."

Jeanette scratched her ear.

The two elevators arrived simultaneously, one going up and one going down. Christopher Fortune had already left the Hall of Dinosaurs. He was waiting for the down elevator when Jeanette's car ground slowly to a halt.

"Fourth floor," the attendant whined. "Early Mammals and their extinct relatives. Hall of Dinosaurs."

"Going down," the other car's operator intoned.

With agonizing slowness, the attendant pushed back the heavy grating to let the ascending passengers off the elevator. Chris stepped onto the down elevator. Jeanette and Anne Marie stepped into the hall. Both sets of metal doors clanged shut.

Gockie stood in the hallway. He shook his head as he watched the hand on the brass floor indicator over the down elevator spin to the left. Third floor, second floor, first floor. "He missed her," he sighed.

"What?" Lincoln cried. "How could they have missed each other? They were so close!"

Jeanette and Anne Marie entered the Hall of Dinosaurs just as Lamont Feather and Glitter Man came through the wide doorway on the far side of the room. Jeanette waved. She hurried toward the Tyrannosaurus to meet her friend. When she stepped on the fallen piece of sketch paper, she carelessly kicked it aside. Had Jeanette looked down, she would have been surprised to see that it was a drawing of her.

CHAPTER TWELVE

Saturday, October 7, 1973

"What is it about Japanese food that is so comforting?" Glitter Man asked.

"You probably had a former life in Japan as a concubine," Lamont said dryly. He drained his cup of sake. "It must have been a good life. No doubt you loved it when the Emperor chose you for the night."

"You should know," Glitter retorted, "since he probably had you first."

"Ah so?" Lamont raised his cup in a mock toast, blew Glitter a kiss, and bowed. "Don't touch my moustache, because I was his favorite."

"Can we all be grownups now?" Jeanette begged.

The sweet sounds of koto music drifted through the air. There was a small fountain in one corner which created the illusion of a miniature waterfall cascading at the feet of a smiling bronze Buddha.

"This is a groovy place," Anne Marie said. "Man, do they put out a feast. I can't believe you get all this for six bucks. Most restaurants these days have such exuberant prices." She bit into a piece of shrimp tempura. "Yum. If I eat much more, I swear I won't be able to get up off this floor."

The Aki Restaurant's family dinners included a sampling of nearly every item on the menu. The foursome had already devoured generous helpings of sushi, sashimi, tempura, yakitori, teriyaki, and sukiyaki.

A waitress in a beautifully embroidered kimono opened the screen to their private tatami room. She stepped out of her slippers and knelt at their table to serve the next course. She set down a huge platter of fresh fruit arranged in the shape of flowers on a bed of ice garnished with daisies.

Lamont lifted his sake cup, "More all around, please," he said. The smiling waitress bowed as she backed out of the room. She closed the screen behind her.

"How did you ever find this place?" Anne Marie asked Jeanette. "You would never know it was here unless you knew it was here. I mean, who ever heard of a restaurant in the basement of an apartment building?"

"Is she always so articulate?" Lamont said. Anne Marie threw a grape at him. He countered by throwing one back that landed in her cleavage.

"Bulls eye!" Lamont exclaimed.

"Touchdown!" Glitter Man cried.

Anne Marie fished the grape out of her bosom, taking extra pains to expose as much of her loose breast as possible.

Glitter and Lamont made eye contact and burst out laughing. "Who is she trying to impress?" Glitter had a dazzling smile.

"Maybe Jeanette," Lamont countered. "She is wasting her time with either of us."

"Oh you're just jealous 'cause you wish you had boobs," Anne Marie teased.

"Well if I had boobs," Lamont said, "I would wear a bra. I think I would like one of those German bras, 'der schtoppem fum floppin.'"

"Are they always this rude and crude?" Anne Marie asked.

"Ignore them," Jeanette advised.

"So how did you say you found this restaurant?"

"Chris and I used to come here when he was a student at Columbia University. It was our special place. Chris proposed to me here." Jeanette tried unsuccessfully to hide the sadness in her face when she spoke of Chris.

The waitress opened the screen. She placed more containers of hot sake on the table. Jeanette drained her cup. Lamont promptly refilled it with steaming hot rice wine.

"I would like to propose a toast," Lamont announced.

They raised their cups expectantly.

"To Richard Nixon."

Jeanette burst out laughing. She downed her sake.

"Come on, drink up, Lamont insisted, "to Tricky Dicky."

"Are you out of your mind?" Glitter protested. "Why on earth would you propose a toast to Nixon?"

"For giving us those fun-filled Watergate hearings."

Glitter Man looked horrified. "I hate the Watergate hearings. I haven't seen 'All My Children' in weeks. I don't give a rat's ass about the boring Watergate hearings. Like lying and spying in the political arena hasn't been going on for decades. So the dick head got caught? Who cares?"

Lamont grinned. "And I haven't had to hear about Erica Kane's love life since the hearings began. Personally, I'm grateful to Nixon for screwing up. It gives me a chance to check out Maureen Dean's latest hairdo."

Lamont downed his sake and poured another. "But seriously, I do care about this fiasco. The government may actually be overthrown. I think it's fascinating. But then, I have always preferred reality to fantasy."

"That wasn't what you said last night," Glitter pouted.

Anne Marie said, "I like Pat Nixon. I think she's so brave. A woman must stand by her man, you know. And Tricia's wedding in the rose garden was so beautiful. At least Nixon loves his family, even if he is a lying pig. Anyhow, all men are lying pigs."

Glitter rolled his eyes. "I think I'm flat lining."

Anne Marie turned toward him. "You watch 'All My Children' too? Erica's my favorite."

"Darling, nothing interferes with Glitter's Erica Kane obsession," Lamont said.

"Well excuse me," Glitter retorted, "but I hate to miss my show. I go home for lunch every day so I can see it."

"That soap opera is like a religion with Glitter Man." Lamont laughed. "He won't answer the phone between noon and one o'clock. Nothing must interrupt that sacred hour."

"Well, no kidding," Anne Marie said. "In the matter of fact, I feel the same way."

"Thank you," Glitter replied. He kissed her hand. "It's nice to know I'm not alone."

"Ooh, how chivalrous." Anne Marie giggled. "Has anyone ever told you that you look like Richard Chamberlain? What's your real name anyway?"

"I don't remember," Glitter muttered. His green eyes turned dark. He popped a slice of apple in his mouth.

"Don't bother," Jeanette quipped, "he won't tell."

"Why not?"

"It's a Biblical thing. Don't pursue it," Lamont cautioned.

"How ridiculous. What is your real name, Glitter Man? I promise I won't tell."

"You promise?"

She raised her right hand. "I swear on my father's grave." Glitter leaned over and whispered in her ear. Anne Marie burst out laughing. "Herod Caesar Romero? You're making that up, right?" Glitter Man looked horrified and hurt. "Oops, Herod," she said, "I mean Glitter, I'm sorry. I swear I'll never bring it up again."

"Shall we change the subject, please?" Lamont looked at his watch. It's ten o'clock. Does your husband know where you are?"

Anne Marie shook her head. "What Joseph don't know won't hurt him."

Jeanette shook her head. "Batten down the hatches," she muttered, "we are sailing into choppy water here."

"It was a joke," Lamont said.

"Joseph is out of town," Anne Marie explained. "This weekend he is racing his Bultaco and Ducati in the dirt bike races upstate in Fishkill."

"Who are Bultaco and Ducati?" Glitter Man asked. "Sounds like a news team."

"They're motorcycles." Jeanette laughed.

"So why didn't you go with him?" Lamont asked. "Don't you like motorcycle races?"

"Oh, no, I love them, but Joseph won't let me go. He says it would embarrass him, and he doesn't like me to be around his friends. He says I inhibit him. Joseph would have a fit if he knew I came here today without his permission. He says a wife's place is in the home, and I agree with him. I think the man should make the rules."

"So he makes the rules, and you break them? Do you get to make any rules in this relationship? What if he calls?"

"I left the phone off the hook. I won't get in trouble if he thinks I'm on the phone."

Lamont looked concerned. "Are you serious? You really had to sneak out?"

She nodded.

"I can't believe this!" Lamont exclaimed. "So your husband can go away for a weekend with bikers in the woods doing God knows what, and you can't leave the house? You live with a man you have to lie to? And you put up with that?"

"But it's okay, Lamont," Anne Marie said defensively. "I agree with Joseph. You have to be a snoopy for your man. I'm happy being a house mouse. So there."

"A what?" Lamont looked like he might explode.

"Have you been to the top of the new World Trade Center?" Jeanette attempted to change the subject.

"That abomination," Glitter said disgustedly. "$750 million dollars for two ugly buildings that look like saltine boxes. The World Trade Center has nothing on the Empire State Building, or the Chrysler

Building. Those buildings have character. I mean, if you insist on constructing the most gigantic phallic symbols in the world, at least give them good heads."

"Oh God," Lamont groaned. "Don't get him going on the World Trade Center. Talk about something else. Has anyone seen any good movies lately?"

"Joseph let me go to see '*The Way We Were*' with my girlfriend, Linda," Anne Marie replied.

Glitter sighed. "Oh, Streisand is so fabulous. I love her. You know, I saw her on stage in 'Funny Girl.'"

Lamont looked relieved. "*Memories*," he sang, "*light the corners of my groin*." He refilled everyone's sake cups.

"You sound more like her than she does." Jeanette giggled.

"You should hear his rendition of '*Don't Rain on My Parade*'," Glitter said dryly.

Lamont stuck out his tongue. "You only love me because I remind you of her."

"It's your nose, baby, and the way you cross your eyes when you hit a high note."

Oblivious to their playful banter, Anne Marie continued, "I thought '*The Way We Were*' was so romantic. Who wouldn't fall in love with Robert Redford?"

"Who indeed?" Glitter agreed.

"Oh, I know what you mean," Lamont sighed.

"Did anybody ever tell you, you kinda look like him?" Anne Marie asked Lamont. She held out her cup for a refill.

Lamont's face glowed. He proposed another toast. "To Bob and Babs."

"I'll drink to that," Glitter Man said. "Which one do you want to be tonight?"

"I thought it was a stupid movie," Jeanette observed.

"Well, snoopy for your man, whatever that means," Glitter said, "since this is your big night out, I think we should make it a classic."

"How intriguing. What did you have in mind?" Lamont leaned across the table.

"I'm thinking 42nd Street. I'm thinking Hubert's Flea Circus."

Jeanette shuddered. "Oh no."

"Oh yes!" Lamont cried, clapping his hands together. "Marvelous! An adventure!"

"What's Hubert's Flea Circus?" Anne Marie's eyes were wide.

"An education," Lamont replied.

*   *   *

A large mullioned window framed the cushioned window seat where the angel Mario sat. He leaned against the sill with his legs stretched out comfortably in front of him. The angel looked out at a mist-covered moor that bordered on a sparkling sea. A fragrant breeze dancing through the open window ruffled his rosy wings. The child Isabelle snuggled on his lap. She rested her curly head on the angel's shoulder as she gazed dreamily at the swirling fog and the pounding tide. The angel sang softly.

"*We will know…life has nothing sweeter than its springtime…*"

"Can we really see them if we want to?" Isabelle asked.

"*Golden days…When we're young…*" he warbled.

"Please, Mario. I want to see them."

"*Golden days…*"

A peach colored cloud picked up the last three notes of Mario's song. It swept them out the window toward the sea. The notes cut through the clouds like bright arrows. The arrows became a graceful golden sea gull that soared above the waves.

Isabelle clapped her hands. "I love it when you do that!" She giggled. "Now let me see them, please, Mario." She tugged on his wing.

The angel pointed out the window. "Gaze until you see the waves breaking through the mist. Can you see that?"

The fog began to swirl and dissolve until an oval frame of swirling clouds surrounded a clear space.

"I don't see anything," Isabelle complained.

"Focus on what you want to see. That is all you have to do. Later I will show you how to create your own reality by using the same principle."

"All right. I want to see the mother and father I have chosen," the child said wistfully.

"Look again," Mario whispered. He waved his hand toward the sea.

The child concentrated her gaze intently. Vague shapes appeared in the water like a movie projected onto the surface of the sea.

Isabelle saw a small fountain in a room ringing with laughter. It looked like a restaurant. The laughter came from the four people who were finishing their meal. They were obviously enjoying each other's company.

"Your mother is having dinner with some of her teachers," Mario said.

"There she is!" Isabelle cried, pointing excitedly to Jeanette. "I can see her! Oh, Mario, isn't she beautiful? I love my mother already."

"Yes, she is lovely, but you mean if she becomes your mother," he gently chided. "Remember, destiny is not carved in stone, dear Isabelle. Free will is involved. Jeanette Lightly Fortune is the strong, spiritual woman you need for your soul's nourishment and support, but she may not choose to have you. Right now she is very confused about a lot of things. Her fear is very strong."

"I think my grandfather will not fail me," Isabelle said confidently.

Mario sighed. "Even the prophets with all their wisdom and psychic abilities could not predict what will truly be. We shall know in the fullness of time."

"Oh, I hope he will not fail, Angel. It is such an important life. I was reading the Great Book of Possibilities in the Hall of Akasha, and do you know that if I get this lifetime as Isabelle Fortune I may have the opportunity to contribute in a vital way to putting an end to war?"

The angel laughed with a sound like wind chimes.

"The Book said that by the time I become President, there is a very good chance that the consciousness of the world's people may have evolved enough to fulfill some of the old prophesies. So true brother-hood and beating weapons into plow shares and the lion lying down with the lamb could really happen. And I could have a part in manifest-ing that peace."

"I know." Mario smiled. "I read the book."

"Did you read the part about the treaties and the powerful Alliance of All Nations? I shall initiate the Alliance in the name of the world's children when I become the first woman President."

"Well it certainly sounds good to me. Isabelle, listen to me. You must understand that even if your window closes on this particular path, there are many others you can choose from. You must understand that you con-trol your own destiny. There is a potential for greatness in every person born on earth. There are unlimited ways to express one's greatness. There are countless unique opportunities to give the gifts you have to share. This is true no matter what personality you choose for your incarnation."

"May I see him now?" she pleaded. "Please may I see my father?"

Mario sighed. He waved his hand, and ripples passed across the sea. When the water calmed, the child saw Christopher Fortune.

"Doesn't he look wonderful?"

"He is wonderful," Mario agreed. "Fortune is an extraordinary man."

"Tell me what he does again?"

"Christopher teaches Political Science and History at Bloomfield High School. He's a simple man, a modern philosopher, and a talented artist. As a teacher, he has the gift of infusing his students with a passion to learn more, to never stop questioning. That is his gift."

"He is thinking about her, isn't he?"

The angel nodded. "You have tuned into him very well. You are an old soul, aren't you?"

"That is what I hear." Isabelle laughed. "Is she thinking about him?"

"Much of the time, although she will never admit it."

"What is that place he is sitting in? What is that he's eating?" Isabelle leaned out the window so she could see more clearly. "It looks like…Mario? Is he where I think?"

The angel nodded. "Chris and Jeanette may have missed each other in the museum, but who said two coincidences cannot happen in one day?"

Isabelle hugged Mario. She jumped up and down on his lap. "It could happen! It could really happen!"

"There are no guarantees," Mario cautioned.

Isabelle leaned back out the window. "I want them so much for my parents. I know what you say is true, Angel, but oh, I hope I get this path. If I miss it, another century will pass before the opportunity comes again."

✳   ✳   ✳

The four friends emerged from the tatami room into the main restaurant. Lights made out of blowfish that looked like aquatic porcupines hung from the ceiling. Candles flickered on all the tables. Delicious aromas permeated the room. The same sweet koto music drifted through the air.

Jeanette could not resist looking over at the small booth in the corner where Chris had proposed to her. She was taken aback to see Chris sitting there alone. He was reading a book and nursing a cup of green tea. A plate of half-eaten sushi sat on the table. Jeanette blinked, certain she was imagining things. Christopher Fortune looked up and saw her. His face registered the same surprise she felt.

Before she realized what she was doing, Jeanette had crossed the room to his table. She reached out for his hand. He rose to greet her, his copy of Aldous Huxley's "*Island*" falling to the floor. They both stooped to pick it up. He had half the book in his hand. She held the other half. Their eyes locked, and they smiled at one another.

"I see you're reading one of my favorite books," Jeanette said.

✳   ✳   ✳

The angel saw the sparks ignite. He danced around the room with the child in his arms. His feet never touched the floor. His joy was contagious. "*Gaudiamus igitur,*" Mario sang.

"*Juven estum sumus.*" Isabelle Fortune joined in.

"Let us rejoice while we are young," they sang.

CHAPTER THIRTEEN

Saturday, October 7, 1973

Lincoln Lightly rubbed his palms together gleefully as he and the ghost of his grandfather followed Jeanette and her friends down Broadway. "I've got to hand it to you, Gockie. Knocking Chris' book off the table in the restaurant was a stroke of pure genius."

"It worked, didn't it?"

"Yes." Lincoln smiled. "It worked like a charm. No one was more pleased than I when Lamont convinced Chris to join them."

"Except maybe your daughter," Joseph Stoeckel teased.

"Be serious, Gockie. The angel warned me that I must not interfere in trying to bring Jeanette and Chris back together."

"And you did not interfere," Gockie chuckled, "I did." He pointed his cane toward the people they were following. "Your daughter really loves this man, doesn't she?"

Lincoln nodded as he watched Jeanette and Chris steal glances at one another. The ghost could read their thoughts. He knew how much they longed to reach out to one other, and how stubbornly Jeanette blocked that possibility. But they seemed comfortable talking and laughing within the safe cocoon of the group, like the old friends they had always been.

"Look how beautifully their auras blend," Gockie observed.

Lincoln was new at seeing auras, but the way Jeanette's and Chris' danced with one another lit up Times Square brighter than the neon lights for which the street was famous.

"Your daughter and her husband are powerful people," Gockie remarked. "Jeanette does you proud. She is so lovely. She has my Annie's beautiful green eyes, and your mother's careless grace."

"Jeanette is your descendent, too." Lincoln slapped his grandfather on the back. "She has good genes."

Gockie stopped in the middle of the street. He leaned on his cane and looked around "What happened to Times Square? Where are Childs, and Toffenettis? Where are the Astor Hotel and Jack Dempsey's? And I don't see the Paramount Theater."

"Oh, there have been a lot of changes since the last time you saw New York," Lincoln replied. "They closed your favorite restaurants long ago. The Paramount and the Astor Hotel have been gone for over thirty years."

"Tell me they didn't ruin the theaters," Gockie sighed.

"Oh, no, the Broadway stage is still thriving." Lincoln pointed down the street toward the shining lights of the theaters. The audiences were arriving, some in limousines and furs. "Do you remember when you took me to see my first Broadway show?"

"Yes I do. It was 'Roberta'," Gockie recalled, "with that young British actor, Robert Hope. Whatever happened to him?"

"He did quite well for himself," Lincoln replied.

Gockie continued, "I remember taking the train and the Hoboken ferry into the city every weekend when I lived with you and your mother. How you and Billy loved to tag along."

"Those weekends have always been some of my fondest memories, Gockie. Remember how you taught us to gargoyle hunt, and Bill got so good at it he could spot a rooftop gargoyle from blocks away? And I always loved it when you took us to the Fulton Fish Market."

"What a stink," Gockie said.

"Oh, but New York is always full of delicious, exotic smells too. You can eat your way around the world in this city."

Gockie stroked his beard. He tipped his hat to a pale ghost who was hurrying into the glistening Shubert Theater. She was dressed in a white, shroud-like dress, a Saturday night frock from the 1930's. Her transparent silver bobbed hair glistened in the lights of the Great White Way. She raised a bony arm and waved to them.

"Someone you knew?" Lincoln asked.

Gockie shrugged. "I knew many like her, son. The world is full of beautiful women, but I only loved one. I lived many years missing my Annie."

Lincoln put his arm around his grandfather's shoulder. "I know. I felt the same way about Lizzy." They walked silently toward 42nd Street.

"When I had my first stroke, and I could not come into the city anymore, it almost broke my heart," Gockie sighed. "Oh, but I was left with such memories."

"I always wondered what you were thinking," Lincoln said softly, "when you could no longer tell me. I watched you gaze out the window for hours, and I wondered where your mind was taking you."

"Many of those times, son, my mind was bringing me back here, back to Vaudeville, and Broadway shows, and pretty ladies on my uniformed arm. I was thinking about the amazing Hippodrome Theater down on 14th Street, the Ziegfeld Follies, and Minsky's Burlesque. On rainy days, my mind took me back to Luchows, with the trains from Grand Central Station thundering by outside the restaurant. On just such a day I looked up from my table by the window into my future wife's amazing eyes. She was so beautiful, I stammered when I gave her my order."

*　　　　　　　*　　　　　　　*

The gaudy theaters that lined both sides of 42nd Street in 1973 no longer ran current films. Their marquees displayed titles like "*Sinners in White*", "*Deep Throat*", and "*Wild Beavers*". Jeanette was certain the latter was probably not an Alaskan documentary.

A soapbox preacher standing on an old wooden Alderney Dairy milk box had gathered a fair-sized congregation under the old Ben Franklin clock on the corner of 42nd Street and Eighth Avenue. A man without legs, on a wheeled board, propelled himself along the sidewalk with his padded knuckles. He panhandled the crowd while the preacher thundered a dire warning that the end of the world was at hand.

"Except for all the electric lights and neon, this could be Ancient Rome," Chris observed, "around the fall of the Empire."

"That's weird," Anne Marie said.

Lamont replied, "Chris sees everything through the eyes of history." Lamont and Chris had been friends since the sixth grade. Lamont swore he had turned gay because of the regular beatings he had received at the hands of Sister Mary Alexandrine. While it was true, Chris conceded, that the nun had a penchant for breaking long wooden blackboard pointers over the backs of young boys, he hardly thought that she caused Lamont's homosexuality. They had been good-naturedly debating the point for years.

The group stopped for a moment to listen to the soapbox preacher. He was quite a showman. They listened as he exhorted his audience to repent, for they were all sinners doomed to eternal damnation.

"So, since this reminds you so much of Rome, Chris, do you think the American Empire is falling?" Glitter Man asked.

"I'm not sure I would go that far, but you can draw your own conclusions. Look at the soapbox prophet. All he needs is a toga. We could be standing in the Roman Forum." Chris pointed across the street. "Look at how our society's decadence is reflected in the trashy movies, shops, and peep shows on this street."

"Yeah, isn't it great?" Lamont laughed. "All we need is to go to the Coliseum and watch the lions eat some Christians. Now that I think of it, gladiators are playing our version of the Coliseum tomorrow, although we call them football players now."

"Did you see where O.J. Simpson rushed more than two thousand yards this season?" Anne Marie said.

"So you compare football players to gladiators?" Jeanette asked.

Lamont nodded. "Of course. I just love their buns in those tight uniforms," he sighed.

Glitter Man groaned.

"Oh, tell me you don't look," Lamont protested. "So, Professor, tell me more. I find t his Ancient Rome analogy interesting."

Chris laughed. "All I'm saying is that Rome's fascination with decadence contributed to its ultimate decline. The Empire's downfall finally came from within. It follows then, that if decadence is one of the symptoms of a dying culture, perhaps we need to take a closer look at our own society. Here, in the microcosm of the city, decay is pretty obvious. 42nd Street wasn't like this when we were kids."

"That's true," Jeanette said. "My father used to take me to see Roy Rogers and Abbot and Costello movies in that theater across the street. They only play smut there now. You're right, it has become decadent."

"Well, personally I'm all for decadence." Lamont laughed. "I think it's time we all lighten up. Thank God it isn't the '*Father Knows Best*' fifties anymore. The sixties finally gave us permission to be depraved, which is one of our constitutional rights, isn't it? Life, liberty and the pursuit of pornography?"

"I do agree that the sixties had to happen," Chris observed. "The turbulence of that decade brought a lot of things out in the open, like lancing a wound so the infection can rise to the surface and ultimately be healed. People say we lost our innocence, but I think we simply opened our closets so the skeletons could come out into the open."

"Yes, well more than skeletons came out of my closet," Lamont teased. "So you think our society has become a pus hole?"

Glitter looked up at the movie title on the marquee they were walking under. "Make that pussy hole," he quipped, "starring Harry Reams and Linda Lovelace."

        ⋆   ⋆   ⋆

"Where are the double-decker buses? Where are the trolleys?"

"There has not been a double-decker bus or trolley in New York since the early fifties, Gockie."

"The early fifties," the old ghost said dreamily. "I was born in the early fifties, in 1851." Gockie looked up at the towering skyscrapers that surrounded them. "What a difference a hundred years makes. My family came to this country in 1856, in steerage. We crossed the Atlantic from France during the great European immigration. It was before Ellis Island. Immigrants were funneled through Castle Garden down by the Battery, the old music hall where Jenny Lind, 'The Swedish Nightingale', had sung. Even then New York had a heartbeat, and an energy that was contagious. We were welcome, for we had come to help build the country.

"I thought this was the most exciting city I had ever seen, with its cobblestone streets full of horse drawn carriages. New York teemed and buzzed with life. Its high buildings awed us. Some of those same buildings still stand, but now they are dwarfed by skyscrapers and concrete canyons."

"It must have been something in those days," Lincoln said.

His grandfather nodded. "We sailed in on a wave of hope, my beautiful gypsy mother, my proud father, my older brothers, my baby sister, and me, all of five years old. This is where my family first set foot on American soil. We had never seen so many nationalities in one place. We came in with Italians, who dug the ditches and later built the subways. And with the Irish fleeing the famines, and the Germans. We met Jewish stone carvers, who came to build and carve their artistry and their philosophy into America.

"My father stood us all on the dock, and we watched the sun rise over our new world. 'Remember this sunrise,' my father told us, 'for this day dawns on a man who has been blessed to be given his dream.' Yes," Gockie sighed, "New York was something back then, when men believed in dreams that could come true."

"I think it still is something," Lincoln agreed. "It is still a city of excess, still a melting pot for all the world's people and cultures. New York may be constantly changing, but that is part of what makes it so wonderful. And if you listen closely, you can still hear the heartbeat."

The ghosts followed along as the group crossed to the other side of the street, where a blind street musician stood, wailing a plaintive song on his harmonica. An old beat up hat with a few coins inside sat on the sidewalk in front of him. His tired looking guide dog guarded both man and hat. Jeanette dropped some change into the old fedora.

"Why do you give beggars money?" Anne Marie complained. "Let them go out and get jobs like the rest of us. That guy's probably as blind as I am. Joseph says you should never give beggars money."

"Yeah, 'let them eat cake'," Jeanette retorted. She was tired and feeling the effects of too much hot sake. "Oh, well if Joseph says so," she snapped, "then wait here and I'll go back and get my thirty-five cents. You didn't used to be like this, Anne Marie. What happened to you? Do you ever have a thought of your own anymore, or has your husband taken over your mind?"

"Hey, I want for nothing because my husband works for a living. Why can't that faker?"

"They're not all fakers, Anne Marie. And anyway, even if he is faking, that's on his soul, not mine."

"Oh, excuse me, Saint Jeanette. I bet he's watching us behind those sunglasses right now. Watch." Anne Marie walked up to the beggar, pulled up her shirt, and flashed her bare breasts. There was no reaction from the beggar; however, everyone else in the immediate vicinity stared at her in wide-eyed disbelief.

"Put those things away," Glitter Man complained. "Talk about decadence."

"Beggars are just lazy, and some of them are schizophreniacs," Anne Marie said.

"Just ignore her," Chris sighed. "Let's move on."

They stopped in front of a shop between two theaters. Its windows displayed some of the bizarre novelty items commonly found on the streets of New York. A sun-bleached sign proclaiming "Giant Close Out Sale" had stood in the window for years. Next to it was a group of multi-colored skulls with blinking red lights for eyes, surrounded by assorted knives and whips. "Genuine" Prussian helmets hung in the window next to "genuine" Pennsylvania Dutch tablecloths. Pictures of Jesus, whose eyes followed you everywhere, were propped up next to fake vomit, "genuine" shrunken heads, and trick dog droppings. The store also carried "genuine" oriental carpets depicting cigar-smoking dogs playing poker and shooting pool. A small worn sign with a red arrow pointing inside the store read *"Hubert's Flea Circus. The Smallest Show on Earth."*

CHAPTER FOURTEEN

Saturday, October 7, 1973

Christopher Fortune looked at the sign for the "Smallest Show on Earth." He leaned over and whispered to Jeanette, "Have you been here before?"

"Yes." She smiled at the horrified look on her husband's face. "I know it's twisted, but aside from the fact that it's an old time freak show which exploits unfortunate people, it is harmless, Chris. The sad thing is this is the only way they can make a living."

They followed Lamont and Glitter inside the store, past the novelty counter and the old penny arcade with its outdated pinball machines and curtained "flicker" booth. In the far right corner of the store, a dark enclosed stairway led down to the flea circus.

"Down there? The flea circus is in the cellar?" Chris looked a little uneasy.

"To paraphrase Auntie Mame," Lamont said, "'Life is a banquet', and I for one refuse to starve to death. Just think of this as an opportunity to observe twentieth century American decadence first hand, Chris."

Jeanette took Chris' hand, pretending she did not feel the electricity pulse through her body when they touched. She avoided his bemused expression. She didn't trust herself to look into his eyes. "Perhaps it is symptomatic of our dying civilization that the freaks have moved out of the open and into the cellars," she teased. "You want to see decadence? Ancient Rome had nothing on this." She pointed to Lamont and Glitter Man. "Let the masters lead the way."

A woman who looked like an aging vampire in a tight black mini skirt sat at the ticket stand filing her blood-red nails. Her fishnet stocking-clad legs were crossed. She wore bright orange shoes with four-inch stiletto heels. "Twenty five cents," she whined. She batted her fake eyelashes and popped her gum. She tore their tickets in half, gave them the stubs, and pointed down the stairs. "Well? Waddaya waitin' for? Show starts in two minutes."

The two ghosts followed the group down the damp stairway, which smelled like stale urine. They entered a dark rectangular room. There were four stages, two on each side of the tented flea circus itself. Admission to see the fleas under the miniature big top was an extra quarter. The vampire who had taken their tickets emerged from behind tattered red and white striped curtains. "That'll be another twenty five cents," she said, popping a big pink bubble. "Each."

They were ushered into the small enclosure, which contained a low white table covered with a pane of magnifying glass. A scratchy recording of the soundtrack from "*Ben Hur*" played in the background.

"Speaking of ancient Rome," Glitter laughed.

"I was thinking more along the lines of an LSD flashback," Lamont whispered.

The rest of the audience, if you did not count the assorted ghosts, including Lincoln and Gockie, consisted of three young sailors in uniform, and two young Puerto Rican couples on a double date. In the back corner sat a hippie with long unkempt hair. He had the disoriented look of the drugged. The Latino couples made out noisily while they waited for the show to begin.

A short odorous man with a toothless grin entered the tent. He placed three matchboxes on the edge of the table. He opened the matchboxes and freed half a dozen hopping fleas. The sweaty ringmaster manipulated tiny brass harnesses and chariots with jeweler's tools. Using minuscule tweezers, he harnessed the fleas to the chariots and placed them in the center of the table under the magnifier. The audience watched the tiny chariots move around every time the fleas jumped.

"Shouldn't we place bets or something?" Lamont laughed. "I'll put my money on Messala."

Anne Marie looked confused. "Who?"

"You know, Messala? Stephen Boyd? Charlton Heston? The chariot race? '*Ben Hur?*'"

The music swelled into a trumpeting fanfare.

"Loved Ben," Glitter Man remarked, "hated Hur."

Lincoln nudged his grandfather's shoulder. He pointed to Jeanette and Chris, whose hand still rested casually in hers. Their auras had blended into a warm, sensual deep rose color. "Look how she leans toward the table, pretending she's watching the fleas," Lincoln whispered.

Gockie nodded. "And see how Chris leans back and fills his eyes with her."

"It won't be long now," Lincoln predicted.

After a few minutes, the toothless man used the tweezers to put everything back into the matchboxes. He bowed deeply while the audience applauded.

"What?" Anne Marie said. "No trapeze? No clowns?"

The two couples were still making out. They had missed the show.

"Take it home," Glitter said dryly.

"Oh, wow," the hippie slurred.

The group left the flea circus tent to watch the main show. The left hand stage lit up. Out stepped the vampire woman, dressed like a belly dancer. A transparent veil covered her mouth. A sign over the stage proclaimed that she was "Scheherazade, Princess of Bagdad."

"I'll say she's a bag, Dad," one of the sailors joked.

"I escaped from the harem of the evil Bagwan Ben Mumtaz," she announced solemnly, popping her gum.

"Does the Shah of Iran know?" one of the sailors heckled, provoking a round of laughter.

The Princess of Bagdad ignored him. "Now I must dance and remain in hiding until the day when my father's throne is once again freed from the infidel." She placed a brass bowl on the stage in front of her. "Alms," she begged, "alms for the love of Allah, and to feed the Royal Python of Derriobar."

"She saw that movie too," Lamont remarked.

Glitter Man nodded. "Douglas Fairbanks Junior and Maureen O'Hara. Cool flick."

The cud chewing belly dancer opened a basket from which she removed an eight-foot python, which she wrapped around her neck.

"Unbelievable," Glitter gasped.

"Oh wow," the hippie said. "Groovy snake, man."

The Puerto Rican girls squealed. "Ay Dios mio!" one of them screamed. She buried her face in her boyfriend's shoulder.

"Right on, Mama," one of the sailors cheered.

Scheherazade had removed her shoes, revealing large holes in the toes of her fish net stockings. Her costume did nothing to hide a mean looking purple scar that ran straight down from her exposed navel. She began an undulating dance, encouraging the snake to crawl over her pendulous breasts. An old recording of "*The Sheik of Araby*" scratched away in the background. The snake looked like it had seen better days. No amount of coaxing seemed to motivate it to do anything remotely python-like.

"Only twenty five cents," she whined, "and I will drape the Royal Python of Derriobar around you." She held the head of the snake toward the audience. The Princess popped her gum.

"The snake looks stoned," Anne Marie said.

The hippie piped up, "What's he on, man? Can I get some?"

One of the sailors tossed his quarter into the bowl. The belly dancer bent over, thrusting her wrinkled cleavage in the sailor's nose, and nearly suffocating him. She placed the snake around his neck. The sailor's buddies cheered and whistled. The reptile hung limp.

"Is it dead?" one of the boyfriends asked.

"I don't think so," Chris said, "just bored. And probably overfed." He pointed to the large lump three quarters of the way down toward the tail. "I imagine there is no shortage of rats in this building to keep the Royal Python of Derriobar full."

Scheherazade took her bows, and the curtain closed.

The next stage lit up. It was the half-man-half-woman's turn to be in the spotlight. Its face looked like it had been split with an axe, reminiscent of the Frankenstein monster. A bluish shadow suggested a third eye just above the bridge of the nose. One side of its hair was grown long, and died blonde with a permanent wave. The other side of its head had a man's crew cut.

Like the snake lady, the hermaphrodite placed a jar for tips on the edge of the stage before telling its sad story. Being two-faced from the womb had labeled him/her a freak, a reject of society, and this was his/her only way to make a living.

Then he began to dance with her, swirling the hot pink chiffon dress on her woman-side, slapping the tuxedoed knee on his male side. The old record player behind the curtain scratched through a record of Judy Garland singing, "*They're writing songs of love, but not for me.*"

The third stage in Hubert's Flea Circus belonged to Zombie the Jungle Creep. Someone behind the curtain changed the record, and while Screaming Jay Hawkins wailed "*I'll Put a Spell on You,*" a black man wearing only a leopard skin loincloth jumped onto the stage. Zombie waved a spear in one hand and a human skull in the other. Bones pierced his nose and hung from his ears. His hair was a wild Afro, complete with pigeon feathers. His body was oiled, painted with garish symbols, and covered with baby powder.

Zombie danced wildly around the stage. He shook his ankle bells in time with Screaming Jay Hawkins, all the time screeching like a lunatic.

Zombie the Jungle Creep was the only performer in Hubert's who did not beg for money. He didn't have to. The crowd loved him. They whistled, clapped, screamed, and threw change onto the stage.

Zombie pulled up a ladder-like rack with saws set in it instead of rungs, their teeth facing up. He climbed on each saw in turn, stamping on the jagged teeth, holding up his feet to show they weren't cut. "Zombie got de world's hardest feets!" he shrieked. The audience cheered and threw more change onto the stage.

For his finale, Zombie swallowed a lit cigarette, went into convulsions, and brought it back up, still lit, all the time rolling his eyes crazily and screeching. His performance done, the Jungle Creep took his bows.

The last stage lit up, revealing the man with the "little handsies." The dwarf had no arms, just hands protruding from his shoulders. He related the heart-rending story of his deformed birth and childhood. Then he shuffled to the edge of the stage, bent over and set his tip bowl down with his teeth. The dwarf proceeded to untie and remove his shoes with his teeth. He used a combination of toes and teeth to light and smoke a cigarette, all the while singing "these are my little handsies," and waving his strange hands that were where armpits should be.

Anne Marie's mouth gaped open. The dwarf got down from his stool and shuffled to the edge of the stage. "What's the matter?" he shouted at her. "Don't you think I'm funny?"

Anne Marie tried to hide behind Lamont. "Laugh at me, Goddammit!" the dwarf shouted. He danced around the stage singing "these are my little handsies...handsies...handsies..."

Anne Marie screamed and ran up the stairs.

"Well, there are some things that have not changed in over a hundred years," Gockie observed. "I saw a show just like this at Coney Island around the turn of the century." He and Lincoln watched the people and the other ghosts drift out of the flea circus.

"Marone! That was sick!" Anne Marie exclaimed, when the others caught up with her outside on 42nd Street. Lamont and Glitter Man doubled over, laughing hysterically. Anne Marie punched them both.

"Is this your idea of some bizarre kind of initiation for Anne Marie?" Chris asked.

Anne Marie was waving her arms and cursing in Italian.

"Yeah," Lamont choked. "Now she's come of age. No true American should die without seeing Hubert's Flea Circus."

"You guys are really twisted," Jeanette said sardonically.

"Marone! That guy singing 'these are my little handsies,'" Anne Marie blustered. "That's just sick! I'm so depressed! Ba Fongool!"

"Remind you of Ancient Rome?" Lamont said.

Chris laughed. "Maybe a little too much," he agreed.

"Truth, Contessa," Glitter demanded, "you were fascinated, weren't you?"

Anne Marie blushed.

"I knew it. You loved it," he howled.

She put her thumb behind her two front teeth and snapped it forward at him. "Okay, I admit it." She giggled as she gripped Jeanette's arm, "Oh my God, swear on your mother's grave you won't tell Joseph I went to Hubert's Flea Circus. Marone! If he knew I went here with you preverts, he would kill me!"

"We're not 'preverts', we're perverts," Lamont corrected.

"That's what I said, prevert. So there."

Jeanette thought, "Anne Marie thinks Lamont and Glitter are perverts? How ironic." She remembered the weekend she had spent at Anne Marie's house last summer. She had stepped out of the shower to dry herself off. She was standing naked at the sink brushing her teeth when she saw his reflection in the mirror. Joseph Mustaschio was peeking in the window. He must have been there, watching, the whole time. Jeanette had pulled the towel around her with a startled cry. Joseph had ducked out of sight.

Jeanette was mortified, but her cousin had Joseph on such a pedestal, that she had never told anyone. After that, Jeanette was extremely uncomfortable around Anne Marie's husband. At family functions he seemed to leer openly at her. She avoided him.

"I think we've had enough adventure for one day," Jeanette said. "I'm going home now."

CHAPTER FIFTEEN

Saturday, October 7, 1973

"What do you mean the last bus is gone?" Lamont thought that arguing with the robotic ticket agent was going to get him somewhere. "When did they change the schedule?"

"What's the problem?" Anne Marie asked.

Glitter fidgeted nervously. "We missed the last bus back to Bloomfield. There won't be another one until morning."

"Well, what are we going to do? We can't stay here!" She looked around at the beggars and panhandlers that filled Port Authority Bus Terminal. It was after midnight. Creatures that hardly looked human were crawling from the subways and sewers to prey on the provincials who were stupid enough to be in the bus station at this hour because they missed the last bus home.

"Are any buses still running to Newark?" Glitter asked.

Lamont wrinkled his nose. "Oh, yeah, let's go to the only place more dangerous than here. Anyway, the last bus to Newark is gone, too. I'm afraid we're stranded."

"Well, we certainly can't spend the night here," Chris said. "Come on, I'll get us a cab."

"Are you crazy?" Lamont protested. "Do you know how much it costs to take a taxi from the City to New Jersey?"

Glitter spoke up. "Wait a minute, I have some friends in the East Village. We can crash at their pad tonight and head home in the morning."

"Greenwich Village?" Anne Marie looked uncomfortable. "Isn't that where they found Uncle Danny's body?"

Jeanette nodded. "Yes, Anne Marie." She turned to Glitter. "You have friends you can just drop in on in the middle of the night?"

"Oh, really, it won't be a problem for Fagatha and Fathom at all. It isn't the middle of the night for them. The commune won't be asleep. Saturday is party night. So who's game?" Glitter Man took Anne Marie's hand and led her toward the Eighth Avenue subway station.

Chris leaned against the black iron grating at the top of the subway stairs. "Look, guys, I'm not comfortable with this idea. I'm just gonna grab a cab and head back home."

"Oh, come on, Chris," Lamont urged. "The night is young."

"I'm pretty tired. I think I'll pass," Chris insisted.

"Well, you do what you want," Lamont said. "I'm not tired. I'm heading for Fagatha's."

"Fagatha?" Anne Marie said, "You know somebody named Fagatha? Is he gay?"

Glitter laughed. "What was your first clue, Contessa?"

"Does he know you call him that?"

"He calls himself that."

Jeanette yawned. "I'm really tired, too. I want to sleep in my own bed. I would really rather go home."

Chris put his arm around his wife's shoulder. It was a gesture that seemed as natural as breathing. With some amusement, the two ghosts who were still following the group watched Jeanette and Chris struggle to appear cool and casual as they attempted to ignore the sparks of their chemistry.

"Would you care to share my cab?" Chris offered.

Jeanette nodded gratefully. "This has been fun, but I think I really have had enough adventure for one day. Thank you. I will share your cab. But only if you let me chip in."

"We can work that out later." Chris turned to Anne Marie. "Are you coming with us?"

Anne Marie looked back and forth from Jeanette and Chris to Lamont and Glitter Man. "Well, I don't know," she hesitated. "If Joseph ever found out…"

Lamont poked her in the ribs and whispered, "Go with us. Let Jeanette and Chris be alone."

Anne Marie's eyes shone at the idea of conspiracy. "Well, in the matter of fact, what Joseph don't know won't hurt him, right? He won't be home till tomorrow afternoon anyway. I just have to get there before him."

"We'll leave first thing in the morning," Glitter promised, "Scouts honor."

"Okay. I'm going with you," Anne Marie announced.

"Are you sure it's safe?" Chris looked anxious.

"Is the Pope Italian?" Lamont retorted. "Anne Marie is safe with us. Glitter Man happens to be a third degree black belt. Don't' worry, we'll stay at Fagatha's until the monsters go back in their underground caverns."

Glitter straightened to his full six and a half foot height and executed a couple of karate chops in the air.

"Okay," Chris laughed. "You're sure I can't convince you to come with us?"

"Nope. So we'll see you at Eddie Lightly's wedding next week?"

"Right. See you at the wedding."

*　　　　　*　　　　　*

Jeanette felt the effects of the sake and the long day. She was sleepy and fuzzy headed. All she could think of were her warm bed, clean sheets, and a big glass of fresh squeezed orange juice in the morning. "Goodnight," she mumbled.

Lamont winked. "Ciao, Baby Cakes."

Jeanette watched Lamont, Glitter Man, and Anne Marie descend into the labyrinth of the New York City subways. Chris took her hand. It felt comfortable and familiar. He hailed a cab.

"Where to, Bud?" the gum-chewing cabby asked.

"Can you take us to New Jersey?"

"Where in Joisy you headed?"

"Bloomfield and Montclair."

"Cost you double fare, Bud."

"Fine." Chris opened the taxi door. They climbed into the back seat. "Let's go."

"Yeah, sure. I'm on duty all night," the cabby shrugged. "Why not?"

The driver skidded away from the curb. Eighth Avenue was a two-lane street that even this late at night was congested with four lanes of cars. New York drivers made their own rules, as well as their own lanes. The cabby weaved through the honking, exhaust-fume filled mess. He leaned heavily on his horn as he gestured wildly out the window, shouting epithets at the other cars and hapless pedestrians. The cab careened toward the entrance to the Lincoln Tunnel.

"Strange weather we're havin' ain't it, Bud?" The cabby lit a cigarette and offered one to Chris, who declined. "So waddaya think of this Watergate fiasco? Think they'll impeach Nixon?"

Soon the yellow tiles of the Lincoln Tunnel sped past them, casting a hypnotic spell on Jeanette. She rested her head on Chris' shoulder. He casually put his arm around her. It seemed so natural. How long, she wondered, had it been since she had felt this relaxed?

"Honeymooners?" the cabby guessed.

"Kiss her," a ghostly voice whispered.

"No," Chris replied softly.

Jeanette heard their far-away voices in the drowsy world between sleeping and waking. The cabby carried on a conversation with Chris that swam like music inside her head. Jeanette dreamily thought she had all the time in the world to divorce Chris. It would not hurt to be friends for this one night.

She was sorry that she had said such vicious, cutting things to him the past few months. She had said things to Chris that he did not deserve. She would not have blamed him if he never spoke to her again. Yet he continued to be there for her. When her father died, she had welcomed the sanctuary of Chris' protective concern. She knew that he had loved Lincoln, too. Regardless of what happened between them, Chris had become a part of the family. Jeanette was grateful for Chris' generosity of spirit, but she had not told him that.

In her shock and grief, Jeanette had set aside the pain of what happened to the baby, the pain that was breaking them up. What had been damaged between them could never be mended because it was all her fault. But none of that seemed to matter tonight. Somewhere in the middle of the Lincoln Tunnel, Jeanette Lightly Fortune fell asleep with her head on her husband's shoulder.

           *   *   *

"Oh, wow! Psychedelic, man!"

A beautiful naked black woman, whose entire body was painted dayglo paisley, knelt in front of Anne Marie. She stared into her eyes, exclaiming repeatedly how psychedelic they were. Anne Marie thought the woman's long dread locks hairdo was fascinating.

"Check it out," the black girl called to Fagatha, "She has the trippiest eyes!"

"You have great boobs," Anne Marie blurted. "Oh, God, I hope you don't think I'm gay. I mean I have never seen blue flowered tits before."

The hunk with the hearty laugh must be Fagatha. Now he was kneeling in front of Anne Marie gazing intently into her eyes. Fagatha was exotic looking and handsome. He had dark smoldering eyes and long curly black hair. Since he was naked too, Anne Marie did not hesitate to check out his perfect proportions. She was impressed. Fagatha was blessed with a flawless physique. What a shame he was gay. What a waste. Anne Marie felt somewhat disconcerted when he echoed his sister's observation.

"Psychedelic, man!" Fagatha exclaimed.

Anne Marie wondered what was so different about her eyes? They always looked pretty ordinary in the mirror. Lamont passed the joint that was making the rounds to Anne Marie. Unsure what to do, she tried inhaling it. It made her cough. After a moment, her head buzzed pleasantly. She saw a bright blue jewel gleaming in the black woman's navel. It was really beautiful how it caught the light.

Lamont said, "This is Fathom."

"Hi," Anne Marie said. She felt stupid. "I like your paint. How long does it take to do your hair?" Fathom's laugh made Anne Marie picture silver droplets rippling on water. She wondered if she was stoned.

The open loft where Fagatha and his sister Fathom lived with their friends was furnished with mattresses, overstuffed pillows, and beanbag chairs. An easel with a painting in progress stood in a corner by the window. Paintings in the same surrealistic style, full of bright, swirling colors, adorned the walls.

"Who is the artist?" Anne Marie asked.

"That's Phoenix' work," Lamont replied.

"Which one is Phoenix?"

"I don't see him here. Maybe he'll show up later."

There must have been at least 25 people in the loft, and most of them were naked. Lamont and Glitter had stripped down like the others.

"I hope you're not gonna pressurize me to get naked," she had whispered to Lamont, as she admired Glitter Man's ass.

"Don't worry about it," Lamont had assured her. "Everyone does their own thing here. Nudity is optional. No one cares if you keep your clothes on."

"Then I'll keep my clothes on. So there. So is this a real commune? Do all these people live here?"

"Not all of them. People pass through here all the time. Fagatha has an open door policy. It's hard to keep track of who lives here and who doesn't."

Music blared from a stereo in the corner. "Acid rock," Glitter called it.

"Acid rock?" Anne Marie said, her eyes wide, "LSD?"

"Sure," Lamont laughed. "Most of the people here are tripping. Why do you think Fathom and Fagatha think your eyes are so 'psychedelic'?"

"Really? Are you going to pop some LSD?"

"That's 'drop', not pop." Lamont shook his head. "I'm not into it, but if you want to try some, feel free. There is more than enough to go around."

"No way!" Anne Marie was horrified. "Marone, Joseph would kill me!"

"From what I have heard, darling, Joseph might kill you anyway." Lamont moved away before she could react.

"This place has the weirdest interior decorator," Anne Marie thought. A strobe light hanging from the ceiling sent rainbows dancing through the room. Fagatha's coffee table was made out of two wooden milk crates pushed together. Dairy cows were painted on the crates. Someone had painted red smiles on the cows' faces and joints in their mouths. Rabbit fur covered the top of the crates, with a sheet of glass over the fur to create a smooth surface. The table was covered with Rheingold beer bottles and a big green mound of marijuana. Every few minutes someone rolled another joint and passed it around.

Off the main room was a smaller room set off by hanging glass beads and lit by dim red lights. The floor of that room was covered with wall-to-wall mattresses. A peace sign hung over the doorway proclaiming, "Make love, not war." Apparently, the couples and threesomes who were in the red light room were doing just that. Anne Marie thought she wouldn't mind getting a little piece herself. She giggled. What would her mother think?

"Marone, is this some kind of orgy?" she asked Glitter. "Is this a bordello?"

"No, this is free love, Contessa." Glitter laughed.

Fathom moved gracefully to answer the door. The paisley designs on her body rippled as she walked. She unbolted several locks and opened the door to reveal a tall dark-haired man wearing a black velvet floor-length cloak. He had thick black eyebrows that met in the middle, fiercely framing his penetrating, glassy eyes. The corners of his mouth turned up slightly, suggesting a permanent smile.

"Phoenix!" Fathom exclaimed. She embraced him. "Welcome to the happening!"

Phoenix entered the loft, smiling broadly, shaking hands, and hugging everyone. "Peace and love," he proclaimed in a deep voice.

Someone changed the record and switched off the lights.

"Marone!" Anne Marie exclaimed.

"Just watch, Contessa," Glitter Man whispered.

The strobe light took over. Fathom moved directly beneath the light. Her amazing day-glo body glowed in the dark. Everyone gathered around, gasping "oh wow, man!" and "psychedelic, man!" Phoenix approached Fathom. He shed his cloak to reveal his own human canvas. His body had been similarly painted in Salvador Dali-like designs. Anne Marie could not take her eyes off him. She had never imagined a man would paint that part of his body.

Phoenix and Fathom began to dance to the music. They swayed gracefully, undulating sensuously beneath the flashing strobe light.

"That is the most amazing thing I have ever seen," Anne Marie whispered to Lamont. "Does he have a license to carry that?"

Lamont choked on his beer.

"Is Phoenix gay?" Anne Marie asked. She hoped the answer would be negative.

"Bi," Glitter answered, sucking in the smoke from a joint and passing it to her.

"What do you mean, bye? You're not leaving me alone here are you?"

"No, Bi," Glitter explained. "Phoenix is Bi. He's AC/DC."

"He's from Washington, D.C.?"

"No, Contessa. Phoenix is bisexual. He swings both ways."

"Oh." Now she really felt stupid. The combination of pot and the strobe light made Anne Marie dizzy, but she couldn't take her eyes off Phoenix. She took another hit on the joint. "Wow!" she exclaimed, "Psychopathic, man!" Phoenix and Fathom danced erotically into the red light room. Lamont and Glitter Man followed them.

Anne Marie sat in the beanbag sipping her beer. She fantasized how she would look painted, and how she could get Phoenix to go to bed with her. A hippie with daisies woven into his beard knelt down in front of her and held out a tray of cookies and brownies. Suddenly she was starving, so she helped herself to a handful of each. They tasted delicious, although they were a little grainy. She washed them down with more beer. Finally, Anne Marie dozed off. She dreamed erotic, paisley dreams.

CHAPTER SIXTEEN

Sunday, October 8, 1973

"Do you mean I can actually enter Jeanette's dreams?"

Gockie smiled and patted his grandson on the back. "It is done all the time. Dreaming is one of the ways the dead can communicate with the living. Did you ever dream about Lizzy after she passed on?"

"Constantly," Lincoln sighed. "Especially when Jeanette was a teenager. Lizzy was in my dreams almost every night, like she was helping raise the girl."

"And in the morning did you feel comforted, and perhaps have fresh insight on how to relate to your daughter?"

"Well, yes."

"So it is. We do not stop loving and looking after the people we leave behind just because we are on the other side of the veil," Gockie said gently. "The vividness of those dreams of your dead wife was not a figment of your imagination."

Gershwin sat between Lincoln and Gockie. He looked from one to the other as he listened to their conversation.

The only thing the dog did not like about the ghosts was that they never ate. Here they were at the kitchen table in the middle of the night, and neither Lincoln nor Gockie made a move toward the refrigerator full of meat, cheese, and pickles. It made his mouth water just thinking about it.

In an attempt to give them a hint, Gershwin trotted over to the counter and stared up wistfully at the loaf of bread that was next to the toaster. He gave a little whine and wagged his tail, but the ghosts ignored him. Gershwin lay down. He rested his head on his paws and heaved a big sigh. He looked over at his food bowl, which held nothing but kibble. Boring. Gershwin wanted a big fat people sandwich.

"I'm hungry," he whined. The ghosts remained oblivious. Gershwin rolled onto his back, waved his feet in the air, and wagged his tail. He stared upside down at them until his eyes crossed. Nothing.

"It takes a great deal of love and a strong connection," Gockie was saying, "but it can be done. It remains up to the dreamer, of course, whether or not to be influenced by the dream. I see no reason, however, why you should not pay a nocturnal visit to your daughter. See if you can talk some sense into her."

"Well I'll be damned!" Lincoln exclaimed.

"Actually, you have not been damned, or you would not be here."

Gershwin chuckled. He padded back to the table and sat next to Gockie's chair. "I like Gockie," he barked. "Your grandfather has a good sense of humor."

Joseph Stoeckel smiled at the dog. "You are a good dog, Gershwin. Have you always been so smart?"

"I am pretty intelligent as dogs go," Gershwin agreed. He bit a flea off his paw. "I don't miss much." Gershwin looked up at Lincoln adoringly. Lincoln bent down and kissed his snout. The dog grinned broadly, thumping his tail on the floor. "How 'bout a sandwich?" he begged.

"Not now, boy, we're busy."

"That's fine for you," Gershwin complained, "but I'm still in a meat body. If you' are going to wake me up in the middle of the night, the least you could do is feed me."

"I think I see some food in your bowl," Lincoln chided.

"Next time around," Gockie laughed, "remind me to get a dog. Now about entering dreams. I do it all the time. I have been visiting with my great grandson Eddie ever since he got drafted and sent to Vietnam. Been trying to help him deal with his war issues."

"Eddie Lightly? My nephew, Eddie?"

Gockie nodded. "He is having a hard time of it. Eddie does not know who I am, but I show up in his dreams a lot. He thinks of me as 'the old soldier'. I have been helping to guide him, but Eddie is a real challenge. He clouds his mind over so much with booze and drugs, that I am never sure I'm getting through to him."

"I had no idea. Why didn't he come to me? Eddie always came to me with his problems."

"He was planning to come to you. He was planning to talk it all out. He didn't expect to lose you. Eddie feels isolated and alone. He does not realize that there are thousands just like him, struggling with what we used to call 'shell shock'. Who knows what they call it now? Eddie suffers in silence, thinking no one understands. He is a lot like his father."

The lonely whistle of a freight train cut through the night. The Erie Lackawanna tracks ran only three blocks behind the house, so close they could hear the wheels clacking along the rails.

Gershwin ran over to the window and stood up, front paws on the windowsill, sniffing. He could hear the train, but he could not smell it. No need to bark at it unless it got closer, he decided. He curled back up under Lincoln's feet.

Lincoln sighed. "Yes, my brother Bill was a handful. The sound of that train brings back memories. When I left the seminary to handle my father's death and settle his affairs, Bill was a fool street kid. He was running wild with the wrong crowd. And Mama, well Mama was not in her right mind."

Gockie nodded. "I know. Odella was never the same after your little brother Wally died. You were only a boy then; maybe you don't remember. Odella set a place at the dinner table for Wally every night. She talked to the empty plate, admonishing the child who was not there to eat his supper."

"I do remember that. But when my father was hit by the train and killed, Mama really began to unravel. She smashed every bottle of liquor in the house. Bill and I were forbidden to ever touch a drop of alcohol. Bill just laughed and ran off."

Gockie looked wistful. "I hated it when you had to leave the seminary and come home. I felt so old and useless. I had so much anger and frustration about my helplessness after the stroke. I couldn't help my daughter. I could not even communicate with you. There I was, calling out to you in my head. I longed to say the words that were clear in my mind. I wanted to say that I loved you, and everything would be all right. But all I could do was make animal noises. I felt like I was an added burden, and you were already overwhelmed. You had made such a sacrifice."

"I never thought of you as a burden, Gockie. I saw your heart in your eyes. I did what had to be done out of love for all of you. There was no sacrifice involved. Anyway, some good did come out of my leaving the seminary," Lincoln reflected. "If I had not come home to take care of my family's crisis, I would never have met Lizzy. I would have become a priest, and never have fathered Jeanette. She was the most precious and joyful part of my life."

Gershwin lifted his head off his paws and rested it on Lincoln's foot. All these things had happened before his time. They were part of Lincoln's life before he had such a faithful dog to love and comfort him. "It must have been a lonely time for Lincoln," Gershwin thought.

"Bill was too much for your mother to handle," Gockie remarked.

"Bill is still too much for anyone to handle." Lincoln chuckled.

Gockie smiled. "God knows I loved my daughter more than my life. I would have done anything to help Odella. But my time was up."

"More than once," Lincoln recalled, "I found Mama in her nightgown, running through the dark streets of Newark. She would be calling Wally's name, hysterically insisting he was still out playing. At night she ran through the streets, and all day she sat rocking in the chair by the front window, crocheting and talking to herself.

"Mama still set a place for Wally at the supper table. Every time she looked at the empty plate and said 'eat this' or 'eat that, Wally,' Bill burst into tears and bolted outside. My living brother was running wild, and Mother was so focused on my dead brother, she did not seem to know Bill was there.

"Night after night I set up your old army cot in the room next to Mama's bed. I tied our ankles together with clothesline rope. I would wake up in the middle of the night to find the rope untied, and Mama gone. I was so worried about my mother that I could not tolerate Billy's nonsense. When he and his no-good friends tried to rob the liquor store down on Market Street, I snapped. I beat the crap out of my brother."

"And Bill worshiped the ground you walked on after that, Lincoln. Right up until the day you died."

Lincoln looked out the window at the dark night. "Gockie, it broke my heart to have to put my Mother in Overbrook. Mental institutions back in the 1940's were cold, horrible places. I just could not work, keep on top of Bill's schooling, and be her jailer all at the same time. It was not safe to leave my mother alone. And at the end she hardly even knew me."

"I know, Lincoln. Son, we all have different reasons for the way we leave a lifetime behind. When you get to the other side, you will come to understand this. I was close to you back then, you know. You were the first one whose dreams I learned to enter."

Lincoln's eyes widened. "So you guided me from the other side?"

Gockie nodded.

Gershwin nuzzled his knee.

"I felt responsible for Mama's death."

"Those primitive mental institutions were breeding grounds for the tuberculosis that killed Odella. You should not have blamed yourself for that."

"Will I see my mother on the other side, Gockie?" Lincoln asked longingly.

Gockie shook his head. "She is not there."

"What do you mean she isn't there?"

"Odella has already begun a new life. Would you like to see her now?"

Lincoln did not know a ghost could find it hard to swallow. How could his heart be pounding when he no longer had one?

The old ghost read his mind. "We take our emotions with us when we go," he said softly. "So, son, do you want to see your mother now?"

"Oh, yes," Lincoln breathed.

"All you have to do is think of Odella," Gockie said, taking hold of his grandson's hand. "Focus on her soul and spirit."

*   *   *

Gershwin shook his head when the two ghosts disappeared. "Where did you guys go?" he barked. He ran around the kitchen, sniffing and barking.

The kitchen light came on. Jeanette stumbled sleepily into the room, rubbing her eyes. She was still half asleep. "What's the matter, Puppy?" She yawned. "It's the middle of the night. Why are you barking?"

Gershwin stared at the empty table and yapped. "The ghosts were here. They just disappeared."

Jeanette knelt down and hugged the dog. "Shh," she whispered. "You'll wake up everybody in the neighborhood." She shuffled over to the refrigerator and opened the door. Gershwin's ears perked up. He sat at attention. Things were looking good. Yes! She got the mayonnaise and the bologna out.

"Don't forget the pickles," Gershwin arfed. "Good. Now the cheese, not the yellow cheese, the white kind with the holes."

She reached for the bread. "I'm in luck!" Gershwin quivered with anticipation. "Thank goodness Jeanette is not a ghost. She still likes sandwiches."

Gershwin sat barely leaning his furry body against Jeanette's leg, so she wouldn't forget he was there. He assumed the irresistible puppy face and wagged his tail.

     *   *   *

"Where is she?" Lincoln Lightly searched the faces of the sleeping patients. They were in some kind of hospital. It appeared to be a primitive, tropical place. Mosquito netting gracefully draped the beds.

The night was alive with cricket song and buzzing insects. The air was fragrant with pungent tropical flowers. In a corner of the room a young doctor with bright red hair and a full beard sat at the bedside of an emaciated black man. He held the sick man's hand and spoke softly to him. The patient moaned, tossing feverishly in his bed.

"There she is," Gockie said.

"Where? I don't see her."

"There." Gockie pointed to the doctor. "Odella has chosen a solitary life devoted to service. This time around she is a man, a missionary doctor. He specializes in tuberculosis cases. He is working on a cure for the most virulent strains of TB, and this is his first laboratory. There is a very good possibility that he will be awarded the Nobel Peace Prize around the turn of the century."

Lincoln looked at his grandfather incredulously. "This is unbelievable!"

"Believe it. This is the soul who once lived as my daughter and your mother. Odella learned some great lessons in her troubled and tragic life. Look how tenderly she, now called 'Patrick', is helping that patient cross the threshold between this world and the next. Just like I used to help the soldiers," Gockie said proudly.

Lincoln drifted forward tentatively.

"Go ahead, he cannot see or hear you. Go as close as you want."

Lincoln approached the bedside of the dying man. He looked closely into the eyes of the red headed doctor. They were, indeed his mother's eyes. The same sweet soul burned within this young man's body.

The patient coughed up blood and shuddered. His spirit, still attached by the silver cord, grew brighter. The man's body sank back with a sigh. There was not much life left, but still he clung to life. The young doctor took the skeletal man in his arms and rocked him. Softly, he sang an old Irish lullaby in a sweet tenor voice. It was the same lullaby Lincoln's mother used to sing to him.

"*Toora loora loora,*" the doctor sang.

"Odella learned that song from your grandmother, Annie," Gockie murmured. "Some of the happiest days of my life were spent watching Annie as she rocked our baby and sang that song to her."

"Where did he learn Mama's lullaby?" Lincoln wondered.

"Oh, Doctor Loftus was born and raised in Ireland. He is a proud son of County Mayo."

"Where Gramma was born?"

Gockie nodded. "My Annie's homeland."

"But I don't understand. If Mama has taken on another life, why haven't you?"

"I don't think I was very good at life. I chose to be a guide. I get along real well with angels, you know. I enjoy working with them. For now, my choice is to remain in spirit. Maybe if Annie decides to take on another lifetime, I shall go back too. We like to stay together. Now what about this dream thing, Lincoln? Do you want to try it?"

"Can I enter Jeanette's dreams tonight?"

"I don't see why not."

The dying man relaxed in the doctor's arms. "*Hush now, don't you cry,*" Doctor Loftus sang. An orchestra of insects and wind blowing through the trees accompanied him.

"Interesting, isn't it, Lincoln, how music can have the same continuity as the soul? Maybe that is why we respond so purely to it. We can carry the same music in our hearts through many lifetimes."

CHAPTER SEVENTEEN

Monday, October 9, 1973

Jeanette stood at the dining room window where she waited every day for Dad to come home from work. The clock chimed five. He would come around the corner of Henry and Thomas Streets any minute now. But the figure that turned the corner wasn't Dad. Instead a huge polar bear, bigger than the grizzly in the Natural History Museum, came up the street. The polar bear wore roller skates, the old kind that you put on over your shoes and tighten with a key, the kind of skates that get rusty when you leave them out in the rain. As the bear got closer, Jeanette could hear the rough wheels scraping along the sidewalk. The bear was coming, Jeanette knew, to get her.

She ran out the kitchen door into the back hall. Smitty was there, pasting potato chips on the wall. Quacks picked up the chips one by one in his beak and handed them to Smitty.

"Run!" she screamed, but Smitty just looked at her and smiled as he took another chip from Quacks and pasted it to the wall.

Jeanette could hear the metallic sound of the old roller skates coming down the driveway. The bear was almost to the back stoop. Panicked, she pulled open the cellar door. She ran down the steps into the musty basement. Terrified, she hid in the dark space under the steps. The bear opened the door, and she heard the skates clattering down the stairs.

*   *   *

Jeanette waltzed in Chris's arms through a beautiful sunny garden in full bloom. Nothing mattered but being in his arms. Her dress was pale blue chiffon trimmed in ostrich feathers. The gorilla musicians up in the monkey tree played Irving Berlin's *"Always"*, as she and Chris glided gracefully in circles around the tree. Chris pulled her closer and kissed her.

*   *   *

The village was dark and deserted. It looked like Pinnochio's village, with cobblestone streets, quaint stone thatch-roofed buildings, and gaslights dimly lighting the foggy night. Jeanette sat down on a green park bench. She smoothed out the skirt of her lovely ostrich-feather gown.

Someone was approaching through the fog. She squinted her eyes, trying to see clearly. "Daddy!" Jeanette cried. She jumped up and ran into his arms. He hugged her warmly. Tears spilled down her cheeks. They sat down on the bench, and she hugged him again. Dad smiled radiantly.

"I thought you were dead!" she exclaimed.

"I am. I am dead, but not gone."

"I don't understand, but how are you? What is it like?"

He smiled a bright smile. "Pardon the pun, but I never felt better in my life."

"I miss you so much."

"I know, dear. I don't have much time. I just want you to know I am here, close by you always. Now I want to talk to you about Chris."

Jeanette turned away. She didn't want to talk about Chris. Dad took her chin in his hand and turned her face toward him. "Do you still love him?"

"Yes," she sobbed. "I shall always love him."

"Then why don't you forget about this divorce business and go home to him?"

"I can't, Dad. I don't deserve Chris."

"Is that what you really think?"

"Yes!" she cried, and her feelings spilled out all at once. "I killed my mother. I killed her by being born. That is why my own baby died. I punished Chris because he was alone with the baby when it happened, but I know the punishment was meant for me."

"You are wrong about your mother, Jeanette. You were not responsible for her death, or your baby's. And what do you mean, you punished Chris?"

"I stopped sleeping with him, Dad. I was afraid to make love. I was afraid to get pregnant again, and I could not bear to lose another child. I could not bear to be responsible for the death of another innocent. It was easier for me to pretend to fall asleep on the couch in front of the T.V. every night than to try to explain how I felt. It had the inevitable effect. We lost each other."

The fog began to swirl in, and Dad started to fade. "I have to go," he said in a hollow sounding voice. "Chris loves you, Jeanette. It is not too late."

Lincoln disappeared, leaving Jeanette alone in the fog. She ran blindly down the cobblestone street, falling to her knees in wet grass, her hand touching cold stone. It was the baby's gravestone.

"It **is** too late," she sobbed. "It is too late."

＊   ＊   ＊

Jeanette opened her eyes to see the early morning light pouring through her bedroom window. She squinted at the clock. It was six o'clock in the morning. Gershwin lay curled up on the floor next to her bed, snoring. Jeanette turned her head into the pillow and let her tears flow.

Suddenly, Gershwin's head jerked up. He barked. Someone was knocking insistently at the kitchen door. Jeanette pulled on her robe. Who could it be at this early hour? She opened the door, and Aunt Teresa grabbed her by the arms. Jeanette was alarmed. It wasn't like Teresa to be hysterical. Her aunt was already dressed.

"Jeanette!" she cried. "It's Anne Marie! She has been taken to the emergency room. Please, can you drive me to the hospital?"

"What happened?"

"I'm not sure," Teresa sobbed. "Joey said she fell down the stairs. She's hemorrhaging."

*   *   *

Eddie Lightly sat on the roof of his apartment house. He lit up a cigarette. The New York skyline kissed the horizon, as the sun rose behind the Empire State Building. Eddie came up here a lot when he couldn't sleep, when the dreams of blood and death woke him up, when he was afraid to go back to sleep.

The old soldier had appeared in his dreams again last night, and for awhile it didn't seem so bad, until the skeleton faces showed up, their flesh hanging like sliced meat from their bones.

Eddie had left Olivia sleeping while he pulled on his jeans and headed up to the roof to clear his head. If he could only banish the night mares…

The weight inside Eddie's chest felt like an anvil. He walked over to the edge of the roof and looked down. He was high above the trees, their colorful leaves breaking loose and spiraling slowly to the ground. The ledge came just to his knees. It would be so easy to just step up and out. No more bad dreams. No more memories. No more anvils crushing his heart. He could be just like one of the fallen leaves.

Eddie put one bare foot up on the ledge and took a drag of his cigarette. The early morning air was cold, but even though he was bare-chested and barefoot, Eddie did not notice the chill. It would be so easy…

"Eddie!" Olivia called.

He turned, startled, afraid for a minute that she knew what he was thinking, and how did she know? She came running onto the roof in her nightgown, the outline of her body showing through the nearly transparent fabric. "Eddie, Jeanette just called from the hospital. It's Anne Marie."

His thoughts of suicide evaporated as Eddie ran for the door. "Where is she?"

"Mountainside Hospital. She's in the emergency room. Do you want me to go with you? Should I call in to work?" Olivia ran down the steps to their apartment behind him.

"No, honey, you go on to work. I'll be fine." He struggled into socks and boots. He ran out the door, pulling a tee shirt over his head. Olivia tossed him the keys to his motorcycle, and his leather jacket.

"I'll call you as soon as I can," he promised. Olivia blew him a kiss. Dear God, how he loved her.

*   *   *

Jeanette leaned over the gurney, holding Anne Marie's hand. Her cousin's broken left arm had been set in a plaster cast. Anne Marie's face was whiter than the sheet that covered her, except for the horrible purple bruises around her eyes, and the blood crusted on her split lip.

"Can you hear me, Annie? I'm here. Eddie is on his way. You hang on, okay? We'll be waiting for you. Everything's gonna be okay, Annie, I promise."

Anne Marie whispered something weakly, and Jeanette leaned closer to hear.

"Joseph," Anne Marie rasped.

"He's here, too, Annie. Joseph and your Mom are here. We're all here. You're gonna be fine, okay?"

"We have to go now," the orderly said.

Joseph Mustachio, looking crestfallen and concerned, stepped forward. He held Anne Marie's hand as the orderly wheeled her into the elevator to take her to surgery. Anne Marie closed her eyes and turned her head away from him.

*   *   *

Jeanette and Eddie watched as the surgeon spoke to Joseph Mustachio and Teresa Tempesta. Joseph revealed no emotion. Teresa's face registered shock. She walked over to Jeanette and Eddie. She sat down heavily in the chair next to them.

"What is it?" Eddie asked. "Is Anne Marie all right?"

Teresa burst into tears.

"I'm going outside for a cigarette," Joseph mumbled. He left them alone in the waiting room.

"The doctor said he removed a three-month old fetus from Anne Marie," Teresa sobbed. "My daughter was pregnant."

"What!" Jeanette exclaimed.

"Is she going to be all right?" Eddie asked.

Teresa nodded. "The doctor says Annie will be fine. They stopped the hemorrhaging. She suffered a miscarriage, the broken arm, and contusions. Luckily, she is not more seriously injured. It could have been worse. He says she'll be back on her feet in a few days, and thank God she will able to have more children."

Jeanette swallowed back tears. "I didn't know Anne Marie was pregnant."

"I know," Teresa moaned. "I didn't either. Oh, God, my poor baby."

Eddie put his arm around his aunt. "There now, Aunt Tee, the important thing is that Annie is going to recover. How did the accident happen?"

Teresa blew her nose. She dabbed at her streaming eyes with a crumpled Kleenex. "You know how clumsy she is. Joseph said she wasn't paying attention. She tripped at the top of the stairs. He came running when he heard her scream."

Eddie wondered how a fall down the stairs could blacken both his cousin's eyes in the shape of a man's fist, and split her lip.

✻   ✻   ✻

Later that night, Eddie sat next to Anne Marie's bedside. Jeanette sat on the edge of the bed next to him. Anne Marie was still very weak and pale.

"So, kiddo," Eddie said quietly, "What's the story?"

Anne Marie's eyes were painfully swollen. She spoke with difficulty. She was still a little groggy from the anesthetic and the painkillers. "Joseph," she whispered. "I told him I wouldn't do it."

"Wouldn't do what?" Jeanette asked.

Tears flowed down Anne Marie's face. "Eddie, I didn't want Jeanette to know. I didn't want her to know what Joseph was pressurizing me to do…what I was going to do."

"Anne Marie," Jeanette sighed, "it's okay. Tell us what really happened."

"Swear," Anne Marie sobbed, gripping Jeanette's hand, "swear on your mother's grave you'll never tell."

"I swear," Jeanette promised.

"On your mother's grave."

"On my mother's grave."

"Musketeer promise, both of you," Anne Marie begged. "Remember, we're the 'Three Mosquitoes.'"

"We're not kids anymore," Eddie protested.

"I don't care. You have to swear, or I won't tell you."

"All right, calm down," Eddie said quietly. "Musketeer promise."

"It was my own fault. Joseph came home from the motorcycle races. He wanted to know where I was, 'cause he was trying to call me all weekend. I told him I didn't know the phone was off the hook. He said I was lying, which I was. He was right, but I couldn't tell him I was in New York, or that I spent the night in a hippie commune. So I stuck to my lie. Then he asked me if I made the arrangements for the abortion yet."

"Abortion?" Eddie and Jeanette looked horrified.

Anne Marie coughed. Eddie held her water glass with the straw up to her lips.

"I found out I was pregnant two weeks ago. I was so happy. Joseph went through the roof. He said it wasn't a convenient time. We had a terrible fight. 'Why not?' I wanted to know. God, I wanted the baby so bad. 'We have our own home,' I said, 'You make plenty of money. We want for nothing.'"

"Joseph got really mad. 'We don't have the boat', he argued, 'I don't have the money in the bank I told you I wanted to have before we start a family. I will not give up my plans to get a Porsche'. He called me a self-ish 'ef-ing bitch' for getting myself pregnant."

"Oh, Annie," Jeanette sighed.

"Joseph always calls me that. He demanded I have an abortion. Last night when the fight broke out about my being gone all weekend, he threw it in my face. He said, 'this proves you're not ready to be a mother. You're too irresponsible to have a baby, you stupid ef-ing bitch!'"

"I screamed, 'I don't care! I want this baby, and I'm not going to kill it.' So, see? It's my own fault. I should never have defied my husband like that. I provoked him."

Eddie's eyes turned black. The color drained out of his face. "Are you telling us that Joseph did this to you?"

"Marone!" Anne Marie cried. "Please don't say anything. If you do, he'll kill me. It was my fault, Eddie. I asked for it. Joseph didn't mean it. He was drinking."

"I'll kill the bastard," Eddie said.

"You don't know him. Joseph had such a horrible childhood. He just needs love. You don't understand. It's only when he drinks. In the matter of fact, Joseph was right. I lied to him. I wasn't a good wife. You have to be a snoopy for your man. Really, Joseph is wonderful to me, Eddie. I want for nothing. It was my own fault."

"Oh, God, Anne Marie." Jeanette got up and walked over to the window.

A nurse entered the room to check Anne Marie's I.V.

"I'm sorry," she said softly. "Mrs. Mustachio needs her rest. I must ask you to leave."

Anne Marie gripped Eddie's hand. "Eddie, please!"

"Annie, you have to report this. You cannot let him get away with this."

"Please, Eddie, I beg you. Let it go. I cannot shame my family. This is my problem. It's private. I should never have told you. You promised. Eddie, you promised."

Eddie made an effort to control himself. "Go to sleep. Everything's gonna be all right."

"Promise?" Anne Marie choked.

"I really must insist," the nurse said, "Mrs. Mustaschio needs to rest."

Eddie nodded. "Okay, I promise," he whispered. He kissed his Anne Marie on the forehead. "We'll be back tomorrow, okay? You rest now."

Eddie and Jeanette left their cousin's room. They rode the elevator downstairs and walked out to the parking lot in silence.

"What are we going to do?" Jeanette finally said.

"What the fuck can we do?" Eddie sighed. "Annie will never press charges against that son of a bitch, and no one else can. There are no witnesses to her 'accident'."

"Why can't the hospital report this to the police? Why can't they demand an investigation?"

"The hospital has Anne Marie's report and her husband's, both confirming that it was an accident. What more can they do? Maybe someday the laws will change and make the hospital report this kind of 'accident' to the police." He slammed his fist into the roof of Jeanette's car. "Damn it, Jeanette!"

She leaned over and kissed him on the cheek. ""Night, Eddie. Thanks for being here."

"Annie is wrong about one thing. The 'Three Mosquitoes' were children, and we are not children anymore. Musketeer promise or not," Eddie said grimly, "if that mother fucker touches Annie again, I'm gonna waste him. I swear, Jeanette, if he ever hurts her again, Joseph Mustachio is a dead man."

Eddie got on his motorcycle, revved up the motor, and roared out of the parking lot.

Jeanette sat for a long time behind the wheel of her car, so blinded by her tears that she was unable to drive.

CHAPTER EIGHTEEN

Thursday, October 12, 1973

"I really appreciate you helping me, Eddie." Jeanette laid another of her father's suits on the bed. She was attending to the difficult business of sorting through Lincoln's things.

"I wasn't about to let you do this alone, or worse yet, leave you to have to deal with Aunt Teresa by yourself."

"Thank goodness for the holiday, and that Teresa is busy bringing Anne Marie home from the hospital. Columbus Day gives me a chance to pack up Dad's things without her interference. I don't mean to be disrespectful toward Aunt Teresa, but…"

"No need to explain to me," Eddie said wryly. He took a swig from his beer bottle and wiped the back of his hand across his mouth. "Why the fuck is Anne Marie going home to him? It's like everything we said to her went in one ear and out the other."

"I know," Jeanette sighed. "If only we could have convinced her to press charges. I could not believe it when she said, 'Why should I press charges against Joseph when it was all my fault?' How can you reason with someone who thinks like that, Eddie?"

"I don't know," Eddie groaned. "She continues to defend the bastard. If I hear one more time how Joseph is just a victim of his abusive childhood, and when he drinks then she becomes his victim, and all this is perfectly normal and acceptable, I'll go ballistic. She swears he's a good man, just misunderstood. Joseph beats the crap out of her, says he's sorry, and she acts like nothing ever happened. Annie seems to really believe that everything will be fine, as long as she doesn't defy him again. And when Annie said she should have obeyed her husband and gotten the abortion, I thought I was gonna puke."

"I know, me too."

"I still don't understand why she puts up with it."

"Annie says it is because she loves him. She says she has to be a 'snoopy for her man.' She 'wants for nothing,' and she is afraid to be alone, afraid she will be poor without him. Annie would rather have Joseph's money than her own self-respect."

"Yeah," Eddie said, "that's the saddest thing of all, that she thinks that's what love is. I wonder if Aunt Tee dropped her on her head when she was a kid?"

"I hate to say this, but Aunt Teresa is part of the problem. Last Thanksgiving, when you were in Nam, Anne Marie got up the courage to divorce Joseph. She told her mother what she was planning, and Aunt Teresa was furious. She said she wouldn't hear of it. She told Annie that when you vow to God for better or worse you cannot leave just because it turns out worse. She said Anne Marie had always been too headstrong and wild, so if her husband had to punish her, she deserved it."

"No! I don't believe it. How could Aunt Tee be so cruel?"

"I don't think she saw herself as cruel, Eddie. I think Aunt Tee really believes all that. And unfortunately, Anne Marie believes it too."

"Shit."

"I know. Even worse, Aunt Teresa reinforced Annie's belief that, since a woman's duty is to her husband, if she got divorced she would go to hell. She said she would never forgive Annie if she shamed the family by getting excommunicated from the Church. By the time she got done with her, Anne Marie was convinced she already had one foot in hell, and to leave Joseph would make her a complete failure as a wife and a woman."

Eddie grimaced. "There's not enough booze in the world to deal with this shit."

Jeanette continued. "My father was furious when he found out what Teresa had done. He insisted there was no way the Catholic Church would condone what is happening under Joseph Mustachio's roof. He told Aunt Teresa to stop making the Church her scapegoat."

"Ripped her a new one, eh?"

"Oh yeah. Dad said he thought one of the goals of parenting was to teach children to rejoice in their God-given strength to rise above their lower selves, and that nothing was lower than Annie's husband. He said he thought the idea was for people to learn to strive to be more than they think they are, and more than they think they can be. He said the sin was Teresa's for making Annie think taking abuse was the right thing to do."

"Good for Uncle Lincoln."

"Dad told Aunt Tee that to glorify emotional martyrdom and encourage her daughter to be a victim was to misunderstand the whole point of her religion. Teresa would not speak to him for weeks after that."

"I still do not understand why Anne Marie won't listen to us now? She nearly died at that bastard's hands."

"Eddie, you're talking about a grown woman whose heroes are Vinnie Barbarino and Horshack from "'Welcome Back Kotter.'"

*   *   *

Lincoln Lightly sat on top of the sizzling radiator in the corner of the room. Gershwin lay curled up at his feet. Gockie sat on the edge of the bed, leaning on his cane.

"Jeanette is right," Lincoln said. "I did read Tee the riot act. She was irate. I could not make her understand she could be endangering her own daughter's life."

"You're a regular philosopher, Lincoln," Gershwin woofed. "I'm really gonna miss that when you're gone."

Gockie sighed. "Anne Marie's situation is frustrating," he agreed, "but she is a lot like her mother. She will not listen to anyone. In Teresa Tempesta's defense, I don't believe she comprehends the very real danger Anne Marie is in as long as she stays with Joseph Mustachio."

"Why, Gockie? Why is this horror happening to my niece?"

"Anne Marie chose this lesson before she was born, son. Sadly, she is not learning it very well. It is possible that Anne Marie may die because of the choices she has made in her life. She has always had the choice to move toward life or death."

"How terrible," Lincoln sighed.

"On the other hand, who are we to judge?" Gockie said. "That is the first thing I learned when I crossed over. The whole picture is not in yet."

*   *   *

Eddie took a joint out of his pocket. "Wanna burn one?" he asked.

Jeanette reached into the large walk in closet and took her father's favorite shirt off its hanger. It still smelled like him. Sudden tears burned her eyes. "Why not? God, Eddie, I miss my father." She sat down on the bed, next to the ghost of her great-grandfather.

"I know," Eddie said. "I miss him too." He passed her the joint. She choked on it. "All right," Eddie laughed. "You ought to get a good buzz off that one."

Gershwin sniffed the smoke that filled the room. The dog sneezed. "They always laugh a lot when they smoke those wrinkled cigarettes," he observed.

"I never knew," Lincoln said, "until I entered her dream the other night, that my daughter feels responsible for her mother's death. It is something we never discussed. Jeanette never knew about Lizzy's heart. It never occurred to me that the child would blame herself for being born."

"Hey, you got another beer?" Eddie asked.

"Eddie is so like Bill," Lincoln sighed.

"You don't understand Eddie," Gockie said defensively. "You have never been in combat. Eddie has had many lives as a soldier in wars that go back to the beginning of time. He has a lot built up inside. He runs away from facing himself by seeking oblivion."

"I suppose so."

"Vietnam was the last straw for Eddie. Your nephew is struggling with an ancient soul challenge that is every bit as difficult as Jeanette's and Anne Marie's."

Gershwin scratched at a flea behind his ear. "In other words, they're human," the dog remarked. He yawned, giving everyone a good view of his many sharp teeth. "Personally, I like Eddie."

Eddie took a toke of the joint, passed it to Jeanette, and absent-mindedly patted the old dog on the head. Gershwin nuzzled his head in Eddie's palm. Eddie hugged the dog and kissed his snout.

"See what I mean?" Gershwin woofed. "You gotta love him. I wish there was something I could do to help Eddie. I wish I could help Jeanette, too."

Lincoln scratched his beard. "You know, Gershwin?" he said thoughtfully. "There just might be something you can do."

Gershwin and Gockie watched as Lincoln floated up to the top shelf of the closet and drifted in and out of the various boxes stored there.

"What's he doing?" Gershwin asked.

Gockie shrugged his shoulders.

*   *   *

"Gershwin is such a crack up," Eddie said laughing. "Look at him."

The dog was sitting in the closet staring at the ceiling. He moved his head back and forth like he was watching something.

"Is he sniffing the smoke?" Jeanette asked.

"Think he has a contact high?"

"I don't know," Jeanette replied. "Maybe. So what about you, Eddie? Are you all right?"

"Me? Why wouldn't I be?"

"I don't know. You seem preoccupied. You've been different somehow since you got out of the army. What happened to the carefree Eddie I used to know?"

Eddie turned his head away from her like he was trying to hide the shadow that crossed his face. "I guess I've had a lot on my mind, that's all."

Let me tell you about the Tunnel!

"Are you having doubts about the wedding?"

It's not the wedding; it's Nam; it's war; it's death! I'm different all right. Can you help me die? "I'm not sure I'm such a good catch," he said. He took another swallow of beer. "I don't deserve Olivia."

"Why wouldn't you deserve happiness, Eddie? Why would you think that? Olivia adores you. Pull yourself together. You just have pre-wedding jitters. It happens to the best of us."

"Did it happen to you?"

She shrugged her shoulders. "Well, maybe nothing is forever, Eddie. That's all the more reason to 'seize the day' as they say. That's what Dad would tell you to do, only he would say it in Latin."

"Cave canem," Eddie quoted.

Jeanette giggled. "That means 'beware of the dog.'"

"Are you talking about me?" Gershwin ran out of the closet and sat at Jeanette's feet, thumping his tail on the floor. "What? What?"

They ignored him, so the dog went back to watching the ghost of his master drift in and out of boxes.

"It's 'carpe diem,'" Jeanette said. "'Carpe diem,' Dad would insist, and he would be right. You and Olivia have as much chance at this marriage thing as anyone, probably more. Don't throw away the happiness you can have now because you fear tomorrow."

"It's not tomorrow I fear," Eddie murmured, lighting a cigarette. "It's yesterday. It's what yesterday is doing to tomorrow."

"What do you mean?"

"Considering how things turned out, do you regret marrying Chris, Jeanette?"

Jeanette inhaled the joint he passed her and thought for a moment. "No. You know, when I was younger I promised myself that no matter what happened to me in my life, I would never regret any decision I made. I would forge ahead and pay the consequences for my mistakes. I would harvest the joy of my successes. And, of course, my successes would be many, and there wouldn't be any mistakes. I was so smart. I had it all figured out. Do I regret marrying Chris? How could I regret having known that love? How could I regret having experienced, even for a short time, that connection, that friendship? Some people go through their whole lives never having that."

"Sometimes you amaze me, Jeanette."

"What I do regret is how I treated Chris when the baby died. I was so selfishly wrapped up in my pain, that I didn't see his until it was too late to repair the damage, and too late to rekindle the fire that had died inside us. I was a fool to think the fantasy was real. So I lost the dream. No, I destroyed the dream."

Eddie put his arms around her. "I guess when it comes to fucked up families," he sighed, "we're right up there with the best of them. You know what my problem is? I'm nothing but a weak coward. I wish I was as strong as you."

Jeanette laughed bitterly. "Oh, everyone thinks I'm so strong. I've got a news flash for you, Eddie. Since Dad died, I don't feel very strong at all." The tears came, and she buried her face in Eddie's shoulder and let them flow. Eddie rocked her in his arms, lost in his own private pain.

*   *   *

Gershwin sniffed around the floor of the closet. From the farthest, darkest corner, he heard a muffled cry. "I found it!" Lincoln appeared in the dust motes before him. "Okay, Gershwin, old boy, here's what I want you to do."

*   *   *

"What are you doing? What's the matter with this dog?" Eddie pushed Gershwin away. Gershwin flew at him, yanking on the leg of Eddie's bell-bottom jeans with his teeth.

"Gershwin, no!" Jeanette cried. "You'll rip Eddie's pants!" She tried to push the dog away too, but he bared his teeth and growled, as if to say, "don't do that again."

"What the fuck is wrong with him?"

"I don't know. Gershwin never growls at me like that."

The animal attacked her pants leg. Then he ran in and out of the closet, barking insistently.

"What is it, Lassie?" Eddie said laughing. "What are you trying to tell us? Is Timmy in trouble? Did he fall down the well again?"

Gershwin sat on his haunches. He looked disgustedly at Lincoln. "I want to help you," he barked, "but must I be insulted like this? Lassie? How much do you expect me to tolerate?"

"It's okay," Lincoln said. "Don't take Eddie seriously, Gershwin. It's nothing personal. Try again. You have got to get them to find the box."

"Okay, but one more comparison to Lassie, and I'm gonna bite him."

Gershwin renewed his efforts. He tried to pull the box out by the handle with his teeth, but it was too heavy.

"Look, Eddie," Jeanette said. She stood up and followed the dog into the closet. "I think he is trying to show us something."

Gershwin bounced up and down yapping. "Yes! Yes!" He nosed the box and put his paw on it. "Here! Look here!" he pleaded.

Jeanette pulled the container into the light of the room.

Lincoln clapped his hands delightedly. "Good work, Gershwin," he said.
"It's an old strong box!" Jeanette tried to open it. "It's locked," she said.
"Let me see that." Eddie pried at the lock with his Swiss army knife.
After a little effort, it sprang open. "It wasn't locked, just a little rusty."

Jeanette leafed through the old papers in the strong box. There were
birth and baptismal certificates, her parents' marriage certificate, and
her mother's death certificate. Jeanette unfolded the latter and read it.
She had never seen this document.

"What is a 'myocardial infarction'?" she asked Eddie.

"A heart attack. Why?"

"It says here that my mother died of a myocardial infarction, and
according to the date I was two months old. I don't understand; I
thought she died in childbirth."

A weathered piece of parchment fell to the floor. Eddie picked it up
and unfolded it. It was a letter of commendation issued to Joseph
Stoeckel during the Spanish American War. In the bottom of the
strongbox they found his purple heart.

"Now the journals," Lincoln whispered. "Find the journals."

Jeanette set the papers aside. She removed two small books from the
strongbox. She opened one of them. The pages were filled with her
father's familiar handwriting. "It's a diary!" she exclaimed. "My father
kept a diary!"

She flipped through it. The entries were sporadic, spanning over a
decade, from 1928 through 1940. The first entry was dated September
10, 1928.

"Today," she read, "I am leaving Seton Hall behind and entering
Darlington Seminary. I pray for the strength and wisdom I will need. I
hope I will be a good priest. It is in God's hands."

She turned to the last entry, May 21, 1940, two months after she was
born. She read it aloud. "I have just buried my wife. I should say I have
just buried my life. But I cannot be weak and give in to the despair that
overwhelms my soul, because the baby needs me. I have to go on for her

sake, even though saying goodbye to the only woman I will ever love has broken my heart. Even though God has forsaken me."

"Wow, that's heavy. What's the other book?" Eddie asked.

Jeanette set her father's journal aside and opened the other volume carefully, for it was very old. The yellowed pages were fragile. "It's another journal," she said.

"Of your father's?"

"No." Jeanette looked at Eddie. "This one belonged to our great-grandfather. It is Joseph Stoeckel's."

He reached out his hand, and she handed him the book. "Wow. Gockie's journal." It opened to a page spattered with dried mud, where a sprig of lily of the valley was pressed.

"Her name is Annie Ryan," he read. "I promised her that when this is over, I will come back for her. I am going to marry her.

"God help me, I must somehow live through this blood and pain. I must first survive the mud, and horror, and the tropical Cuban heat. I pray to God to let this be my last war. But I am never sure anymore if God hears me. I'm not even sure there is a God. I think somebody made Him up. I think He's just a lie.

"The firing is getting closer. Sometimes we cannot tell the difference between the cannons and the thunder that heralds another storm. I am so tired. Maybe it is because I am getting too old to fight anymore. Maybe it is because the wound in my leg is on fire, and the fever is making me so sick. But when I think of Annie, I think I have to hold on so I can get back to her, back to my lily of the valley. Just got to hold on a little longer."

Eddie looked up, blinking back tears. "I wish I could read this whole journal."

"Take these with you," Jeanette said. "I think Dad would have wanted you to have them." She handed him the journal, along with Gockie's commendation, and his purple heart.

Jeanette stood up and started pulling things out of the closet with a vengeance. Suddenly she was all business. "Come on, Eddie, let's get this project finished, before I have to think too much about what I'm doing. I want to curl up with Dad's journal knowing this is all behind me."

She filled up boxes and shopping bags with shoes, ties, and shirts. "If you can use any of Dad's clothes, help yourself. Are you sure you don't mind dropping everything off at the Salvation Army on your way home?"

"No problem," Eddie replied. "I've got plenty of room in Olivia's car. Like I said, I'm glad to be of help."

*   *   *

Over in the corner of the room, Lincoln Lightly danced a jig and saluted his grandfather, who tipped his cane to his hat brim and smiled.

Gershwin curled up in front of the radiator with a big grin on his face, feeling very much like an exceptionally good dog. "You guys can thank me later," he woofed. He reached his hind foot up behind his ear for a good scratch.

CHAPTER NINETEEN

Saturday, October 14, 1973

Jeanette followed a path past the old farmhouse to a clearing by a moss-covered waterfall in the woods. It was a beautiful afternoon, full of the music of the gurgling stream and bird song. The warm sunny day was a welcome respite from the early cold spell that had brought the first snow.

Children ran around the trees, playing tag and laughing The wedding guests who waited in the clearing for the bride and groom were as colorful as the autumn leaves drifting down around them. The bride's parents looked askance at the hippies. Like something out of a medieval faire, Eddie and Olivia's friends were like a kaleidoscope of color. They were decked out in flowers, feathers, and love beads. In contrast, Olivia's aunts looked like crows in their traditional somber black widows' weeds.

The Dragons thundered up on their motorcycles, shattering the serenity of Hacklebarney Farms. They stomped down the path in their black leather "colors," their chains rattling. Eddie's friend, Pagan, the leader of the gang, wore a Hell's Angels patch across his butt. Jeanette had heard that the only one way for a biker to get such a patch was to kill its original owner. She did not know if that was true, but if so, that feat alone would have earned Pagan his rank in the gang. Pagan's status as the son of his hometown's Chief of Police couldn't hurt either, since it shielded the Dragons from the long arm of the law.

It was obvious to Jeanette that the Dragons' arrival made the more conservative guests uncomfortable. In fact the whole scenario presented a problem for both the bride's and the groom's parents, who were already upset with them for not getting married in a church by a priest.

Eddie's mother, Faye, wore a formal chiffon and lace mauve dress with matching silk shoes, and pristine white gloves. An old fashioned white straw hat with a veil perched precariously atop her Phyllis Diller hairdo. Faye's eyes were red from crying. She dabbed at them with her damp lace handkerchief.

Bill Lightly stood unsteadily by his wife's side, chain-smoking his Chesterfields. He nervously shifted from one foot to the other. The way Faye clutched his arm, Jeanette wondered if she was holding Bill up, or vice versa.

Eddie's twin sisters, Mary and Terry, looked sweet and demure in their matching flowered granny dresses. Pagan, a huge hairy bear of a man, moved behind the twins and whispered something in Mary's ear. She blushed, but Terry giggled and moved closer to him, brazenly rubbing her breast against his tattooed arm. Pagan grinned, revealing two missing teeth. Faye saw their flirtation and burst into a new frenzy of tears.

Teresa Tempesta nervously fingered her rosary beads as she stood between her daughter, Anne Marie, and son-in-law, Joseph Mustachio. Anne Marie's broken arm was in a cast and sling. She looked pale, but her makeup covered the bruises on her face, and her long dress hid the contusions on her legs.

Only Teresa, Jeanette, and Eddie knew that Anne Marie's fall and miscarriage had not been an accident. The incident was already a dark family secret, which had been safely tucked away in the closet where all the moldy skeletons lay rotting.

Jeanette was sure that Joseph had counted on the security of that closet when he beat his pregnant wife, threw her down the stairs, and killed their unborn child. It sickened her to look at him.

She smiled and waved to her aunts, Rose and Irene, who stood in the shade of a tree, away from the rest of the group. No doubt they had never envisioned such a gathering. The old dears had never socialized with hippies and bikers, especially the likes of the Dragons.

Jeanette sniffed the fumes in the air. There was so much marijuana smoke wafting through the forest, that it created a haze in the branches of the trees. She would not be surprised if a stoned rabbit or deer stumbled into the clearing, or birds fell from branches.

Christopher Fortune arrived, looking handsome in a comfortable flannel shirt and jeans. Jeanette's heart skipped rope when she saw him. She watched her estranged husband greeting everyone, smiling his Cary Grant smile. She longed to run over to him and take his arm as if they still belonged together. He was being so charming to Rose and Irene, making them laugh and feel comfortable.

Chris looked up and saw Jeanette. He smiled and waved, and she smiled and waved back. She took a step toward him, but a shadow hand bolted the door that had almost opened. She stepped back into the safety of her self-made fortress.

Olivia's brother, Arlo, sat tailor fashion on an old tree stump. With his long hair in his eyes, Arlo resembled Cousin It from "*The Adams Family*". He strummed "*Scarborough Faire*" on his guitar. His pregnant wife, Tranquility, daisies braided through her long blonde hair, sat adoringly at Arlo's feet, accompanying him on a silver flute. They wore matching tie-dye tee shirts and torn hip-hugging jeans. Tranquility's swollen belly protruded between the bottom of her shirt and the top of her pants, revealing an inside-out navel.

In the silence following their song, Eddie's friend, Jude, the mail-order minister, walked up the path. His bare feet rustled in the autumn leaves that carpeted the forest floor. Jude wore purple striped bell-bottom jeans and a bright purple Nehru jacket embroidered with grape vines winding around Celtic crosses. Several strands of different colored love beads hung around his neck. Jude had long, curly red hair, and a bright red beard. He had tucked a daisy behind his left ear. His eyes looked glassy behind granny glasses with pink lenses.

Jude stepped up onto a flat granite rock by the waterfall and faced the wedding guests. "A wedding is happening," he announced.

One of the hippies played Tibetan finger cymbals while. Arlo and Tranquility launched into their rendition of Olivia and Eddie's favorite song, John Lennon's "*Imagine*".

The barefoot bride and groom walked up the path hand-in-hand. Eddie's hair was pulled back in a ponytail. He smiled sheepishly. He was wearing a flowing white gauze tunic and matching pants.

Olivia was a radiant vision in her hand-made gown trimmed with purple ribbons. A wreath of purple and white mums and autumn leaves framed her lovely face. She carried a single daisy.

The couple spoke their vows, borrowed from the poetry of Kahlil Gibran. As they exchanged jade rings, rays of sunlight poured down through the trees, bathing the forest in the warmth of an Indian summer day. When Jude pronounced the couple husband and wife, Olivia threw her flower into the water.

"*Relax, turn off your mind, and float downstream,*" Arlo sang.

Eddie kissed his new wife. Faye sobbed audibly. Bill hiccupped. Both sets of parents stepped forward to embrace the bride and groom. After congratulating the happy couple, their guests followed them back down the path to the yard behind the old farmhouse. Long tables covered with quilts and decorated with vases full of mums and autumn leaves had been set up in the yard. Rock music blasted out of Arlo's stereo, which had been moved outside for the occasion.

The hippies provided the food. They all had contributed their cooking skills to this communal "happening". Within minutes the table was overflowing with stuffed turkeys, hams, roast beef, lasagna, mouth watering vegetarian casseroles, corn muffins, loaves of home made breads, and a variety of salads, cakes, and pies.

"It looks like the first Thanksgiving," Jeanette said.

Anne Marie agreed. "All that's missing are the Indians."

"Maybe not." Jeanette laughed. She pointed to a young woman with long black braids, wearing a beaded head band and fringed deerskin jacket."

Arlo and his friends tapped the kegs of beer, popped the champagne corks, and poured liquid refreshments. The guests toasted the happy couple, drank to excess, and devoured the delicious banquet.

The shadows grew longer, the air grew cooler, and the afternoon waned. Jeanette and Anne Marie sat under a big tree in the corner of the yard watching the children playing. People were dancing, and a ball game had started in the side yard.

Eddie staggered over to them, knelt down, and hugged his cousins warmly.

"Congratulations," Jeanette said. She kissed him affectionately on the cheek.

"Thanks." Eddie turned to Anne Marie. "How are you doing?"

"I thought your wedding was just super, Eddie. The doctor says my cast can come off in six weeks, and then I'll be good as new."

"Annie, are you sure you're all right?" He pointed to her broken arm, and the bruises on her face that were beginning to show through where her makeup had faded.

"I got adjida. I think I ate too much. I might have a hiatus hernia."

"No, I don't mean that," Eddie said. "I mean what happened with your husband."

"Oh. Joseph and me made up. We're working out our differences. We have our problems, but who don't? I hate to bust your bubble on your wedding day, Eddie, but nobody's marriage is perfect." She glanced at Jeanette and said, "At least I have my man. I can't complain. I want for nothing."

Jeanette looked away. "Shit, Annie," Eddie said, "you are about as sensitive as a piranha."

Anne Marie shrugged. "I didn't say nothing that's not true, and you know it. In the matter of fact, Joseph wants to put the past behind us and move on. So there."

"Are you going for counseling?"

Anne Marie shook her head. "Joseph don't believe in it. He says those people are full of shit. But that's okay."

"I swear to God," Eddie whispered, "If he ever lays a hand on you again…"

"You look stoned," Anne Marie said bluntly. "What are you on?"

"Oh, I'm just a little punch drunk." Eddie smiled and rolled his eyes.

"There you are, darling!" Olivia glided over to them.

"I hope you'll be as happy as me and Joseph," Anne Marie gushed.

Eddie looked at Jeanette and grimaced.

"Olivia, you are such a beautiful bride," Jeanette said. Welcome to the family."

"Thank you," Olivia smiled. She took Eddie's hand. "Darling, dance with me."

The bride and groom danced across the yard.

"Aren't they a beautiful couple?" Anne Marie sighed.

Jeanette nodded. Maybe it was the champagne that made her blurt out, "Anne Marie, I'm really worried about you. I don't believe you are all right."

"Oh, get off it, will you, Jeanette? I was just upset that night at the hospital. I should never have told you and Eddie what happened. They gave me drugs, and I just exasperated is all. It was no big deal, really."

"Anne Marie, this is not the right time or place, but we really need to talk. I think you need help. What Joseph did to you is a very big deal."

"I wish you would stop pressurizing me. I said I'm fine. Except my gentiles are still sore, and Joseph is getting really impatient."

"Your gentiles?"

"Yeah, you know, my private parts. Joseph says since I don't have any stitches from my miscarriage, he don't see why he has to wait. He says if I make him live without sex, he'll get it somewhere else."

Jeanette was appalled. "Please tell me you're joking."

Anne Marie shook her head. "Well, what is he supposed to do? Joseph's all man. They need it more than we do, you know. Personally I hate sex. It's sweaty, and sticky, and disgusting. I only put up with it because it's my duty."

"Anne Marie, this is your life we're talking about! You just had a miscarriage. Say no."

"Oh, I couldn't do that, Jeanette. That would be wrong. Maybe you can't understand because yours was a failure, but the way to have a happy marriage is to be a snoopy…"

"Don't say it," Jeanette snapped. "Sometimes I think you are just as sick as that creep you married."

From the far end of the yard, Joseph caught Anne Marie's eye. He raised one eyebrow and snapped his fingers.

"Excuse me," she said, struggling to her feet, "I have to get my man a beer."

Jeanette sat in the shade of the tree and took deep breaths in an attempt to calm down. She felt so helpless where Anne Marie was concerned She did not want to accept that getting through to her cousin might be hopeless.

She watched hippies and bikers going in and out the back door in a steady stream. She needed to use the bathroom. Jeanette rose and headed into the house.

The house reeked of marijuana smoke. No wonder the few conservative relatives who had been invited to the wedding were staying outside. The downstairs bath was busy, so Jeanette used the one upstairs. On her way out, she heard laughter coming from behind the closed door of one of the bedrooms. The door opened, and two Dragons rattled into the hall, grinning.

"Looking for the punch?" the one who looked like a yeti growled. He nodded toward the door and laughed. "Go on in."

Jeanette opened the door that led into Arlo and Tranquility's library. Built-in shelves held an extensive and eclectic book collection. A dulcimer sat on the cushioned window seat in the gable. Two comfortable looking old stuffed chairs covered with Indian print bedspreads flanked a round table. In the center of the table was a large punch bowl. A half dozen or so people crowded the small room.

"Have some punch," one of the biker mamas said. She smiled and handed Jeanette a cup full of the pink concoction.

"What's in it?" Jeanette asked.

They all laughed. A man with pheasant feathers in his hair said, "A little bit of everything. Classic punch, man. This stuff is definitely not for the fossils. Arlo set it up here for the hard-core partiers. Go ahead, try some."

Jeanette was thirsty. She tasted the punch. It was delicious. It seemed to be a mixture of Hawaiian punch, soda, and rum. She thought the hippies and bikers must be naive if they thought a "fossil" like Uncle Bill couldn't handle this. The punch did not taste as potent as the high balls Uncle Bill liked to drink. It seemed pretty benign and refreshing. Jeanette emptied the cup and drank another.

"Not bad," she said. "Thanks." She opened the door to go back downstairs.

"Have a good trip," the biker mama called.

CHAPTER TWENTY

Saturday, October 14, 1973

Joseph Mustachio took a bite out of a turkey drumstick. Jeanette thought he looked like Henry the Eighth, if Henry the Eighth had looked like an ape, that is. He waved the drumstick around in the air. She saw streamers, like rainbows, trailing after the meat. She felt a little dizzy, and leaned against the door.

"May I have this dance?"

Where did he come from? Chris seemed to materialize out of thin air. He held out his hand. Jeanette felt like she could see through his eyes right into his soul, and it was a place that was full of light, a safe place. He smiled. Dazzling. Gorgeous. God, but she loved him.

She was in his arms, gliding, the Righteous Brothers singing "*Unchained Melody*". Where were the Righteous Brothers? She didn't see them among the guests. It didn't matter. All that mattered was that she was where she belonged, and she never wanted to leave. Chris swirled her through rainbow streamers all around the yard.

Jeanette laid her head against Chris' chest. She could feel his heart beating beneath her ear. She could hear the blood coursing through his veins, like a gentle waterfall. Christopher was warm and vibrant. He was everything wonderful.

"*I need your love,*" the Righteous Brothers sang.

"Are you all right?" Chris asked. He sounded concerned. Why did he sound that way?

"I've never been better," she sighed. "Don't you just love weddings, darling?"

"*I've hungered for your touch,*" the song proclaimed, echoing her feelings.

Chris laughed as he swung her around, making her feel dizzy again.

"You stupid fucking bitch!"

Everything stopped as the wedding guests stared at Joseph and Anne Marie. She had tripped and spilled beer on him. Joseph looked more like the gorilla in the Natural History museum than ever to Jeanette. In fact, he looked like a monster. His eyes were black with rage.

The warmth she had felt in Chris' arms turned to a sudden chill. Jeanette could see auras around people, and the one surrounding Joseph Mustachio was murky and dark, like congealed blood, but with flames shooting through it.

She leaned back into Chris, and he folded his arms protectively around her. Jeanette was grateful for the sanctuary of his arms because Joseph was really scary looking.

She watched the scene play itself out in slow motion. Joseph stood up, swung his arm toward Anne Marie, and hit her across the face so cruelly that she fell, hitting the ground hard. Anne Marie struggled to her feet sobbing, and ran, a blue aura trailing behind her, into the woods.

Then all hell broke loose. Eddie Lightly went crazy. He jumped on Joseph Mustachio, pummeling him and screeching like a wild animal.

"Call the Red Cross!" someone yelled.

One of the hippies reached into his pocket and pulled out some pills. "I have white cross, man," he responded.

"You fucking bastard!" Eddie screamed at Joseph. "I'll kill you, you filthy fucking bastard!"

They rolled on the ground, and in spite of his weight and strength, Joseph seemed helpless as Eddie pinned him down, sat on top of him, and punched his face. Blood spurted from Joseph's mouth. Joseph threw his hands up, trying to protect his head, but it did no good. He squirmed and screamed under the mad man who was beating the crap out of him.

Jeanette muttered something under her breath.

"What did you say?" Chris asked.

"I said don't fuck with Tarzan."

No one made a move to stop Eddie, until Olivia, who was in tears, begged Pagan to do something. Pagan moved to pull Eddie off Joseph, but Uncle Bill stepped in and grabbed Pagan's arm.

"Leave him alone," Bill said grimly. "Joseph has been asking for this."

Pagan looked surprised at the old man's passion, but he nodded and stood his ground.

"Get him, Eddie!" Bill shouted. "Use that left hook I taught you." Bill punched the air and hopped around like a boxer.

Finally, Bill nodded to Pagan. "Okay, he's had enough," he said. Pagan signaled the Dragons, and three of them pulled Eddie off Joseph.

"Let me see what I can do to help," Chris said softly.

"Go ahead." Jeanette nodded. Her head was spinning.

She watched Chris help Olivia wrap ice in a towel and hold Eddie's bruised knuckles against the pack. No one made a move to help Joseph. He lay curled up in a fetal position, puking blood and beer into the dirt.

Jeanette turned toward the woods, where Anne Marie had run. The sun was going down, and the trees looked dark and menacing in the twilight. She shivered. The day had turned cold.

"Annie," she whispered. This was like one of the games they used to play when they were kids. When they pretended they were the "Three Mosquitoes," she and Eddie always rescued Anne Marie from monsters.

"Are our childhood games a prophesy of our future?" Jeanette asked herself. "Is all this happening because we created it with our thoughts?"

Somehow real adventure lacked the charm of pretend games. She thought it strange that at this moment she would be entertaining such philosophical reflections, which seemed to her to be quite profound.

Jeanette ran into the darkening forest, determined to find Anne Marie and rescue her from the horrible monster, her husband. It shouldn't be too hard to find her. Anne Marie was the one who, because of her cast and sling, looked like a mummy.

∗   ∗   ∗

"William Lightly, this is none of your business!"

"I think it is my business. I care about your daughter, even if you don't. How can you even consider letting her go home with that son of a bitch? Are you really that fucked up? Are you really that cold hearted? I can't believe you would defend that asshole against your own child!"

Pagan had retrieved Anne Marie from the edge of the woods, where he found her sitting under a tree crying pitifully. Her mother was now trying to convince Anne Marie it was time to go home with her husband. There had been enough embarrassment for one day.

"You have been drinking too much as usual," Teresa Tempesta sniped. "Keep out of this. Joseph is her husband. Her place is with him, right or wrong. Your son did not help matters losing his temper like that."

"My son made me prouder than I have ever been in my life," Bill retorted. "My only regret is that he didn't kill the bastard."

Teresa turned disgustedly and walked away.

Most of the guests had said their goodbyes. Olivia and the Dragons were keeping Eddie on the side of the yard farthest away from Joseph Mustachio.

Joseph picked himself up. Bruised and bleeding, he stumbled to his car. Teresa Tempesta sat primly in the back seat. Joseph cringed when he saw the anger in her eyes.

"Get your wife, and take me home," his mother-in-law said. She glared at him. "We will deal with the way you treat my daughter later. You two are a disaster waiting to happen. This is going to stop."

"We're leaving, Anne Marie," Joseph called. "Get in the car."

Christopher Fortune took Anne Marie's hand. "Don't go with him. You don't have to go with him. If you need a place to stay, I have an extra room at my house. Please, Anne Marie, you have got to get out of this situation for your own safety. Can't you see what you're doing to yourself?"

"It's okay," Anne Marie sobbed. "It was my own fault. Please, Chris, this is embarrassing enough. Just let me go home with my husband. I just want to go home."

"Get in the car," Joey called, starting the motor, "or you can fucking walk home, bitch."

"You see how he is," Anne Marie whined. "I have to go, or it will only get worse."

"Anne Marie," Chris said, "this is not about Joseph; it's about you. Why do you let him treat you like this?"

"Because I love him. You don't understand, Chris. Joseph is not like this when we're alone. He just had too much to drink, that's all. Joseph is never comfortable in a crowd. I shouldn't have forced him to come today. He wanted to stay home and watch the ball game. It's my own fault, can't you see that?"

Chris threw his hands up in a gesture of hopelessness. Anne Marie got into the car with her husband and mother, and Joey burned rubber down the quiet country road.

Eddie walked over to Chris and shook his hand. He winced from the pain of his bruised knuckles. "Thanks for trying, man."

"You okay?"

Eddie nodded. Pagan and the Dragons approached Eddie. "We're getting on the road, man," Pagan said. "You want we should take that bastard out?"

"Don't tempt me," Eddie said grimly.

"Where's Jeanette?" Chris asked.

Eddie held the ice pack against his bruised cheek, where Joseph had landed a blow. He shrugged his shoulders.

"What does she look like?" Pagan asked.

"Long black hair, blue flowered dress…"

"Oh, she had some of the orange sunshine," Pagan's girlfriend said. "I saw her head off into the woods."

"Orange sunshine?" Christopher looked puzzled.

"It's in the punch," Eddie muttered.

"What's in the punch?"

"Orange sunshine, you know, LSD…and a couple other things."

"What? What other things?"

"Yeah, man, the Dragons spiked the punch with LSD, mescaline and magic mushrooms."

"What!" Chris exclaimed. "Are you saying Jeanette drank that?"

"Yeah, man," Pagan replied.

"Oh my God! Are you all crazy? Jeanette has never tripped before!" Chris was furious. "If anything happens to her…did you see where she went?"

Pagan's girlfriend pointed to the place where Jeanette had disappeared into the trees.

"Don't sweat it, man," the leader of the Dragons told Chris. "She'll be fine. It's all harmless shit. She'll just have a groovy trip, that's all. Chill out, man."

Christopher didn't wait to reply. He was already in the woods calling her name.

*   *   *

Jeanette was lost. There were so many trees, and it was getting dark. She thought she had turned around and headed back to Arlo's, but the farther she walked, the farther in the woods she found herself. She must have become disoriented somehow. Where was the stream? She could trace it back to the waterfall and find the path that way, if she could just find the stream.

Jeanette sat down under a huge old tree, whose branches touched the ground all around her. It was the kind of tree she used to play house under when she was a kid. Its branches were like the walls of a shady room. The light of the setting sun still shone weakly through the leaves. Jeanette could see their veins. She could hear the tree breathing. She could smell the dirt beneath her, and the autumn fragrance in the air.

Suddenly, just at the moment the sun passed over the rim of the earth, leaving a trace of pink in the sky, the tree came to life. Thousands of tiny birds burst into song. Where had they come from? She had not seen them before. Jeanette wondered what kind of birds they were? They were all different colors, their music sweet and bell-like in the twilight, like vespers. As quickly as it began, the song ended, and the birds all flew away. Jeanette parted the branches of the tree to resume her search for Arlo's house.

She came to a clearing on the edge of a high granite cliff. The sight of the full moon took her breath away. A cartoon path led up to the moon. The path was lined on either side with brightly colored cartoon flowers. Jeanette sat down on the rock and looked up the pathway to the moon. The man in the moon winked his eye and laughed. He rocked back and forth in the sky as he sang, *"I'm in love with the man in the moon, and I'm going to marry him soon…"*

"Sing with me," the man in the moon called to her, and Jeanette sang along with the stars and the flowers with faces that lined the cartoon path.

"How funny, that the moon knows that silly song, too," Jeanette thought. She watched the cartoon stars dance around in the sky when they sang.

Jeanette looked up at one particularly bright star. "Must be a planet," she thought. No sooner had she focused on it then she seemed to be sitting on top of it. It was a very small mauve-colored planet, and she had to struggle not to fall off into the vast blackness of the universe, where she would be lost among the gazillions of twinkling stars.

She held tight to a little flowering bush, hoping its roots were a strong enough anchor to hold her on the planet. Far away in the dark night sky she could see Earth, and she thought it really did look like the big blue marble from the children's television show.

Suddenly, Jeanette was aware that she wasn't alone. Someone was sitting next to her, someone not entirely solid. "Dad!" she exclaimed, recognizing his dear old face.

Lincoln Lightly embraced her and smiled. "Hello, pussy cat."

"Is it really you, Dad?"

"It is, really. I don't know how long this trip of yours is going to last, Jeanette, but for the time being you can see beyond the veil."

"I'm having a hard time keeping my balance on this little planet," Jeanette complained.

"Take my hand," her father urged, and when she did, she did not feel frightened anymore. "You don't ever have to feel afraid," Lincoln told her. "Everything that happens in your life has a reason, a lesson, a beauty beyond your comprehension."

"Why do you shine like that?" she wondered, reaching up and touching Lincoln's glistening beard.

"It's my light body. I'm beginning to get used to it. It is really quite wonderful, not heavy and clammy like a solid body."

"Sometimes I am afraid, Daddy. Life does not seem very beautiful to me. It's lonely and painful, especially since you're gone. I miss you. I miss Chris."

"You don't have to miss him. Why don't you go back to him? He loves you a great deal."

Jeanette sighed. "You don't understand. I have hurt him too much. Chris deserves happiness, and I can't give him that. He wants children, and I can't give him that, either."

"Why not? You are still young and healthy. Why can't you give Christopher another child?"

"I'm jinxed, Dad. Besides, I can't go through it again. I can't carry a child inside my body, only to lose it. I can't stand any more loss. It all hurts too much."

"Jeanette, it is time to break that cycle. You need to change your focus. You need, what is it you always call it, 'an attitude adjustment'? You are not the only one…"

"Oh, don't give me that 'you're not the only one' crap. Yes I am the only one, Dad. I am completely alone in this. No one understands my pain. How could they? You have never been in my shoes, so don't tell me how to walk in them." The tears burned her eyes like fire.

"There once was someone who would understand your pain, dear. Did you read my journal yet?" he asked softly.

She shook her head. There was a loud rustle of wings…big wings.

"Now I know I'm dreaming!" Jeanette exclaimed when the angel landed next to them. He bore a striking resemblance to Mario Lanza, except for his rosy wings that almost matched the color of the little planet.

"Color coordinated angels," she mused, watching her dead father talk to the seraph. They stood a few feet away from her, occasionally glancing her way. It looked like they were arguing. Only Dad would have the nerve to argue with an angel. He was waving his arms around and gesturing, with that passionate expression on his face she remembered so well. Finally, the angel nodded, spread his wings and flew away.

"Nice company you keep, Dad," she remarked.

"That's Mario. He's my guardian angel. Isn't he wonderful?"

"Incredible! Do I have one?"

"Of course! Didn't those nuns teach you anything? She's right behind your left shoulder, and she's incredibly beautiful. She looks a little like my Lizzy."

Jeanette strained to see behind her shoulder, but all she got a glimpse of were some sky blue and white wings. She had the feeling the angel was giggling.

"She looks like my mother?"

Lincoln nodded. "The angel is a little taller. She looks very powerful to me, and very wise. You should pay more attention to her."

"Wow!" Jeanette whispered. "I wish I could see her."

Lincoln beckoned to the angel. "Come on," he urged. "What can it hurt to let her meet you just this once?"

A whisper of music tickled Jeanette's ear.

"She is a little shy," Lincoln explained. "Come on, then," he entreated, "Jeanette will probably think this is all a dream later."

The angel stepped around her and faced Jeanette, gently fanning her wings and bowing gracefully. "Hello," she said, with a voice like liquid moonbeams. She was blue and white, with long white gossamer hair that was stirred by a perpetual breeze. Her most striking feature was her eyes, blue as the ocean, with kaleidoscopic flower-like irises. Her smile made Jeanette feel as if everything in her life had a reason.

Jeanette was speechless.

"What is your name?" her father asked the angel.

"I am called Reliance," she said in her lilting voice. She reached out her hand and Jeanette took it. When she touched the angel, she felt like she was infused with light.

"You…you are so beautiful," Jeanette said awkwardly.

Reliance laughed. Jeanette heard a harp glissando. "Are you always this happy?"

"I am happiest when your heart is full of joy," Reliance replied. "But, yes, I am almost always this happy. You might say joy is my job."

The angel addressed Lincoln. "Are we going now?"

He nodded. "I convinced Mario it would be a good idea. We must hurry, before Jeanette gets back to normal."

"Where are we going?" Jeanette wondered.

"Remember, I am always with you." Reliance smiled and resumed her place behind Jeanette's left shoulder.

Lincoln took his daughter by the hand and pulled her to her feet. "Come on," he urged, "there is someone I want you to meet."

They left the little mauve planet and flew into the void.

CHAPTER TWENTY ONE

Saturday, October 14, 1973

Jeanette looked at the little girl who sat on the window seat. Outside the window, clouds swirled in a beautiful blue sky.

"Cute kid," she thought. "I wonder who she is?"

"Hello, Mother," Isabelle Fortune said, smiling broadly.

Jeanette looked at Lincoln. Her face registered the confusion she felt. That rosy-winged angel named Mario stood behind him, smiling. "Why don't you two get to know one another?" he suggested.

Mario Lanza and Lincoln Lightly faded into the mist.

She sat down on the window seat. The little girl smiled and handed her a lily of the valley. "My father always told me this was my mother's favorite flower," Jeanette said. "He used to call her his 'lily of the valley.'"

The adorable child giggled.

"Who are you? Why did you call me 'Mother?'"

"I am one of your possibilities, and you are mine. If you will let me, I would love to be your daughter."

"I don't understand."

"There are many things we do not understand in this vast universe, and many things we have no need to understand, only to accept," the child said, with a wisdom belying her apparent age. "I only know what could be, if you are willing to let it be. And, oh, Mother, it would be so wonderful! I do not think I am allowed to say more than that."

A golden mist swirled around them. The little girl's eyes filled with tears. "You have to go now, Mother." Isabelle touched Jeanette's face longingly.

"Oh, don't cry!" Jeanette exclaimed, instinctively putting her arms around the child. "Why are you crying?" She was such a beautiful little thing. It felt so natural, holding and rocking her like this. It was like some horrible dark void inside Jeanette filled up. It felt like a miraculously healing balm.

"Please want me," Isabelle pleaded. "Please, Mother, take a chance on me. I promise I won't die."

                *   *   *

"Jeanette! Jeanette!"

She heard the words as if from a great distance. Suddenly she was the child; she was the one being comforted and rocked. Jeanette opened her eyes and looked into his. She saw the moonlight reflected in Chris' eyes.

She was lying on the granite rock ledge. It was cold, but Chris' arms were warm and strong. He was kissing her face, and caressing her hair. "Chris!" she whispered. "I was dreaming."

"Thank God I found you," he murmured. "Thank God you're safe." He leaned over and kissed her very gently on the lips.

Jeanette had forgotten how his kisses drove her wild. She grabbed him around the neck and kissed him back, passionately. She was starving for him. She needed him more than warmth, more than food.

A shooting star crossed the sky. "Take a chance," the night wind called. "Come on, darling," Chris said huskily, "I'm taking you home." "Make love to me here," Jeanette whispered.

Chris looked up at the moon. His jaw was tight as he struggled to bring himself under control. The night air was cold, but he was sweating.

"When I make love to you again," he sighed, "I want you in full control of your faculties. I am not going to take advantage of your vulnerability."

"Take advantage!" Jeanette wanted to cry, but she knew he never would. He was too chivalrous, too noble, and that was one of the things she loved about him. Chris was a man of honor.

Jeanette felt dizzy. She shivered as she rested her head on Chris' shoulder. "I'm glad you found me, too," she whispered.

Chris picked her up in his arms and carried her into the woods, back toward Arlo's farmhouse.

*   *   *

Monday, October 16, 1973

"Come on, wake up!"

Gershwin pulled the covers off the bed. Jeanette had already thrown the alarm clock into the wall. The broken clock lay on the floor next to the bookcase. The dog jumped up on the bed and licked her face. She pushed him away and rolled over, moaning.

"Come on, you're gonna be late for work!" he woofed.

"Some days Jeanette makes things rough," Gerswin thought. She had spent all of Sunday in bed, and she was still groggy and miserable.

"What did you do to yourself?" he barked. "Come on, I want to walk you to work, and I can't hold it in much longer. Wake up! Wake up!"

Finally, eyes still closed, Jeanette rolled out of bed and headed for the bathroom muttering, "I think I'm dying."

Gershwin padded down the hall after her. Satisfied that she started her shower, he skipped his daily mouse check and dashed out the doggy door for the tree, where he lifted his leg with a sigh of relief.

Indian Summer was surrendering to cold, cloudy days. The air smelled like rain. A bright orange and gold leaf fell on the dog's head while he was doing his business. If Jeanette had slept any later, he would have had an accident in the house. That always got him in trouble.

A gray and white shadow moved on the other side of the picket fence. Was that who he thought it was? Gershwin fairly quivered with excitement. Igor was on his way home from a night of cat debauchery. The cat had not seen or smelled him yet.

Gershwin looked up at the bathroom window. It was steaming up. Jeanette was still in the shower. He had time. He hid behind the tree and waited, ears trembling, tail twitching.

Finally, Igor, looking somewhat haggard and mangy, got within pouncing distance. The cat looked exhausted. He was limping slightly, like he had been in a fight. His fat furry tail was matted. "Perfect," Gershwin thought. "The idiot is off his guard."

As Igor staggered toward the back stoop, Gershwin jumped out yapping. Igor froze, his body arched, his fur stuck straight up. The cat hissed and bolted. Gershwin had to give him credit; the moron was really fast. Igor was up the tree in a flash, spitting down at him. He looked freaked out and really pissed off. Gershwin was so pleased with himself he rolled over on his back and laughed hysterically.

"You rat fart!" the old cat hissed. "You're road kill, dog!"

That made Gershwin laugh so hard he had a coughing fit. "Well, enough fun," he thought. He had a job to do. He had to get Jeanette to work. The dog ran back inside and gobbled down his breakfast.

Jeanette was already struggling into her clothes, holding her head and chug-a-lugging a Pepsi. "I need a jump start today, Gershwin," she groaned. "I can't believe people deliberately do this to themselves. This must be what they mean by 'crashing.'"

Gershwin nuzzled her knee. "I don't know what you're talking about," he barked, "but if you don't feel good, I'll take care of you."

She patted his head as she reached for her shoes.

Gershwin saw the ghost of Lincoln Lightly sitting on the dresser. "Hi, Lincoln," he barked.

"Good morning, Gershwin," Lincoln said. He pointed to his journal. Jeanette had set it on the bedside table. "See if you can get her to take that with her."

Gershwin ran over to the table and took the journal in his mouth.

"What are you doing?" Jeanette cried. "Here, Gershwin, bring that here."

Gershwin dropped the book obediently at her feet. She picked it up and brushed it off. It wasn't too wet. "No!" she said. "Bad dog!" Jeanette stuck the journal in her purse.

Mission accomplished.

"Don't pay any attention to her," Lincoln said from inside the mirror. "You're a good dog."

"I know," Gershwin said, calmly licking his paw. He followed Jeanette to the front closet and watched her put on her coat.

"Think I'll need my umbrella?" she asked.

The dog looked up at her and grinned. He followed her to the front door.

"Are you walking me to work today?"

Gershwin woofed.

"Okay." Jeanette laughed. "I'll enjoy the company."

The dog followed Jeanette down the front porch steps. Gershwin heard scratching on the upstairs window. Igor was glaring down at him. Igor raised a paw, claws unsheathed. "Just wait until I get my claws on you," the cat growled.

Gershwin laughed and turned his butt to the cat. Tail in the air, he trotted happily down the street next to Jeanette.

He walked her all the way to Bloomfield Center and left her at the front door of the bank where she worked. Jeanette bent down and patted him on the head. She smiled at an approaching coworker.

"Did Gershwin walk you to work?"

"Oh, wow," Gershwin yapped, "it's Gloria Osky."

Gershwin thought Gloria was an amazing looking woman. She was six feet tall, and she always wore four-inch spike-heeled shoes. Gershwin kept a good distance from Gloria's lethal feet.

He remembered Jeanette telling her father that Gloria had been a model back in the fifties. She had discovered her style then, and had never changed it. Gloria never wore any color but black, and her dresses were always skin tight. She liked tight clothes because they emphasized her gigantic bosom.

Gloria wore her jet-black hair in a tight bun at the nape of her neck. Her makeup style had gone out with the fifties, along with her wardrobe. Her face was very white with no rouge. Ignoring the current fashion, she wore no eye makeup and blood red lipstick.

Gloria Osky looked like a big black predatory bird to Gershwin, especially when she leaned over and petted him with the bright red claws she called fingernails.

"Be a good boy today, okay, Gershwin?" Jeanette bent down and gave him a warm hug. She giggled when he licked her face.

"I'm always good," he barked.

CHAPTER TWENTY TWO

Monday, October 16, 1973

"I think what Anne Marie needs is an 'Eyerectomy.'"

Jeanette gave Lamont a puzzled look. "A what?"

"You know," he explained, waving his fork with a flourish, "that's when you have your eyeballs removed from your rectum so you won't have a shitty outlook on life."

Glitter Man raised his glass. "I'll drink to that!"

They were having dinner in Lamont's elegant dining room. As usual, Lamont was entertaining in style. The sweet strains of a Chopin prelude filled the house. The table, covered with an exquisite French lace tablecloth, glistened with Lamont's best china, silver, and crystal. Tall candles matched the beautiful white roses in the centerpiece.

"Doesn't Glitter look like Peter O'Toole tonight?" Lamont sighed. Glitter Man seemed to delight in the comparison.

Jeanette speared another piece of swordfish on her fork, popped it in her mouth, and washed it down with vintage wine. She leaned back in her chair. "This is so delicious, Lamont. I feel almost human again. It's just what I needed. Good friends, good food…"

"Fine wine," Lamont finished as he refilled her glass.

"Well, as we were saying," Glitter observed, "as much as we love her, your cousin is the only one who can put an end to her situation. Frankly, as long as she denies anything is wrong no one can help her."

"I know," Jeanette said. "But it is so frustrating, Glitter, not to mention frightening. One of these times Joseph could kill her."

"How embarrassing to create a scene at Eddie and Olivia's wedding like that. He sounds like a first class jerk. This pasta is to die for, Lamont."

"Thank you, darling. Jeanette, Anne Marie knew what Joseph was like when she married him. He did not magically turn into a monster when he put the ring on her finger. I seem to recall hearing more than one horror story when they were still dating.

"Oh, I know. Even in school, everyone knew Joseph Mustachio was twisted, including Anne Marie."

"Then why did she marry him?" Glitter asked.

"She thought he was romantic. She used to call him the 'Wild One'. She begged him to wear leather and get a motorcycle like Marlon Brando. According to Anne Marie, though, Joseph was more interested in wearing her panty hose when they had sex."

"Ooh," Glitter breathed, "Kinky. Now this is getting interesting!"

Jeanette continued, "Anne Marie thought the chip on Joseph's shoulder was romantic, very James Dean and all. She thought it was funny when he called himself a 'rebel without a pause'. I did not agree."

"And after all that, your cousin married the bozo anyway," Lamont said dryly. "Don't waste too much sympathy on her, Baby Cakes."

"I love her, Lamont," Jeanette protested. "I worry about her."

Lamont patted her hand. "I know, Baby, I'm sorry."

"Speaking of engagements," Glitter Man said. He was grinning broadly. He fanned his face with his left hand. Jeanette had not noticed the sparkling sapphire and diamond ring on his third finger. She looked at Lamont, who blushed.

"Tell her," Glitter urged.

"Tell me what?"

Lamont reached over and took his lover's hand. "Glitter and I have decided to tie the knot. We're getting married."

Jeanette emptied her glass and held it out for more.

"Oh, we know it won't be legal in this homophobic society," Glitter said. "But we're having the ceremony anyway. It will be a symbolic way of celebrating our commitment."

Lamont smiled. "We want you to be our Matron of Honor."

Jeanette was touched. "Of course I'll be there for you. When? Where?"

"Halloween," Lamont replied.

"At your annual party?"

"Won't it be absolutely fabulous? Everyone we care about will already be there. And you still have to come in costume, Baby Cakes, just like every Halloween. There is one possible glitch, though. You may not want to do this."

"Why wouldn't I want to stand up for you, Lamont? You are one of my dearest friends, and I have never seen you as happy as you are with Glitter Man."

Glitter kissed her hand grandly. "Lamont was right. You are wonderful," he said.

"Well you see," Lamont explained, "we have asked Christopher to be our Best Man. You know he has been like a brother to me all my life. If that creates an uncomfortable situation for you…I mean, if you don't want to, we will understand."

Jeanette took a big gulp of wine. "Don't be silly," she said. "Chris and I are grown up mature people. Of course I'll be your Matron of Honor."

Lamont's eyes filled with tears. "Thank you, Cakes."

Jeanette offered a toast to their happiness.

$$*\qquad\qquad *\qquad\qquad *$$

Lamont Feather had inherited the estate in Montclair from Mrs. Armistead, who had inherited it from a famous composer. When the aging Mrs. Armistead hired Lamont to be her interior decorator, their association had grown into a close friendship. Lamont had moved in and become her caretaker and companion until she died. Along with Mrs. Armistead's mansion and money, Lamont had inherited her exquisite antiques, paintings, and the famous composer's piano.

Glossy photographs of movie stars from the golden age of Hollywood, autographed with personal messages, lined the wall going up the magnificent staircase to the second floor.

After dinner, Lamont, Glitter, and Jeanette relaxed on velvet couches in front of the blazing fireplace. Lamont's beloved English setters, Sophie and Seymour, dozed on the oriental carpet at his feet.

"So you never knew," Lamont asked Jeanette, "that this journal of your father's even existed?"

She shook her head. "We found both journals when we were cleaning out Dad's things. I gave our great grandfather's memoirs to Eddie."

"Did you read it yet?"

"I started reading it at lunch today. So far, it's just chronicles Dad's feelings about entering the seminary when he graduated from Seton Hall University. He writes about his passion for the priesthood."

"So does your father's diary have any juicy stuff in it?"

Jeanette laughed. "Not what you would call 'juicy', Lamont. It's just the story of a young man in 1928 who is in love with God and the writings of Saint Augustine. The only women he is interested in are the Virgin Mary and Saint Teresa of Avila. He cares about philosophy and theology more than anything in the world. He delights in translating Latin and ancient Greek. He writes about his teachers, and his growing friendship with Monsignor Donovan, who was his teacher. The Lincoln Lightly who wrote down his experiences in the seminary was young and innocent. I guess I never thought of my Dad that way."

"I can just see your father," Lamont mused, "sitting under a tree communing with nature and God. Why didn't your father become a priest, Jeanette? What happened?"

"My father had been in the seminary five years. He was close to taking his vows when his father was hit by a freight train and died."

"Ouch," Glitter shuddered.

"My grandmother was having a hard time. I guess she lost it. She had some kind of nervous breakdown. Dad didn't like talking about what happened to my grandmother. Her invalid father, who they called 'Gockie', lived with her. He needed caring for, and my father's brother was just a kid who was turning into a gangster in the streets of Newark. Uncle Bill was a real 'Dead End Kid' in those days."

"So your father got his first dose of reality, huh?"

Jeanette sighed. "I guess so. Those were hard times for that family. On top of that, the country was going through the Great Depression. There was no money. Dad had to take a leave of absence from the seminary to take care of his family. Anyway, he got a job over at General Electric, and that's where he met my mother."

"Aha!" Glitter teased, "So much for the vow of celibacy."

"I don't know about that. Whose parents ever had a sex life?"

They laughed. Jeanette continued, "When his leave of absence was up and he went back to the seminary, Dad could not get my mother out of his mind. He finally gave up his plans to be a priest because of his love for her."

A log popped in the fire. Seymour lifted a sleepy head and barked at the crackling flames. Sophie rolled over, running in her sleep.

"How romantic," Glitter sighed.

"Did your father ever regret his choice?" Lamont asked. "Did he ever reconcile the conflict between his love for God and his love for a woman?"

Jeanette shrugged. "I haven't gotten that far in his journal yet."

*   *   *

Gershwin snuggled closer to Jeanette. The only light in the room came from the bedside lamp and the green light of the alarm clock that showed it was just after 2:00 a.m. The autumn rain beat softly against the windowpane. Jeanette was engrossed in her father's journal, unaware that his ghost was precariously balanced on the headboard behind her, reading aloud over her shoulder to the dog.

"Mama set a place at the table for Wally again tonight," Lincoln read. "She pointed to the plate and told him to eat his vegetables. I fed Wally's vegetables to Gockie. Billy finally snapped. He jumped up and screamed, 'Wally's dead! I'm alive, Mama! What about me!' Then he and ran outside. Mama didn't even hear Billy. She didn't seem to know he was gone. 'Use your napkin, Wally, dear,' was all she said."

Jeanette turned to another entry. "We found Mama running down Market Street in the middle of the night again, calling for Wally. I have moved my bed into her room, and I've tied our ankles together with a piece of clothesline. If she gets up in the night, it will wake me up.

"I don't think she'll ever get over my little brother's death. Mama talks to Wally all the time now. She told the empty place at the table tonight that if he didn't eat his rice pudding, she would tell Papa when he gets home. She doesn't seem to know Papa is gone, too.

"Gockie sits in his wheelchair watching Mama. Tears run down his face. Sometimes the pain I see in his eyes when he looks at his daughter is like a poison arrow shooting into my heart. Since his last stroke, my grandfather can't talk anymore. He grows weaker every day, like he's giving up on life. I miss Gockie's war stories. I miss his humor.

"Last Saturday, Mama and I wheeled Gockie over to the cemetery and sat him in the shade under the old tree where he used to like to sit every day. He tried to squeeze my hand. I think he appreciated it. I took Mama to Papa and Wally's grave, and she prayed and seemed to understand. That night, though, Mama sat in the rocking chair hugging that old bear of Wally's and singing lullabies. Then she told Wally 'goodnight and God bless you, and don't forget your prayers.'

"Bishop Walsh has granted me permission to extend my leave of absence to a year. Monsignor Duffy set me up with a job interview tomorrow morning over at General Electric in Watsessing. I pray Mama will sleep through the night. If she tries to run through the streets in her nightgown again, the rope will wake me up and I can stop her.

"But, dear God, who will stop Billy? Skinny Gingeleski told me about Billy and the bootleggers. I know I have to confront my brother about that, but right now all I can think of is that my grandfather is dying, my mother has gone crazy, and my brother is alone out there in the night. God help me, how will I endure?"

Jeanette set the journal down in her lap. She looked out the window at the drizzling rain. Gershwin rubbed her tears off his head with his paw.

CHAPTER TWENTY THREE

Tuesday, October 24, 1973

Eddie Lightly sat on the roof of his apartment watching the skyline of New York City take shape along the eastern horizon. First light had brightened the sky from black to navy blue. He watched as each star winked and left the night behind.

Something stirred inside Eddie, something unfamiliar and wonderful that he wanted to grasp and hold onto, but it seemed very fragile and elusive. Eddie felt unsure of himself and strangely shy in its presence.

Ever since he had discovered the legends of King Arthur when he was a boy, Eddie had been fascinated with great leaders, great battles, and great wars. He had not waited to be drafted; he had joined the army the day after he graduated from high school. Eddie had volunteered for Vietnam.

He would be Alexander the Great, Lancelot, and D'Artangnan all rolled into one. He would come home a hero, riding in an open car with ticker tape raining down on him, and crowds cheering. He would grab a pretty woman on the streets of New York and kiss her, and Eisenstadt's picture of them would become eternally famous. People would say, "Who was that handsome soldier?"

Instead, Eddie the romantic came home a broken man. There were no ticker tape parades down Fifth Avenue for Vietnam Vets. There were no cheering crowds, no welcomes home, and no heart-warming photographs for the cover of Life Magazine. Eddie came home to nightmares that drove him to the roof at night.

Only a few short hours before, Eddie had taken a drag on his joint and raised a bottle of vodka to his lips, needing just one more shot of courage to give him the nerve to jump. He had looked over the edge of the roof to the street below, wondering if it would hurt very much. Hell, it couldn't possibly hurt as much as those fucking flash backs. It couldn't hurt as much as Lawton had hurt with that fucking hole blown clean through him.

Only a few short hours before, Eddie had decided he would have one last cigarette before he ended his life, like the condemned man he was. But when he bent down to pick up the pack, his eye had fallen on his great grandfather's journal. *How did that get there?* His mind was fuzzy from the 90-proof Smirnov and the Acapulco gold. Gockie's journal must have fallen out of his pocket, he reasoned. Eddie picked up the weathered old book, sat down on the roof, lit his cigarette, and began to read.

In a sudden moment of clarity that preceded the dawn, Eddie Lightly discovered that the old soldier of his recurring dreams had a name, and a face. The old soldier of his dreams was his own great grandfather.

Eddie hungrily devoured the stained pages of Joseph Stoeckel's journal. He discovered between the lines of his great grandfather's handwriting the same blood and filth and hopelessness of war that had overwhelmed him in Nam. Gockie had put into simple words all that Eddie had experienced and more, from the glory and horror of the Civil War right up through the Spanish American War, when a cannon ball had shattered his leg, ending his military career forever.

In the steaming Cuban jungle, fighting alongside Teddy Roosevelt and his Rough Riders, Joseph Stoeckel had written of his loss of faith, of his conviction that God was a lie that had never existed. At the same time, the old soldier described the men who fought and died beside him. He had rocked them in his arms. He had helped some of them live, and helped some of them die, just like Eddie and Lawton in the tunnel.

Gockie's journal struck a chord in Eddie Lightly that opened his heart. Reading the old soldier's words, Eddie suddenly knew, with a rush that was more than marijuana, that he and his great grandfather had been wrong. God was real, and He was in the old soldier's soul, writing through his pen. And God, through Joseph Stoeckel, was writing to Eddie Lightly.

*   *   *

Eddie could not see what the ghost of Joseph Stoeckel saw at the moment of his epiphany on the roof. The ghost watched in awe as Eddie's powerful angel wrapped her wings around him, raised her voice to heaven, and gave voice to the most indescribably beautiful song he ever heard. She sang with a melody full of sweet gratitude. The angel sheathed her shining sword. She burned with radiant joy.

Gockie leaned on his cane and patted his great grandson on the back. "This is your turning point, son," he said softly. "Well done. Welcome home."

*   *   *

When the sun burst into the sky, reflecting off the glass towers of the great city on the horizon, Eddie burst into tears. He did not know why he was crying, but he sobbed just like a baby. He no longer wanted to die. The morning air tingled with life, and life was the most precious thing he had ever known. He gulped air like he couldn't get enough.

Eddie flung the half-full bottle of vodka off the roof of the building. He heard the bottle shatter when it hit the sidewalk. He knew he would never take a drink again; he would never need to. He sank to his knees, opened his arms, and let the sun shine full on his face.

"Show me the way," he whispered. He closed his eyes, and light flooded through him.

When Eddie opened his eyes, a new passion burned behind them, along with a new clarity. He picked up his great-grandfather's journal and hurried toward the stairway that led down to his apartment. For the first time in years, Eddie moved with purpose. He held his head high. "Don't let me lose this," he prayed. "Don't let me ever slide back." He dropped his baggie full of pot and his cigarettes into the trashcan on the landing.

Eddie was in the shower when he heard Olivia stumble half asleep into the bathroom to get ready for work. He stuck his head out through the shower curtain. Olivia screamed. She didn't recognize Eddie. He had shaved off his beard.

"Good morning, beautiful," he smiled.

"Are you all right, Eddie?" Olivia asked. "You scared me."

Eddie reached out, grabbed her hand and pulled her into the shower with him.

"I'll show you how all right I am."

Eddie took her breath away with his kisses. "You'll drown me!" she gasped.

"That's right. I'm going to drown you in pleasure. I'm going to consume you with love."

✶   ✶   ✶

Later that afternoon, feeling refreshed and alive, Olivia Lightly sat outside the kitchen on the fire escape and watched the last autumn leaves spiral down from the trees across the street. She was not sure she would ever feel the same about soap and water again. Eddie came into the kitchen carrying a pizza. There was a light in his eyes she had never seen before. He looked so different without his beard, like a fresh-washed little boy.

"Eddie," she asked, "are you sure you're okay?"

"Never been better," Eddie smiled, popping the lids on a couple cans of Pepsi. He climbed out on the fire escape and sat down next to Olivia. "I got a job."

"You what?"

"I got a job. You know. You go to work. They pay you."

"What? Where?"

"D'Agostino's."

"Downstairs? The pizzeria?"

"It's good honest work, and it's a start. I have also been to see Monsignor Donovan."

"Eddie, you're scaring me!" Eddie laughed. Olivia thought he was so handsome when he smiled. Without the scraggly beard, you could actually see his dimples.

"Sweetheart," Eddie said, "I'm sorry. I'm so sorry for what I put you through."

"Eddie, you have nothing to be sorry for."

He leaned over and kissed her. "Hear me out, woman. I have been doing a lot of thinking. My G.I. Bill will buy me a college degree. And Monsignor Donovan promised to pull some strings to get me into Montclair State Teacher's College."

"I can't believe what I'm hearing," Olivia said.

"Believe it. I have decided to become a counselor. The Monsignor loved my idea of setting up a support group for Vietnam Vets. He wants to help."

"A support group?"

"Yeah. There must be lots of guys out there who feel isolated and alone like me. No offense, Olivia, God knows I know how much you care about me, and your love means everything to me. But unless you were there, you just can't understand what it was like. I have been locking myself behind a self-centered wall that shut you and everyone who loves me out. I have been so unfair to you, and I am not going to do that anymore. I'm going to get help, and then I'm going to learn to help others. By the way, Olivia, did I mention that I love you?"

Tears streamed down Olivia's face.

"Oh, God, have I hurt your feelings?"

Olivia shook her head. "No," she sobbed. "I'm crying because I'm so happy."

Eddie grinned. "Guess what I would rather eat than this pizza right now?"

Olivia flew into his arms, covering his face with tears and kisses. Eddie climbed in the window, pulled her in after him, swept her up in his arms, and carried her into their bedroom. As they made love, they knocked Gockie's journal off the bedside table. It landed on the floor next to the bed, next to Gockie's purple heart.

*   *   *

Gockie sat on the edge of Lincoln Lightly's bed, leaning on his cane. "I shall tell Lizzy to expect you soon, son," he said.

Lincoln's eyes felt damp. "I didn't know ghosts could cry," he said quietly.

"Are you kidding?" Gockie replied. "Some of those fools have done nothing but cry and moan for centuries. Especially the ones who don't believe they're dead."

Gershwin padded over and rested his snout on Gockie's knee. "It has been nice knowing you," he woofed.

"Thanks for your help, Gershwin." The ghost patted the dog's head. "You are a fine dog."

"I don't feel so fine today," Gershwin sniffed. "I feel kind of tired."

"Take care of my great granddaughter, and keep an eye on this old ghost here until the time comes for him to leave."

Gershwin nodded and sneezed. "I will."

"Well, with Eddie back on track, I have finished what I came for," Gockie said. "Frankly, I will be glad to get back to heaven. You'll love it when you get there, son."

Lincoln was at a loss for words. "I feel like I'm losing you for the second time, Gockie."

"You should know better by now, my boy. You never lost me the first time. What you know in your heart will be clearer to you when you reach the other side of the tunnel. Truly, we are eternally connected. Those we love are never lost."

"Gockie, I'm worried about something."

Gockie tipped his hat back and raised his eyebrows.

"It's just that Mario said I would have to go through the tunnel without a guide. What if I lose my way? What if I can't find heaven? I don't want to be one of the lost souls. I don't want to be a haunting ghost."

"Oh, I would not worry about that if I were you, Lincoln. Love in some form will guide you when the time comes. See you later." The ghost of Lincoln Lightly's grandfather smiled as he dissolved into tiny points of light that gradually faded, leaving Lincoln and Gershwin alone. The dog pawed at the air where the last spark glistened.

CHAPTER TWENTY FOUR

Thursday, October 26, 1973

Anne Marie Mustachio could barely fit into the booth at Gruning's because it was so full of shopping bags.

"It looks like you had a busy morning," Jeanette laughed.

"Marone!" Anne Marie gushed. "Hahnes was having a sale. I saved Joseph so much money! Why don't you knock off the afternoon and go shopping with me?"

"Because some of us have to work for a living. I'm sure Mr. Ferguson would not appreciate my ignoring the report that has to go out this afternoon."

"Oh, it would be worth it, Jeanette. I got the sexiest negligee for tonight. It has a built-in French push up bra that makes my boobs look really groovy. Joseph won't forget this anniversary. And check this out." Anne Marie pulled a pair of bright red panty hose out of one of the bags. "He'll love these. Especially when I rip them off him with my teeth."

"Wait a minute," Jeanette said. "Did I hear you right? Those are for Joseph to wear?"

Anne Marie nodded.

"Isn't that a little strange?"

"Well, Joseph won't have sex with me unless he's wearing panty hose, and these match my negligee."

The waitress asked for their order.

"I'll have a hamburger and a Coke," Jeanette said.

"I'm dieting," Anne Marie announced. "Bring me a green salad, no onions, and be sure the lettuce is fresh. If it isn't crisp, I can't eat it. I want lo-cal Italian dressing on the side, a root beer float, apple pie, make it ala mode with chocolate ice cream, and a double chocolate hot fudge sundae with the works."

"You're unbelievable." Jeanette laughed. "I'd be a blimp if I ate that."

"I'm having salad," Anne Marie retorted. "I'm on a diet. I can't eat any meat or potatoes or bread."

"But you can eat pie ala mode and hot fudge sundaes?"

"Cake and pie don't count as food. I can have as much as I want so long as I cut down on meat, vegetables, and bread. That's where all your fat is. It's a fact, so there."

"And ice cream?"

"Sometimes you are so dense, Jeanette. Ice cream doesn't count as food either. Ice cream is pure calcium, so you don't need milk."

Jeanette rolled here eyes. "And chocolate?"

"Oh, you need the chocolate for flavor. Can you believe Joseph and I have been married five years?"

"No. Actually, I can't believe you're still with him," Jeanette said dryly. "Look, Anne Marie, I have to say this. You're my cousin and I really care about you. Remember the tree house we played in when we were kids? Remember the day we took the Musketeer vow with Eddie?"

"Of course. 'One for all and all for one.'"

Jeanette nodded. "Well, if you were my friend, Annie, Musketeer vow or not, I would have walked away from you long ago. But you're more than a friend to me. We're blood, and we have always been like sisters. So I have to say this. It hurts me to see the way Joseph treats you, and the way you put up with it. Why do you stay with him?"

"Because I took a vow before God for better or worse. I have a duty to my husband. You don't understand Joseph. He had a horrible childhood. He just needs love."

"Anne Marie, he is a violent man."

"If I love him enough, Joseph will change. He just needs time. Sure, we have our problems, but who doesn't?"

"Why do you keep making excuses, when Joseph is obviously one of the bad guys? You need to leave him, Annie, for your own safety."

"I can't leave him. What would I do if I left Joseph, Jeanette? Do you really expect me to give up my house? My car? Just what do you expect me to do?"

"How about get a job? How about take responsibility for your own life?"

"A job?" Anne Marie laughed. "Doing what? I'm not smart like you, Jeanette. I don't have any skills. I don't have an education. How would I live? You don't understand. I can't give up everything. I don't want to be poor."

"He hurts you!" Jeanette exclaimed.

"You always hurt the one you love," Anne Marie replied. "Anyway, I provoke him. It's my own fault that Joseph gets mad."

"So mad that he breaks your arm? Annie, look at what you're doing to yourself!"

"Look, Jeanette, that was my own fault. I shouldn't have got pregnant in the first place. Anyway, Joseph felt so bad about that. He promised he'll never do it again."

The waitress brought their food to the table.

Jeanette struggled to keep her voice low in the restaurant, "I can't believe you. Do you even hear yourself? You are married to a man who demands you have an abortion because having a baby would interfere with his plans to buy a boat. He beats you. He almost killed you, and he did kill your unborn baby. He slapped you around in front of everybody at Eddie's wedding. I just can't believe you're sitting here defending that creep. If you won't leave him, will you at least get counseling? Will you at least think about that?"

"I don't need a shrink." Anne Marie bristled. "Joseph has the problem, not me. I'm not crazy."

"I didn't say you were."

"You should talk, considering your grandmother died in an insane asylum."

"Look, Anne Marie, I don't want to get into a thing with you here. Just answer me this. Are you happy?"

"Is anybody? I want for nothing. Joseph is a typical man. They all suck, and we have to put up with them. Men are all alike. At least I know how to keep my man, which is more than I can say for you. You're just jealous, so there."

"How dare you," Jeanette said darkly.

"You know this argument always gets us nowhere," Anne Marie sighed. "Let's change the subject."

"Fine with me." Jeanette took a bite of her hamburger.

"I have the most romantic evening planned," Anne Marie whispered, leaning over the table conspiratorially. "First, I'm making my famous chicken cacciatore, with plenty of champagne, and lemon marshmallow meringue pie just to warm him up. Then I'll run a bubble bath for Joseph and bathe him."

"Bathe him?" Jeanette couldn't help but wrinkle her nose at the thought of bathing that gorilla.

"Oh, yes. It's very sensual. Anyway, men are so dirty, you have to bathe them before you have sex with them."

Anne Marie pushed her salad aside and dug into the pie. "Now let me tell you," she continued, "how to turn a man on."

"Oh please don't," Jeanette begged

Anne Marie sipped her root beer float. "You start at the toes."

"Oh, is this being a snoopy for your man?"

Anne Marie ignored Jeanette's sarcasm. "First you suck each toe," she continued, "then you lick up his leg until you get to his groan."

"His what?"

"You know, his groan!" Anne Marie pointed to her lap.

"I'm trying to eat here! Can we leave Joey's groin out of this? I swear, Anne Marie, you are the queen of malapropisms."

"Well, you can call me whatever foreign words you want, miss know-it-all-nothing, but if you would listen to me, maybe you wouldn't have a failed marriage."

"I think I'm going to be sick." Jeanette pushed her plate away. "I really have to get back to work, Annie." She waved at the waitress. "Miss? May we have our check please?"

*　　　　　　　*　　　　　　　*

"*Tonight tonight, won't be just any night.*" Anne Marie sang along with the "*West Side Story*" soundtrack. The candles were lit; her chicken cacciatore was done to perfection. It smelled divine. "*Who cares how much he's tired, as long as he's hot,*" she and Chita Rivera sang.

Anne Marie looked at the clock. Joseph was late. He must have run into traffic. She checked herself in the downstairs bathroom mirror. Every hair was in place. Maybe she should just tease the top a little more. Her makeup was perfect. She thought her new neon blue eye shadow made her look like Cleopatra. Her boobs were pushed up nicely. She sprayed some more Shalimar cologne into her cleavage.

The new red negligee looked very sexy. She draped the red chiffon over her cast, so Joseph would not see the reminder of her imperfection. She stepped on the scale. 125 pounds. Damn. Only last weekend Joseph had told her she looked like a fat pig. Well, she would start another new diet tomorrow. No more dressing on her salad. She would be perfect, she promised herself. She would be just what Joseph wanted. He would never have reason to be angry with her again.

Anne Marie heard a car coming down the street. She ran to the window. It wasn't Joseph. "Please come," she whispered. "Please, God, let the next car be Joseph."

It wasn't. An hour and a half went by. None of the cars that turned down South Mountain Avenue were Joseph. She called his office. There was no answer.

Anne Marie poured herself a glass of champagne. She blew out the candles before they melted all the way down. She covered the chicken with aluminum foil. It was probably ruined. She put her favorite Peter Paul and Mary record on the stereo.

"*All my trials, Lord,*" they sang, "*soon be over.*"

Joseph was probably late, Anne Marie told herself, because he stopped to buy her anniversary present. She adjusted her collection of Lladro statues so they were exactly equidistant from one another. She hoped he had gotten her the sad clown one for their anniversary. Or maybe that diamond necklace she had hinted at.

She fluffed up the pillows on the couch. Everything looked perfect. Joseph was so lucky she was such a good wife. You could eat off her floors. The warmth from the fireplace was making her sleepy. She sat down in the wing chair by the window and drank her champagne. Then she got the bottle and poured herself another glass. Anne Marie dozed off with the light of the full moon shining through the window on her face.

When the front door crashed open, it startled Anne Marie awake. She hoped her eye makeup hadn't smudged. Her mind was fuzzy. What time was it? The fire had burned out. Oh, damn, she must have knocked the champagne over in her sleep. Joseph would kill her when he saw the stain on the rug.

Joseph staggered into the room. He was dead drunk, disheveled, and bleary eyed. His shirttails hung half out of his pants, below his jacket. Anne Marie ran over to him and threw her arms around him.

"Happy anniversary, darling."

He pushed her roughly away. "What's in the bowl, bitch?"

"I'll have dinner heated up in a minute. Why don't you clean up, honey?"

"Fuck you."

"Here, let me take your jacket." Joseph reeked of the disgusting, overpowering stench of booze sweat. She smelled something else. Jungle Gardenia. Joseph's secretary, Carol, used that perfume, didn't she? Anne Marie remembered buying it for Joseph to give his secretary for Christmas last year.

Joseph's mouth looked funny. What was wrong with his mouth? It was smeared all red. Anne Marie's stomach flipped over when she realized it was lipstick. A weird buzzing sound filled her head.

"Joseph, where have you been?"

"None of your fucking business. What does a man have to do to get a meal in his own fucking house, bitch?"

Joseph pulled his shirt off and threw it across the room. That was when Anne Marie noticed his fly was open, and he was exposed.

"Oh, God," she sobbed. "Joseph, have you been cheating on me?"

"'Have you been sheeting on me?'" He imitated her in a high nasal whine. Joseph reached into his pocket and pulled out a pair of blue lace bikini underpants. They weren't hers. He threw them in her face. "D'zat answer your question?"

With one sweep of his arm, Joseph cleared her precious collection of Lladros off their shelf. The statues shattered into a million pieces. Anne Marie felt a snap at the base of her skull, like something inside her was also shattering into a million pieces.

"You son of a bitch!" she screamed. "How could you do this to me? How could you do this tonight, on our anniversary? You stupid son of a bitch!"

Joseph moved toward her, his face dark and menacing. His thick black eyebrows had formed one big brow over his cold eyes. "Are you talking to me, bitch?" he said. His voice was so icy calm it terrified her.

She picked up an ashtray and threw it at him. He stumbled forward. His eyes were black with rage.

Anne Marie backed up against the bricks of the mantle.

"I'll teach you to talk to me like that," he growled.

"Joseph, no!" she begged, "Joseph, stop!" she screamed.

He was on her. He had his big beefy hand around her throat. He strangled her with one hand while he slapped her back and forth across the face with the other. The weird thing was, she didn't feel anything. Everything happened in slow motion. She didn't even feel it when he slammed her broken arm against the bricks and broke the plaster cast.

Anne Marie tried to scream, but he was closing off her air. She kicked and struggled, but Joseph was too strong for her. She saw bloody teeth fly across the room and realized from some far away place that they must be hers.

This can't be happening! Dear God, why is this happening? He promised! He promised he would never hit me again!

Joseph had stopped strangling her. Now he was gripping her hair in his two fists and slamming her head against the bricks. Anne Marie's flailing hand closed around something cold and hard. She grabbed Joseph's heavy high school football trophy. She brought it down on top of his head as hard as she could. She heard a loud cracking sound. She flung out wildly and hit him again.

The next thing she knew, she was on the floor, gasping for breath. There was blood everywhere, pouring out of her mouth and her nose. Her hair was caked with blood. Choking on bitter tasting blood and sobbing, Anne Marie used the end of her negligee to try to wipe it up. The blood was ruining her white carpet. Joseph would be so mad. Her arm where the cast had broken throbbed with pain.

Joseph was passed out, lying on his back. Something seemed to be wrong with his head His head looked flat. She crawled over to him. He lay there staring up at her. A dark stain was seeping into the rug under his head.

"Joseph?" she sobbed. "Joseph?"

Anne Marie couldn't say just when she realized her husband was dead. It was all a blur of police cars with flashing lights, and paramedics shining little beams of light into her eyes. They took her pulse. They bandaged her head.

Anne Marie's next door neighbors stood in her living room in their bathrobes. *When did they come in?* They stared at Joseph's sheet draped body with horrified expressions on their faces. Mrs. Webster was talking to a cop, who was taking notes. Anne Marie heard her say, "horrible fight, screaming, breaking things. I called 911."

Another cop was kneeling down asking Anne Marie questions. She couldn't seem to make the connection between her thoughts and her mouth. Her mouth didn't work anymore. A paramedic was arguing with the cop, saying something about head injuries, and couldn't this wait until later?

Anne Marie started screaming. She screamed until whatever was in the needle they stuck in her arm made her not able to scream anymore. Then she dove in to a dark pool where the full moon shone, and her reflection looked just like a Llardo statue.

CHAPTER TWENTY FIVE

Saturday, October 28, 1973

"What is she doing now?"

Mario waved his hand, and the clouds opened up so Isabelle could see clearly.

"Is that my mother sitting in a tree?" She giggled.

"The call it the 'monkey tree,'" Mario explained. "Jeanette has not been up there in years. She is reading your grandfather's journal. See? There he is, sitting on that branch over her head."

"Oh!" the child exclaimed. "I see him now. And there is his dog sitting at the foot of the tree." Gershwin was looking up at Lincoln. The dog grinned and wagged his head back and forth in time with the swaying branches. "Are all dogs that cute?"

"I don't think all dogs are as appealing as Gershwin." Mario smiled. "Although certainly most dogs could teach us a lot about unconditional love. Indeed, that is one of their purposes for existing."

"Can I have one when I get born?"

"I cannot answer that question. Whatever life you live will be governed entirely by your own choices. You know that is why the pages of the Great Book of Possibilities change with each passing moment."

"Angel?" Isabelle asked, "What is my father doing now?"

Mario waved his hand, and the clouds blew across their field of vision. The fog cleared once more, revealing Christopher Fortune.

Chris was helping transform the high school gymnasium into a Halloween fantasy. Bales of hay and sheaves of wheat lined the four walls. Black and orange crepe paper, along with skeletons, spiders, witches, and black cats hung from the ceiling. Chris and his student Dance Committee were putting the finishing touches on artful jack-o-lanterns. Their pumpkins would add an eerie touch to tonight's Halloween dance.

"Is Christopher Fortune going to the dance?" Isabelle asked.

Mario nodded. "He is one of the chaperones."

"I wonder what his costume will be?"

"He's going as Sir Lancelot."

Isabelle's eyes widened.

"Does he remember the time we knew Lancelot?"

Mario laughed. "No, dear. Once you cross the veil, you lose memories of other lives you have lived. Life must be lived in present moments, not the past."

"Oh how sad that Chris has forgotten living in Camelot," Isabelle said.

"Most people do not realize that the times and places which fascinate them come from karmic memories," the angel observed. "This, of course, is one reason why Camelot has always been one of Christopher's favorite times in history."

Isabelle watched as two of his students coaxed Mr. Fortune away from his carving. They begged him to inspect their makeshift haunted house in the corner. It featured a mechanical rat caught in a mousetrap, a creepy willow-the-wisp, and a black light tunnel full of spider webs.

"He looks like he is having a lot of fun," Isabelle said. Chris laughed heartily when the student vampire succeeded in startling him. "He would be a great father, wouldn't he?"

Mario nodded. "He is in his element."

"I remember," the child said wistfully, "when the three of us were together during the reign of Arthur. I remember the magic of the day we pledged to find each other again in future lives. It was the dawn of Hallowmas. We were going to change the world." She turned sadly away from the window.

"What is it, dear heart? Why are you sad?"

"I am running out of time, Mario. There are only three days left, and they are no closer to reuniting as husband and wife than they were when Lincoln Lightly went back there."

She climbed onto the angel's lap. He wrapped his rosy wings around her and began to rock her. "I am going to lose my chance to change the world," Isabelle sobbed. "I remember them, but they have forgotten me."

"Take comfort, Isabelle. You have a trinity of days. You are a trinity of souls. Have you forgotten that Love is the most powerful magic there is?"

*   *   *

Jeanette looked up from her father's journal when she heard a Tarzan call echo through Rossi's alley. Gershwin barked and ran toward the noise she had not heard in many years. Jeanette hardly recognized Eddie Lightly when he came jogging through the lots toward the monkey tree, followed by Gershwin.

"Eddie!" she exclaimed. He nimbly swung himself up into the branches and climbed up to the remnants of their tree house. "What happened to you?" She hugged her cousin warmly. She rubbed her hand on his clean-shaven face. "Where's your fur?"

"I do feel kind of naked. As for what happened to me? I guess you might call it an epiphany." Eddie smiled. "I was sitting under the bodhi tree like Buddha, and a nut fell on my head and knocked some sense into me."

They laughed. "Somehow I knew I would find you here, Jeanette."

"I had to come here," she replied.

"I understand. I also felt drawn to our old tree house. Have you seen her yet?"

Jeanette nodded. Her eyes filled with tears. "Eddie it is so horrible. I can't believe what happened."

"They're taking Anne Marie up to Overbrook Sanitarium today."

Jeanette shivered. "Our grandmother died there."

"I know." Eddie sat down next to Jeanette. He put his arm around her shoulder. Just like when they were kids, she passed him her bag of potato chips. He took a handful and popped one in his mouth. She handed him her Pepsi. He took a sip.

"What's going to happen to Anne Marie?" she said.

"I talked to the doctor this morning, when I went to see her. He said physically she should heal fine. There does not seem to be any brain damage. Mentally is another story. The doctor said her catatonia is not a result of her physical injuries."

"Oh, Eddie, it was so terrible. Annie didn't know me. She just sat there, with her empty eyes staring out from some dark place inside her."

"I know."

"I had lunch with her the day it happened. She was so animated, so excited about her anniversary."

"I should have let the Dragons kill the bastard when I had the chance," he said. "They offered, you know."

"We argued," she said. "We argued about Joseph. I begged her to get away from him. I begged her to get help, but she wouldn't listen to me. I keep feeling there must have been something I could have done."

"Jeanette, there was nothing anyone could do. I don't mean to sound cold, but Anne Marie made her choice, and it was a tragic one. I just left Aunt Tee. She is devastated. She blames herself. My father is taking Tee up to Overbrook to help get Anne Marie settled in. He hasn't left her side since this happened."

"Uncle Bill and Aunt Teresa on the same side? You must be kidding!"

Eddie laughed. "Yeah. Welcome to 'Lightly's Believe It Or Not.' My father brought Aunt Teresa home from the hospital yesterday morning. Neither of them had had any sleep. Mom made them a huge breakfast, and Aunt Tee slept in the guest room. When she woke up yesterday afternoon, Dad got her drunk, and Mom got her crying. Between Dad's booze and Mom's tears, Aunt Teresa's barriers finally went down. She and my father actually made peace with each other."

"Unbelievable."

"I hear Joseph's family is flying in to pick up the body tomorrow. They're taking him back to Oklahoma to bury him in the family plot."

"He can burn in hell for all I care," Jeanette said bitterly. "Eddie, do you think Anne Marie will ever come back to us?"

"I don't know. But I'm not giving up on her. I promised Aunt Tee I'll go up there at least once a week and read to Annie. The doctor says it's a waste of time. He says they don't expect her to ever come out of this."

"Oh, no, Eddie."

"Shit, doctors don't know everything. Maybe we can get through to her somehow. Maybe if I read her some of our favorite books from when we were kids, something will click."

"The Three Musketeers?" Jeanette smiled. "Tarzan?"

"For starters. Hell, if all she can handle is Dr. Seuss, then I'll start there."

"That's a great idea. I'm going to do that, too. Hey, Eddie, if Annie does recover, let's bring her here again. Maybe it will help."

"Make that 'when' she recovers, Jeanette. If there's hope for a fuck up like me, there's hope for Annie. Anne Marie was happiest when we were the 'Three Mosquitoes'. This tree house is our square one. Maybe we should bring her here, like you said."

Jeanette looked up at the tree branches silhouetted against the deep blue of the October sky. The shadows of the children they had been seemed to dance around her. She could hear their laughter in the wind blowing through the golden leaves. The memory was clear and sweet. The wind sent leaves dancing to the ground below.

A squirrel stuck its head out of a knothole high in the tree, screeched, and disappeared back inside the hole. Jeanette could not see what the squirrel had seen. The ghost of her father sat smiling down at her from the high branches.

Eddie said, "I always felt like I could draw strength from the roots of this old tree. I am not giving up hope for Annie, Jeanette."

"Eddie, I can't get over this change in you. What happened?"

"I got tired of feeling sorry for myself. I got tired of wanting to die."

"What do you mean, you wanted to die? Eddie, I couldn't bear losing you, too!"

"It was touch and go for awhile there, Jeanette. I did want to die. I was hiding behind booze and drugs so I wouldn't have to feel anything. I was turning into a pathetic shadow of my own father."

"Don't be too hard on him," Jeanette chided. "I understand a lot about Uncle Bill from reading my father's journal. I think I know why he drinks so much."

Eddie shrugged. "I don't want to go into all the gruesome details," he said. "I almost killed myself the other night. I was standing up on the edge of the roof, drunk and stoned out of my mind. I was going to jump."

"Oh, Eddie, no!"

"Yeah, well, I don't know why, but then I sat down right there on the roof and started to read Gockie's journal. The old soldier's words put so much into perspective for me. He wrote about war, and the reasons for it, and the men who die, and the men who come back. Finally, there was someone who had been through the same shit I had. Anyway, to make a long story short, by the time I was done, not only was I sober, but something had happened to me that I'm not sure I can explain. Suddenly I wasn't alone in my pain anymore. There was more to the world than just me and my self-centered existence. It was like God only needed a tiny chink to open in my armor so He could get in."

"I thought you didn't believe in God anymore."

"I was wrong. God is alive and well, I'm here to tell you."

"I can hardly believe what I'm hearing. This is wonderful! Are you going to join AA?"

Eddie laughed. "I don't need AA. I've got Gockie's words to keep me straight. Hey, look, I'm not going to run around proselytizing, and I'm not going to start going to church or anything radical like that. I'm talking about a personal spiritual experience here. I'm just saying I have found my own connection to whatever that thing men call God is. And when that happened, I didn't want to die anymore. I don't need booze anymore. I don't want drugs."

"Thank God."

"Yeah, well, I'm sick of being selfish. I want to get out there and help other guys who are in the same place I was. I want to let them know they are not alone. I want to let them know there is hope that life just might be worth living. I want to be a man my children can be proud of."

Jeanette threw her arms around Eddie and hugged him tightly. Tears streamed down her face. "Thank God," she sobbed. "Thank God you didn't leave us."

Eddie reached down and picked up her father's journal. "I see you have been doing some reading of your own."

Jeanette took the book out of his hand and held it against her heart. Lincoln Lightly smiled down at them from his perch on the branch over their heads.

"This is almost like having my Dad back again," Jeanette said quietly. "There are things I never knew about him. There are things he never told me. My father wrestled with his own demons, Eddie."

"I think we all do," he said.

"It broke my father's heart when he had to put his mother in the mental institution. Gockie had died, and my father sent your dad to live with their other grandmother so he could go back to the seminary. The problem was, my father had fallen in love with my mother in the meantime."

"Good for him!"

"So Dad went to the bishop, and the bishop told him he could do just as much good in the world being a lay man as he could being a priest."

"Score one for the bishop. Otherwise, you would never have been born, and then I would have been a lot lonelier."

"Well, I wasn't supposed to be born anyway," Jeanette replied. "One of the things my father wrote about is something I never knew. It turns out that my mother had a heart condition. That's why they were married so long and never had children. She was told never to get pregnant. I guess they thought they were too old or something, but one day they were surprised with the news that I was on the way."

"You little dickens."

"Eddie, all these years I thought my mother died in childbirth. My father never talked about her death. He only told me about how beautiful she was, and how much in love they were. I just assumed she hemorrhaged in labor, and I blamed myself for being born."

"Well that was pretty stupid," Eddie remarked.

"Oh, I got even stupider than that, Eddie. My mother's heart gave out when I was two months old. That's when she died. But I never knew that. So when my baby died, I thought it was God's punishment for murdering my mother. I was a jinx."

"Oh, Jeanette, I'm so sorry."

"I thought I did not deserve to be a parent, so I shut myself off from Chris. I was terrified to have sex because I was terrified I would get pregnant again. I didn't want to take the chance of murdering another innocent baby by being its mother. Now I see how wrong I was. And now it is too late. I have ruined everything." Jeanette burst into tears.

Eddie put his arms around her to comfort her. "Shh," he said, "it's okay, Jeanette. It's okay. You should never have kept all that inside all these years, baby. I could have told you how wrong you were."

"Oh, Eddie," Jeanette sobbed. "What have I done to Chris? I destroyed our life together."

"Look at me," Eddie said. He tilted her chin so she looked into his eyes. "Now listen to me. You have a choice here. You can wallow in the bullshit of more useless guilt and erroneous thinking. Or you can decide, like I did, to do something about pulling your life together. What's it gonna be? You're not leaving this tree without deciding."

"Listen to him," Lincoln whispered in her ear. "Listen to Eddie."

Eddie looked so serious. Jeanette felt like a great weight had been lifted from her heart. He was right. She should have unburdened herself years ago. Then maybe her life would not be such a hopeless mess now. "What would I do without you, Eddie Lightly?" she said. "You make me feel like I'm not nuts."

"You are nuts. We're all nuts." Eddie grinned.

She laughed. "I know. You have to let me out of this tree. I have to go somewhere."

"Where?"

"To the cemetery." Jeanette wiped her tears away. "I have to say good-bye to my baby."

"Do you want me to go with you?"

"No," she said. "I need to do this alone."

*　　　　　*　　　　　*

What were those two up to? Humans weren't supposed to sit in trees. They weren't squirrels or birds. Had Jeanette and Eddie lost their minds? Gershwin ran around the base of the monkey tree. "What's going on up there?" he barked. "Are you people ever coming down? Squirrels bite, you know."

He skidded to a halt, panting, in front of Lincoln. The ghost was leaning against the tree with a silly grin on his face. Lincoln patted his old dog on the back. He said, "I think there's hope for my daughter yet, Gershwin."

CHAPTER TWENTY SIX

Saturday, October 28, 1973

Gershwin walked down the street beside Jeanette. After the warm morning, a brisk north wind had turned the afternoon cold. Jeanette tugged the lambskin collar of her warm suede coat up around her ears and pulled on her gloves. By the time they reached the Green, a light snow had begun to fall. Soon the flakes were big and thick, turning the trees to lace and coating the ground with powdered sugar.

Gershwin waited patiently outside the florist on Broad Street while Jeanette went in. Gershwin liked snow, but he could live without the cold that went along with it. His paws ached in the cold. Sometimes it was an effort to wag his tail. Now he knew what Lincoln had meant when he complained about getting old.

Gershwin blinked away snowflakes as a dark shadow came into view. A German shepherd sniffed its way toward him through the snow.

"I hope he's friendly," Gershwin thought. They circled one another tentatively, smelling each other's butts. The shepherd was friendly. The big dog yapped and bounced at Gershwin playfully, and Gershwin bounced back. They chased each other around a tree, sliding in the slippery white stuff.

"Snow is so much fun," the Shepherd barked. "I love to run and dive in it."

"Yeah, it brings out the puppy in all of us," Gershwin agreed.

"Nice to see you," the shepherd said.

"Take it easy," Gershwin answered. The big dog pounced off through the snow, heading toward Bloomfield center.

Gershwin sat on the doormat outside the florist while the snow piled up on his head. At last Jeanette emerged, carrying three white roses. She bent down and patted him.

"I love you, too," Gershwin woofed.

When they got to the cemetery, Gershwin and Jeanette were the only ones in sight, if you didn't count the ghosts. There was a nasty looking one hanging around the old stone mausoleum just inside the iron gate. Flesh hung off the old man's rotting bones. The ghost had a big hole blown through its chest.

"Something terrible must have happened to that guy," Gershwin thought. He ran toward the ghost barking, trying to chase it away.

The ghost leaned over and yelled, "Boo!"

"You don't scare me," Gershwin growled, "You stay away from Jeanette."

The ghost stuck out its rotted tongue and drifted back inside its mausoleum.

The other ghosts in the cemetery seemed more polite. At least they were not grisly. They kept their distance. Most of them sat on their gravestones looking sad.

The cemetery was so quiet in the snow you could hear the flakes falling. Jeanette knelt down at her father's fresh grave. Lincoln Lightly's name and the dates of his life, 1903-1973, had been added to the stone below her mother's name.

"I miss you, Dad," she whispered.

Gershwin watched Lincoln's specter take shape. The dog looked at Jeanette. How odd that she could not see her father's ghost. She was blind to all the wraiths that surrounded them.

"Hi, Lincoln," Gershwin woofed.

"How are you doing, boy?" the ghost replied.

"I'm feeling kind of tired, to tell you the truth. I hope Jeanette takes me home soon. I just want to curl up by the fire and have a good nap."

"I know what you mean."

Jeanette looked down at Lincoln's grave. "This is a little awkward for me, Dad. I am not like Aunt Rose or Aunt Irene. I think nothing is in this grave but the empty shell that once housed your soul. I don't really know why I am here. I guess maybe I need some kind of closure. So here goes.

"I have been thinking a lot these last couple of weeks since you died. Something Eddie said this morning made me look at myself, and I didn't like what I saw. Eddie was talking about being self-centered. I don't want to live my life from that place, Dad. That is not what I learned from you. You taught me that what you claim to believe, or what you say you are has no meaning if you don't back it up with behavior.

"I never understood until I read your journal how much you lived that philosophy. You gave of yourself all your life. You sacrificed your dream to take care of your mother, your grandfather, and your brother.

"You even took care of strangers. I remember you organizing the food baskets and the toy and clothing drives for the poor. You probably wouldn't remember the time you asked me to give some of my toys to the poor children at Christmas. I dug through my toy box until I found a doll Aunt Teresa had given me when I was sick. It was an ugly doll, and I always hated it. And when I handed you that ugly doll, you fussed over me like it was the greatest sacrifice in the world. It wasn't. I was too selfish to give you a toy I liked."

Lincoln looked at the dog. "Apparently my daughter has indulged herself in guilt since childhood."

"I think guilt is her specialty," Gershwin agreed.

"But you were never selfish like I was. Monsignor Donovan told me at your funeral that whenever the church needed money to help someone out, he just phoned you, and you called your friends from college who had become lawyers and bankers. You pulled together whatever was needed. I never knew that, Dad. Monsignor told me that one time you even helped him build a church in a poor neighborhood. You proved that bishop right, you know. You did more good in the world than you ever could have accomplished as a priest."

"I could have told you that," Gershwin whined, sneezing the snow out of his nose.

"Shh," Lincoln chided.

"You gave me so much, Daddy. All those years you raised me alone, always putting my needs before your own. I never said thank you. And I never got to say goodbye." She gave in to her tears and let them flow freely.

"There is no need for goodbyes between us," Lincoln said softly. "I will always be watching over you."

"I just want you to know, if you can hear me wherever you are, that I have thought of a way to honor your memory. I am going to volunteer to take over your work where you left off. I'm going to help Eddie set up his veteran's support group. I'm going to make you proud of me."

"Dear girl, I have always been proud of you," Lincoln said, but Jeanette could not hear him.

"I love you, Dad," Jeanette whispered. She placed two of the white roses on the grave. "Tell Mother I love her too. Her sacrifice was the greatest of all. She gave her life to have me."

"I will tell her," Lincoln promised, "as soon as I see her."

"It won't be long now," Gershwin barked.

Jeanette stood up. She wiped her eyes and nose with her snow-covered gloves, and walked down the snowy road toward the "Grotto of the Holy Innocents". This was the part of the cemetery where children and babies were buried. Jeanette had not come here since the baby's funeral. She took a deep breath and approached the grave. She knelt down in the snow, and placed the last white rose on the ground. This time, Jeanette whispered only one word, "Goodbye," before she broke down completely.

Gershwin watched helplessly as Jeanette poured out all the heartache and pain she had buried inside her. He sat next to her. She put her arms around him and sobbed into his fur. Finally, her tears exhausted, Jeanette stood up and turned her face to the sky. She let the blizzard wash away her tears.

Gershwin struggled stiffly to his feet. The dog shook off the snow that had settled in clumps on his back and head. "Can we go home now, Jeanette?" he begged.

*   *   *

Jeanette and the dog left the cemetery just as the caretaker was closing the gates. It was getting dark, and the snow was getting deep. Jeanette paused on the Green across from the High School to watch the costumed students arriving for the Halloween dance. The sound of their laughter called across to her. The glow from the old gaslights along the street glistened on the newly fallen snow. She felt cleansed by her visit to the cemetery. Finally, Jeanette knew she could put her grief to rest. She had bid them all farewell.

She saw Chris' car pull into the school parking lot across the street. Chris got out, dressed like Sir Lancelot. He looked handsome. "Lancelot himself should look so good," Jeanette thought.

She took a step forward, and almost called out his name. She wanted to run across the street to him. Then she saw him go around to the other side of the car and open the passenger door. Chris helped Debbie Blanco out of the car. Debbie taught Sophomore English. She slipped in the wet snow. Jeanette could hear her squeal all the way across the street. Chris reached out to steady Debbie.

Jeanette knew Debbie. They had gone through school together. Debbie had always had her eye on Chris. She had wasted no time moving in on him, had she? She was dressed like Marilyn Monroe, in a blonde wig, tight red dress, mink stole, and ridiculously high spiked heels, which were deadly for walking in snow. Debbie gripped Chris' arm and gazed adoringly up at him as he helped her up the school steps.

Even from this distance, Debbie's flirtatious game was obvious. Jeanette wondered if Debbie could wiggle her behind just a little bit more, or be more brazen about letting her stole slip so Chris had a good view of her cleavage. Strident laughter and squeals carried across to the Green.

Gershwin barked, and Chris turned toward the sound. Jeanette grabbed the dog and pulled him back into the shadow of a tree.

"Oh, Chris!" Debbie shrieked.

He turned his attention back to her. Good, he had not seen them. As Chris and Debbie went into the gym, a big ice cube froze around Jeanette's heart.

"What was I thinking?" she said.

*   *   *

"I don't know," Gershwin barked. "What were you thinking? Can we go? It's cold out here." He nuzzled her leg with his nose.

As they walked across the Green, Jeanette continued her soliloquy.

"It's too late for us. I have ruined Chris' life enough. He deserves to be happy, although why he would want to date Debbie Blanco is beyond me. But it's none of my business anymore. Chris and I will be divorced soon. I guess I have to let him go, Gershwin."

"I'm freezing." Gershwin sneezed.

Jeanette crossed the street and started up the steps of Sacred Heart Church. Gershwin sat shivering on the sidewalk.

"Come on, Gershwin," she urged.

"Are you crazy?" Gershwin barked. "They won't let me in there!"

"Come on, boy, it's okay. This is half way home. Let's get warmed up."

Gershwin struggled up the slippery steps and followed Jeanette into the church. He shook the cold snow off in the vestibule.

"Good boy," Jeanette whispered. "Now be quiet. No barking."

The church was warm inside, filled with the scent of frankincense. Gershwin had never seen such a high roof. The space inside the church was vast. Everything was made of stone and fragrant old wood. Dim light poured through stained glass windows that were scenes with people in them. Hundreds of flickering candles in red glass twinkled in the shadows. So this was what the mystery building looked like inside.

Jeanette walked up to the front of the church and sat down in one of the pews. Gershwin followed her nervously, his tail between his legs. He curled up sleepily on the floor at her feet.

"I'm not supposed to be in here," he whined. "They don't allow dogs."

"It's okay," Jeanette whispered. "We'll be home soon, boy."

*   *   *

Jeanette felt comfortable sitting in the familiar old church. She had been baptized and made her first communion and confirmation here. She had been married here. She loved being alone in the huge open sanctuary, where whispers were echoes.

Jeanette closed her eyes. She thought of a favorite prayer from her childhood. "Angel of God, my guardian dear," she whispered. "Ever this day be at my side, to light and guard, to rule and guide."

Beautiful blues, like a kaleidoscope, danced behind her closed lids. When she opened her eyes, Jeanette saw a banner on the altar that she had not noticed before. It hung from the marble pulpit, just below the magnificent stone eagle. Just two words were embroidered on the banner, "New Life".

Jeanette thought about Christopher and Debbie Blanco. Maybe it was time she accepted that she had lost her last chance to reunite with Chris. She had destroyed her marriage. He had a right to find happiness in his life. All she could hope for now was to cut her losses and go on with her own life. Maybe it was time to heed the words of the banner. "New Life," she whispered.

"Come on Gershwin," Jeanette said, "Let's go home."

CHAPTER TWENTY SEVEN

Sunday, October 29, 1973

Jeanette glided across the ice. She felt invigorated by the cold air and the beauty of the setting. When Lamont called her this morning to invite her to go ice-skating, she had fought off her desire to crawl back under the cozy comfort of her covers and spend the day in bed. Now she was grateful that Lamont had talked her into coming, because it was a beautiful day.

Icicles hung from the white stone bridge that arched across the lake. Last evening's snowfall had continued until morning, blanketing Verona Park in white drifts that were dazzling in the sun. The lake had frozen thick enough for the season's first skating parties. Fragrant wood smoke from the pot bellied stove and the big stone fireplace poured out of the boathouse chimney.

Lamont and Glitter Man had pulled out all the stops, arriving with sleds in tow, so they could fly down the steep hills that bordered the small lake. As Jeanette skated under the old bridge, she wondered where Lamont and Glitter were. They must be in the boathouse.

Jeanette had not felt so carefree in a long time. It was good to be alive on such a lovely Sunday afternoon. She skated all the way to the end of the lake, carefully avoiding the danger of the thin ice down by the waterfall. She skated back and under the bridge again, enjoying the way the sunlight dappled through the willows, and sparkled on the ice.

Jeanette clumped across the wooden deck into the boathouse to warm her feet by the old pot bellied stove. She saw Lamont and Glitter Man sitting on a bench in front of the flagstone fireplace. They were drinking steaming cups of hot chocolate.

"Hey, chickens," she teased, "afraid of a little cold air?"

"We're just taking a break," Glitter replied.

"Uh, huh." Jeanette laughed. "That's why you're shivering."

"This weather is for polar bears," Glitter man complained. "I would rather be in the Bahamas on a sunlit beach, sipping tall tropical drinks with little umbrellas in them."

She sat down next to them, took off her skates, and wiggled her toes. A waiter came over to them, and she ordered a hot chocolate with lots of whipped cream."

Lamont asked, "Are you ready for Tuesday night, Baby Cakes? Ready for the wedding?"

"I'll be there with bells on, although I still don't know what to wear."

"Well," Glitter Man teased, "if all you wear are bells, I'm sure that will add a nice touch of interest to the affair."

Lamont playfully slapped Glitter's shoulder. "You need a Halloween costume, just like every year, dear."

"What are you two going as?"

"A groom," Lamont responded.

"A bride," Glitter Man giggled.

"Just wait till you see Chris' costume," Lamont gushed. He frowned when he saw the shadow pass across Jeanette's face.

"I already saw it. Last night I just happened to be walking across the Green when Chris arrived at the high school Halloween dance with his date."

Lamont looked confused. "What are you talking about?"

"I saw Chris go into the dance with Debbie Blanco. They looked very connected."

"You must be mistaken," Glitter Man said. "Lamont and I saw Christopher yesterday. He told us he didn't have a date for the dance. He was planning on going stag. He is a fine buck, if you'll pardon the pun."

Lamont slapped Glitter's shoulder. "Behave yourself. The pun is unpardonable. You're mine, sweetie, and Christopher is straight. You can't have him."

"I only have eyes for you, Lamont, you know that."

"Debbie was one of the chaperones for the dance," Lamont said, but she was not Christopher's date."

"Well it sure looked to me like Debbie was Chris' date," Jeanette argued. "She was all over him!"

"I'll tell you what happened. While we were going over our wedding plans with Chris, Debbie called. She was sniveling about being afraid to drive in the snow, and could he give her a ride to the dance? Christopher is too much of a gentleman not to respond to a lady in distress, and too much of a gentleman to think that slut is not a lady. That is how they happened to be together. Are you really that naive, Baby Cakes? Don't you know that Christopher Fortune is still hopelessly in love with you? He is about as interested in dating Debbie Blanco as he is in dating a cobra."

"Interesting analogy," Glitter said dryly.

"Have you ever met Debbie?"

Glitter shook his head.

"Take my word for it, darling. Sorry for insulting the snake," Lamont declared, "but Christopher would no more expose himself to that bitch's fangs than I would turn straight."

"Well, this must be where the elite meet!"

"Eddie!" Jeanette exclaimed. Eddie leaned over and kissed her affectionately on the cheek. "Lamont, you remember my cousin Eddie, don't you?"

"Of course." Lamont smiled, shaking Eddie's hand. "How are you?"

Eddie introduced Olivia. Jeanette smiled at how proud Eddie sounded when he called her his wife.

"Aren't you lovely," Lamont said to Olivia. "Eddie and Olivia, this is Glitter Man. By the way, I love your mittens!"

Olivia smiled. "Thank you. I like yours too."

"It's nice to meet you, Glitter Man," Eddie said, "I've heard a lot about you."

"How's the ice?" Olivia asked.

"Cold," Glitter complained.

"It's beautiful." Jeanette laughed. "It looks like we're having an early winter."

"Well, I'm about ready to brave the elements again," Lamont declared, "Come on, put on your skates and join us. In fact, why don't you two join us for dinner later?"

"Thanks for the invitation, but I have to work tonight," Eddie replied, lacing up his skates. "Olivia and I couldn't miss the first skate of the season. We met ice skating, you know."

"How romantic," Glitter Man sighed.

"I gotta go, guys." Jeanette had retrieved her shoes from under the bench and was pulling them on.

"Aren't you coming to dinner with us?" Lamont pouted.

Jeanette shook her head. "If I'm going to get my costume together in time for your wedding, I have to hurry home and get started on it."

Glitter said, "I thought you didn't know what you were going to be."

"I do now." Jeanette' eyes sparkled. She laughed. "I just figured it out."

"And?"

"You will just have to wait and see."

"Well, be beautiful, and don't be late for my wedding, Baby Cakes." Lamont kissed her on the cheek. She hugged them all and left the boathouse.

Jeanette walked down the path that led out of the park. At the entrance to Verona Lake, she paused on the small bridge by the waterfall to fill her eyes with the timeless picture of the skaters on the frozen lake. Lamont was practicing spins. Glitter Man was gingerly skating toward the bridge. Eddie and Olivia Lightly waltzed across the ice together gracefully.

*   *   *

"I'm a tired old ghost, Gershwin," Lincoln sighed.

Gershwin sneezed. "I know what you mean. I have been feeling a little under the weather myself."

Lincoln Lightly continued, "I just don't know if I'm doing any good here. One minute I can see how much Christopher Fortune loves my daughter, and how much Jeanette loves him, and I think my job is done. The next minute she's pulling away from him, and they are as far apart as ever."

Gershwin nodded.

"I'm ready to go back through the tunnel, Gershwin, especially now that Gockie has gone. I'm anxious to go on to higher things. You can't imagine how much I long to be reunited with my Lizzy again. I know she is there waiting for me; I could see her at the end of the tunnel. Maybe I should have let the angel take me to her. It doesn't seem that I have done much to help little Isabelle."

He had a faraway look in his eyes. "You should have seen her, Gershwin. She was such a beautiful child, all glowing, like an angel herself. She seemed to have such a sense of purpose. Now I fear all this may have been for nothing, and without the angel's guidance, I won't be able to find my way up the tunnel alone."

"Get a grip on yourself, Lincoln." the dog yawned. "Maybe this has all been a fruitless ride on a merry-go-round, or maybe not. Nothing is final until midnight Halloween. You know better than to give up hope before then. Look, the sun is going down already. Halloween will be here before you know it, and win or lose, you will be in heaven soon."

"I hope so," Lincoln sighed. "I don't want to be a lost soul. I don't want to be one of those pathetic creatures hanging around my own grave."

✳   ✳   ✳

"Remember what I told you," the angel Mario said, "You control your own destiny. Destiny does not control you. You have made the decision to incarnate again, and whatever life you choose will offer you many opportunities to learn and grow. More importantly, you will have unlimited chances to share the gifts you have to offer. You don't have to become the first woman President of the United States to do some good down there on Earth. Look at what Lincoln Lightly accomplished in his life, and he was a simple man. His name may never appear in the social register or 'Who's Who,' but he is well known in heaven."

"I know what you say is true," Isabelle sighed. "But I am not going back to the Great Book of Possibilities yet. Not while there is still a chance for me to become Isabelle Fortune."

"I just don't want you to be too disappointed if this thing doesn't work out."

The angel waved his rosy wings, sending a breeze out the open window that was picked up by the wind and carried down to earth. It blew in the attic window on moonbeams. It stirred Jeanette's hair as she bent over her work, guiding the yards of blue velvet carefully through the sewing machine.

Jeanette's grandmother's trunk sat open on the floor next to her workspace. It was filled with old clothes and colorful fabrics, some handed down through the family, some collected at rummage sales over the years to be used for costumes. Jeanette had dug through the trunk. Silken capes and turn-of-the-century lace dresses were draped over chairs and boxes in the treasure-filled attic of her father's house. An old golden hair circlet studded with semi-precious stones rested on top of a silk-lined cloak on the gabled window seat.

From a tape player in the corner, the Beatles sang about a long and winding road.

As Isabelle and the angel watched, Lincoln Lightly gazed out the attic window He was sitting on the window seat next to the golden circlet and silk-lined cloak. He petted the sleeping dog on his lap.

"Lincoln Lightly is dreaming of paradise," Mario whispered. He waved his wings again, and this time the breeze that blew right through the ghost into the attic room carried a tantalizing scent.

Gershwin raised his head sleepily and sniffed. "Do you smell something, Lincoln? What is that?"

"I don't know," the ghost replied, "but it smells heavenly."

CHAPTER TWENTY EIGHT

Tuesday, October 31, 1973

Jeanette walked down the deserted cobblestone street in Pinocchio's village. She stopped to look in the window of Gepetto's toyshop. A toy train with a smiling face crossed miniature mountains, which were just like the real snow-capped mountains that towered over the town. The little train chugged through tunnels. The tiny stuffed animals that rode in the cars were alive, and they waved at her. The toyshop window also displayed dolls, and puppets. A Raggedy Ann and Andy called out "Hello, Jeanette! Hi!" from their tea party in the back corner of the window.

"I have to get a train like that for the baby," she thought. She continued down the street, rubbing her hand across her swelling belly, thrilled and happy to be pregnant.

Jeanette sat down on the green park bench under the streetlight. She had been here before, in a dream. She knew she was dreaming now. An old photo album appeared on the bench beside her. It had a brown leather cover embossed with a golden ship in full sail.

Jeanette opened the album and looked at the pictures inside. There were her mother and father, riding bicycles on the boardwalk in Atlantic City. They were a beautiful young couple. Jeanette remembered these pictures of her parents' honeymoon. On the facing page were photographs of Jeanette's grandparents.

She turned the page and studied a picture of her great grandfather. Dad always called him "Gockie." He had been photographed sitting on a bench under a big leafy tree. The old man was leaning on a wolf-handled cane, his hat pulled low over his face, his overcoat buttoned up against the cold.

Within the pages of the album, Jeanette's life unfolded in pictures. The baby turned into a curly headed child, then a shy awkward teenager. Suddenly, the photographs in the album began to move. Each played out its own movie on the page.

"Wow," she murmured, "living pictures."

Jeanette was inside the album now, inside a picture, waltzing in Chris' arms. As the room spun around her, she saw Halloween decorations. She was at Lamont's party. Someone was playing the wedding march.

She was back sitting on the bench again. "I'm seeing the future!" Jeanette exclaimed. Eagerly, she turned the page to see what came next.

"Why don't you swallow your pride and get back together with Chris?" her father asked. He appeared on the bench beside her. He looked bright and happy.

"I am afraid it is too late for us," Jeanette sighed. The photo album fell off the bench onto the cobblestones. She made no attempt to pick it up.

"Oh, my darling daughter, you are so wrong. Maybe it would be too late for some people, but in your case, as long as you both breathe, as long as your hearts beat, as you long as you both live, it will never be too late."

Jeanette said, "I'm pregnant, you know. I don't remember having sex."

"This is a dream, my dear. Perhaps the dream is reminding you that life is always pregnant with possibilities. Perhaps it is telling you that you have many opportunities for new beginnings, for new life."

"New life," Jeanette repeated. "Why is that familiar? Where did I see that?"

"Life is ever changing," Lincoln told her. "That is both the beauty and the difficulty of it. Accepting this paradox is an important key to happiness. As your generation would say, 'go with the flow.'" He took her hand. "When you were a little girl, you used to scare me to death with your risk taking. You were always climbing the monkey tree or jumping down into the brook. Never mind that you might not be able to climb out again. You were the kind of kid who would leap in the pool without looking to see if there was water in it first, without caring if you knew how to swim."

Jeanette laughed and nodded. "But I never drowned, did I?" she teased. "I must have made your life hell."

Lincoln Lightly shook his head. "You made my life a joy. You gave me a reason to go on when so many times I wanted to give up. You kept me young. You made me believe in magic. You were my greatest teacher."

"How can that be? You were my father. What could you have learned from me?"

"If you open your heart and let a child into your life, you will learn for yourself what you taught me. Just watch a baby who is completely helpless learn to roll over. Watch him push itself up onto his knees and struggle until he finally crawls. And when that baby is learning how to walk, he will fall a hundred times, but he will never give up. He will keep on trying until one day he takes off running.

"I watched you grow from a helpless baby into a child who mastered not only physical grace and coordination, but the wonder of language, and you did it all with such eagerness and joy that I was ashamed for every day I failed to thank God that I could do all those things too.

"You ask me what I learned from you? I learned respect for the human spirit. I learned to embrace life enthusiastically. I learned tenacity. I learned that there just might be some magic in the world, and to look at life with wonder. I learned unconditional love. In all my life, you were my best teacher."

Lincoln pointed at Jeanette's swollen middle. "It is not too late for you to make this dream come true. Why don't you take a chance and embrace the new life that is eager to come into you? Don't close yourself off from the magic of love and the wonder of life. Why did you stop taking risks?"

"I just wanted to protect myself from the pain of more loss."

"You were wrong," Lincoln said gently. "Nothing is ever lost; only changed. Someone very special told me once that we are eternally connected. I think I finally understand what he meant. We are sparks straight from the heart of God. The light and the magic that is contained within our love lasts forever."

"Your words sound so good," Jeanette sighed. "If only I could believe them. But I am here, and you are gone from me, and I miss you. I want to believe, but I reach out, and you are not there. I pick up the phone to share something with you and remember you are gone, and my heart shatters all over again."

"Let your dreams become our phone line, Jeanette. Come to this street in your dreams whenever you need me, and I shall meet you here. Whenever you are confused, whenever you need comfort, come for any reason. We have been given this gift. For the rest of your life you can reach out to me in your dreams, and I can meet you halfway. Like magic."

"Here in Pinocchio's village?" Jeanette giggled.

"Here in the village where my grandfather was born. This is the reflection of a real place. I don't know why you carry this image inside your mind; perhaps it is a gift from your great grandfather. The street where we sit is where Gockie lived and played as a child, before his parents brought him to America."

Jeanette's eyes grew wide. She tried to see more clearly through the rising fog.

"Now go and begin your life again," her father said, his voice fading. "You have important work to do, and important things to focus on. Remember, without risk, there would be no adventure to make life worth living. Remember that I love you, and I am with you always."

When Jeanette opened her eyes, it was Halloween.

CHAPTER TWENTY NINE

Tuesday, October 31, 1973

Cars lined Upper Mountain Avenue as what looked like the whole town arrived at Lamont Feather's Victorian manor. The costumed guests turned their vehicles over to valets to park. They presented their invitations at the gate with the big stone eagles, where they were directed up the long winding driveway. Lamont's Halloween parties were one of the highlights of the season. His guest list included the well-heeled members of the social register, many of whom were his clients.

Behind the high stone wall that encircled the grounds, thick trees blocked the view of the estate from the street. Grinning jack-o-lanterns lined the path that led through Lamont's dormant azalea gardens up to his Gothic front door.

At the entrance to the house, Lamont's guests encountered a life-sized snow lion. Next to the lion stood a classic smiling snowman with a top hat, carrot nose, and mouth and eyes made out of coal.

The old mansion sat on top of a hill just below Eagle Rock. A grape arbor patio extending from the north wing of the mansion afforded a beautiful view of the New York skyline. The city glistened on the far horizon, some fourteen miles to the east. Tonight the arbor was hung with colorful Japanese lanterns. Twinkling white lights reflected off a huge ice sculpture pumpkin filled with orange punch. Trays of black and orange caviar lined a long table. Fountains of pink and white champagne bubbled on either side of the ice pumpkin. Outdoor heaters warmed the patio so that the guests could mingle comfortably, enjoying champagne and caviar under the sparkling lights.

Eddie and Olivia had accepted Lamont's invitation. When they arrived at the party, the dogs were the first things they saw. Sophie and Seymour had been freshly groomed for the occasion. The English setters had yellow tartan bows tied to their collars. They followed the couple through the entrance hall past the Martians, witches, ghosts and ghouls into Lamont's living room with its massive stone fireplace and Italian carved dropped ceiling.

No one saw the real ghost in the room. Lincoln Lightly sat by the fireplace watching the festivities. Classical music consistent with the Halloween theme poured through hidden speakers in all the rooms. Tchaikovsky's dying swan surrendered to Mussorgsky's "*Night on Bald Mountain*".

A sign pinned to Eddie Lightly's back identified him as the Invisible Man. He wore his old camouflage fatigues and combat boots. He had painted his face camouflage.

Olivia, dressed as a gypsy, was awed by the opulence of the home. "This place is unbelievable," she said. She took Eddie's hand and led him through the crowd to the dining room. An exquisite crystal chandelier hung suspended over Lamont's antique round table. A bar had been set up between paintings of the Scottish Highlands. A breeze set the chandelier tinkling and sent rainbows dancing around the walls each time someone passed through the French doors that opened onto the patio.

Eddie asked the bartender for two cokes.

"Those paintings look like Constables," Olivia whispered.

"The whole place is like a museum," Eddie agreed.

"It's more like a castle." Olivia leaned closer to read the tiny brass label on one of the paintings. "Eddie!" she exclaimed. "These really are Constables!"

A massive glowing jack-o-lantern graced the center of the lavishly appointed table. Its face had been carved into the shape of a witch and cat flying on a broomstick The table was laden with trays of jumbo shrimp, crab, and lobster tails. Eddie and Olivia filled their plates with a variety of cold salads. Silver chafing dishes with warming candles contained Lamont's homemade lasagna, turkey, stuffing, roast beef and scallops bordellaise. Fresh loaves of pumpkin bread, golden corn and molasses bread, and crescent rolls completed the spread.

An antique buffet in the corner held a colorful assortment of desserts, including a six-tiered wedding cake topped by two grooms. A vine of tiny orange pumpkins made of icing decorated the wedding cake. In the spirit of the holiday, Lamont also served lady fingers, pumpkin pie, and frosted petit fours decorated with tiny skeletons, pumpkins, and black cats.

Eddie and Olivia found seats on the folding chairs, which had been lined up in rows before the fireplace. The mantle had been draped in Lamont's yellow plaid family tartan and decorated with white and yellow mums mixed with birds of paradise, ferns, pumpkins, and colorful gourds.

"This is almost as good as sex." Olivia swallowed a mouthful of scallops. "Have you ever seen such costumes?"

There were several vampires among the guests, and at least three Cleopatras, including the mayor's wife. The mayor himself was the Wolf Man. A fully set dining room table walked by, the head of its wearer presented on a platter as the main dish. His neck was surrounded by garnish. Several butterflies and a fairy fluttered through the room as "*The Funeral March of the Marionettes*" played on the stereo.

"Eddie and Olivia! We didn't know you would be here tonight!" The Gilberts, Montclair's most up and coming real estate couple, approached them. Anita Gilbert's favorite cliché was that she knew "absolutely everybody who was anybody." She was dressed as a sugar bowl. Her husband, Larry, was a spoon. Anita leaned over and whispered to Olivia, "We weren't sure we should come. We were afraid we might be the only straight people here, and Larry was a little nervous, you know?"

Olivia wrinkled her nose. "There are a lot of straight people here," she replied icily. "Straight, but not narrow, that is." Olivia's sarcasm went right over Anita's head.

"Well," the sugar bowl giggled, "I promised Larry I would protect him if anyone tries to attack him."

"Oh, I don't think he has to worry about that," Olivia observed.

Eddie asked, "If you feel that way, why did you come?"

"Oh, we couldn't pass up an opportunity like this!"

Eddie knew the aggressive Gilberts would do anything to become real estate moguls. Lamont had steered some good business their way already, but the couple were always hustling for more.

"Networking is the name of the game," Larry said, puffing out his spoon chest pompously.

"Everybody who's anybody is here tonight," Anita gushed.

"Well, you know what they say," Eddie said dryly, "it's not who you know, it's who you blow."

Olivia choked on a lobster tail. Larry and Anita laughed nervously.

A seven-foot-tall papier mache penis with eyeholes, feet, and arms walked by. "That must be hot," Larry declared.

"One that big and hard has to be," Olivia agreed.

Eddie looked around the room. "I don't see Jeanette or Chris here."

"Oh, they're upstairs with the homos, helping them get ready," Anita explained. "I understand Lamont Feather is being very superstitious about everything. He won't let his lover see him until the ceremony. Do you think they are flaunting their alternative lifestyle on us tonight?"

"Have you ever met this 'Glitter Man?'" Larry asked Eddie.

Eddie nodded. "Yeah, I met him. Glitter Man is cool. He's really a nice guy."

"What do you suppose his real name is?"

"No one knows," Olivia replied. "I don't think anyone really cares. He's just Glitter Man."

"This is so weird," Larry murmured, draining his glass.

The Pope leaned over and shook Eddie's hand, "Happy Halloween," he said, "I'm Fagatha."

"Eddie and Olivia Lightly," Eddie replied, "and these are the Gilberts, Anita and Larry."

Fagatha shook the Gilberts' hands. "Your outfits are a scream."

"Thank you, your Holiness." Anita tipped her sugar bowl lid."

"I hope you plan to put that tambourine to work later," the Pontiff said to Olivia.

"I will if you dance with me. I have always wanted to dance with the Pope."

They laughed.

"I'm going to get another drink and use the little boys' room," Larry announced.

"Oh, honey," his wife purred, "will you get me another drink?"

"Sure, sugar, but you'll have to wait until later if you want to spoon."

Anita Gilbert had a laugh that sounded like a hyena choking to death. Fagatha and Eddie groaned. A beautiful black panther approached them. She handed the Pope a glass of champagne. "This is my sister, Fathom," Fagatha said. Fathom extended a dainty paw.

In the corner by the black lacquer oriental screen, a male Judy Garland, dressed in a double-breasted tuxedo jacket with black panty hose and spiked heel shoes, tilted back his black felt hat and launched into a rendition of "*Come On Get Happy*".

"He looks more like Judy than Judy did." Olivia laughed.

"Great legs," Fagatha agreed.

A horned satyr took their empty plates, and announced that the wedding was about to begin.

Larry returned, handed his wife's drink to her, and drank his down in one gulp. "My word, have you been in the bathroom? Have you seen the wallpaper in there?"

"Isn't it to die for?" Fagatha said.

"Look, Phoenix is here!" Fathom exclaimed. The panther and the Pope crossed the room to greet their friend.

"Well, tell us," Anita prodded. "What about the bathroom wallpaper?"

"I've never seen anything like it, kitten. It has white Grecian urn figures on a black background, all naked, all men, all in different positions."

"Positions?"

"Sex!" Larry whispered, like it was a dirty word. "They're having sex upside down, backwards, and on swings. I have never seen anything like it!"

"Do you think anyone would notice if we went in there together?" Olivia whispered to Eddie. "Maybe we can get some good ideas."

"Don't start something you can't stop," Eddie warned.

"May I have your attention please?" A "*Hello Dolly*" Carol Channing impersonator clapped his hands. "Everyone!" he cried, waving the guests toward the living room. "Everyone! It's time for the wedding!"

Barbra Streisand lit the thirteen candles on the mantle. The Halloween music being piped through the house went silent. Scarlett O'Hara flounced in, wearing a perfect copy of the white and green "Picnic at Twelve Oaks" dress with a big straw picture hat. Only her five o'clock shadow gave her away.

"Holy shit," Larry whispered to Eddie, "that's a guy! I could have sworn that cleavage was real. How does he do that?"

✷   ✷   ✷

The Pope took his place in front of the blazing fire. At a signal, he nodded to Theatrice Zitzner, from Glitter Man's ensemble acting group. Theatrice lowered her peacock-feathered head and began to play Beethoven's "*Fur Elise*" on the piano. The guests rose and turned to face the doorway where the wedding party would appear.

Christopher Fortune, dressed as Sir Lancelot, was the first to enter the room. Smiling broadly, he walked up the aisle toward the Pope. He wore a white tunic with a red rampant lion sewn on the front. Lamont had designed the costume from the photograph of Robert Goulet on the "*Camelot*" album cover. Chris' red floor-length cape lined in white satin billowed behind him. His tights revealed strong, muscular legs.

"Wow!" Olivia gasped.

"Down, girl," Eddie teased.

The first groom appeared. Glitter Man looked impressive in his impeccable white tuxedo. He wore a single yellow rosebud in his lapel and a cummerbund of Lamont's yellow and black tartan. Towering over everyone in the room except for the big prick, Glitter shook hands and hugged his friends as he walked down the aisle between the rows of smiling guests.

"Glitter looks like Richard Chamberlain tonight," Fagatha sighed.

There was a pause while Glinda the Good changed the sheet music for Theatrice Zitzner. The sequined peacock leaned over the Steinway. Her fingers sent the gentle, ancient melody of "*Greensleeves*" dancing through the room.

The spectators gasped when Jeanette Lightly Fortune appeared. Chris' eyes were riveted on his wife as she glided gracefully toward him. Jeanette looked regal in royal blue velvet. Her scoop-necked gown was fitted in the bodice and waist. The skirt fell in graceful folds to the tips of blue velvet slippers. The sleeves were fitted to her arms, ending in a V at the wrist. A bejeweled golden circlet rested like a crown on Jeanette's long black hair, which hung loose in shining waves like a veil. Wide tapestry-embroidered ribbon created a long V-shaped girdle that hung from her waist to the floor, subtly revealing the soft curve of her hips. She carried an antique golden chalice in her hands. A sapphire teardrop necklace rested against her white skin. Christopher recognized his wedding gift to Jeanette.

"She's Guinevere!" Eddie blurted out.

"Guinevere!" Chris echoed.

"She's yours for the asking," Lincoln Lightly whispered in his son-in-law's ear. "Don't blow it, son."

Jeanette stood on the opposite side of the hearth from Chris. Her eyes were like green fire. His heart beat so hard he could feel it in his ears. Chris hoped he was not imagining the passion and hunger he saw reflected in those emerald orbs.

The ancient melody soared. Lamont Feather made his grand entrance, wearing his traditional Scottish kilts, black velvet jacket, lace trimmed shirt, tartan socks, and silver buckled shoes. The dogs flanked their master as he walked down the aisle. They sat at attention behind him while Lamont stood next to Glitter Man in front of the Pope. He had chosen Robert Burns' words to express his vow, "Till all the seas run dry."

Glitter Man voiced his own commitment. The best man uncorked a vintage bottle of wine and filled the chalice Guinevere held. Chris' hands shook. Lancelot saw only Guinevere as she passed the vessel to the two grooms. She was so beautiful he felt dizzy.

"We celebrate your love and commitment to grow together," the Pope said. The guests applauded as they stepped forward to congratulate Lamont and Glitter Man.

✶   ✶   ✶

Lincoln Lightly glanced nervously at the clock. The hands were moving too rapidly to midnight. Judy Garland launched into his rendition of *"Over the Rainbow"*. A tall man dressed like an angel with realistic rosy wings replaced Theatrice at the piano, and a group gathered around the instrument to harmonize. The angel smiled and waved to

Lincoln. Lincoln, recognizing Mario, chuckled at the angel's ability to manifest and blend in with the crowd. Who would suspect he was real? The Wolf Man mayor swung his Egyptian queen wife into his arms and danced with her.

Jeanette moved through the crowd toward the grape arbor. Lincoln looked at the clock. It was 11:30.

*   *   *

Eddie was helping himself to a piece of wedding cake when he saw Jeanette. He hugged her warmly. "There are a lot of queens here tonight," he grinned, "but none so lovely as you."

Jeanette read the sign on his camouflage costume. "I'm sorry," she teased, "I can't see you. You're invisible."

She stepped outside into the refreshing night air. She filled a glass with pink champagne from the bubbling fountain, drank it down and filled herself another. She stepped gingerly across patches of snow into the back yard.

Lamont's wooden swing hung from the highest branches of the big tree in the yard. Jeanette sat on the swing. She swayed back and forth in time to the music that drifted out to her. The guy in the angel costume was playing "*As Time Goes By*". You could hear his clear tenor voice above all the others. He sang like Mario Lanza, only better.

The music segued into "*The Way You Look Tonight*". She gazed at the night sky, so clear and full of stars. She thought this must be one of the most romantic places in the world. "*I will feel a glow just thinking of you,*" she sang softly.

"You're beautiful in the star light," he whispered as he gently took the champagne glass from her hand. He moved behind her, so close she could feel the warmth of his body.

"Hold on," he said, leaning into her. His voice and his touch set off a chain reaction of electric jolts all through her body. Jeanette grabbed the ropes just in time as Chris pulled her back and let the swing go. He pushed her higher, until she was kicking her feet at the leaves and laughing like a child. She flew on the swing into the star-studded sky. She couldn't remember when she had felt so alive and free.

Suddenly, Chris stopped the swing. He put his arm around Jeanette's waist to steady her. She twisted around and faced him. Everything she needed to know shone in his eyes. He opened his mouth to speak, and she stopped his lips with her fingers. He kissed them. He handed her the champagne, and she took a sip and passed it back to him.

"To us," he toasted. He drank from the place her lips had touched.

Jeanette raised her lips to meet his, and they drank deeply of each other in a kiss so passionate it made her believe in magic again.

"Let's go home," Chris whispered huskily.

"Are you sure you want me back?" Jeanette said.

"Is the Pope Fagatha?"

Jeanette laughed. "Who will live in my father's half of the house?" she teased.

"We'll rent it to Eddie and Olivia. They need a cheap place to live while he gets his degree."

"What about Gershwin?"

"We'll pick him up in the morning."

"You think of everything," Jeanette sighed. She arched her neck as he kissed her throat. His hands moved down to caress her. He lifted her off the swing and set her feet. He embraced her, devouring her with kisses. Her knees buckled.

"Right now," Chris said, "all I can think of is making love to you for the rest of our lives."

Jeanette pushed him back and held him at arm's length.

"Let's slip out the back gate," she said. "Take me home where I can show you how much I love you."

Lancelot swept Guinevere up in his arms and carried her off into the darkness, while the ghost of Lincoln Lightly executed an intricate Irish jig in the snow.

CHAPTER THIRTY

Halloween, 1973

"What time is it down there, Angel?" The child leaned eagerly out the window.

Lincoln Lightly stood just behind her.

"What was Earth time when you left?" Mario asked him.

"A quarter to midnight."

"Less than fifteen minutes to go," the child breathed.

The angel wrapped his wings around her. Lincoln noticed that even angels hold their breaths sometimes. Even angels tremble.

Suddenly Isabelle cried, "What is happening? Something is pulling on me!"

The angel grinned and sang, "*Make your bed and light the light, you'll arrive late one night.*"

Lincoln thought he heard bells ringing.

Isabelle's eyes shone with joy. "Really? Do you mean it?"

Mario took the little girl's hand in his and kissed it gently. "Good luck, President Fortune," he said, bowing formally.

Somewhere a clock tolled midnight. Tears streamed down Lincoln's face. Isabelle ran into his outstretched arms.

"How can I thank you?" she cried. "I love you, so much, Grandfather."

"I love you too," Lincoln replied. "You make the best of your life down there."

"If she accomplishes half of what she has written in the Great Book of Possibilities, she shall have an extraordinary life," Mario said smiling.

Isabelle turned toward the angel. "I don't want to say goodbye to you."

"You don't have to," Mario replied. "You are my next assignment."

Isabelle and Lincoln both looked at the angel in surprise. Lincoln rubbed his glistening white beard.

"Well, how do you like that?" he chuckled. "We share the same guardian angel."

Mario stepped forward and lifted Isabelle in his arms. He stepped up onto the windowsill. His angelic smile radiated light; his magnificent wings were poised for flight. Isabelle Fortune blew her grandfather a kiss. Mario said, "Well done, Lincoln Lightly, well done."

"See you later," Lincoln said. He waved goodbye to both of them.

Mario flapped his rosy wings and flew out the window carrying Isabelle in his arms. Lincoln watched them soar down through the clouds that obscured his view of Earth. The clouds blew in the window, surrounding him.

Lincoln Lightly faced the tunnel again. As before, he saw the brilliant light at its end. The silhouette of his beloved Lizzy stood in its glow, beckoning to him. Next to her, Lincoln could see Gockie reaching toward him. He stepped once more into the darkness. The voices terrified him. He heard the screams and wails of tortured souls. Macabre faces pressed out of the walls. Lincoln shrank back in horror from the groping hands, from the shadows passing through his light body. He was beaten back by the howling wind. The shadows pulled at him from all directions until he was spinning. He could no longer tell which direction he was going in. "Stay with us," the voices of the damned cajoled.

"No!" Lincoln cried, flailing his arms at the phantoms that had no substance. "I will not be a lost soul! I will not be a haunting ghost! Lizzy!" he called miserably.

Without the angel Mario, no light illuminated his way except for the glow at the tunnel's end. No matter how far he walked, his destination appeared no closer. Finally, trembling with fear, the old man sank to his knees, sobbing. He prayed to be guided safely to the other side.

In the cacophony of lost souls, Lincoln heard a familiar voice. "Remember what Gockie told you? He said love in some form would guide you. Well, here I am, Lincoln."

A rough tongue licked the old soul's tear-stained face. Lincoln Lightly opened his eyes to see Gershwin's loveable snout staring back at him, tongue hanging out, irresistible puppy grin.

"Gershwin! What are you doing here?"

The dog bounced backwards, chased his tail and did a somersault. "You're right, Lincoln," he barked, "this light body is really neat! Now come on, you have waited long enough to see heaven. Just follow my nose, and I will lead us home."

              *   *   *

Jeanette lay in her husband's arms. She gazed dreamily out the window at the night sky. Suddenly, she saw a shooting star with a bright tail cut across the heavens. At almost the same instant, another star shot straight upward.

"One coming in, one going out," Chris murmured sleepily.

"What do you mean?"

"My mother used to tell me that when you see a shooting star headed for Earth it is a soul coming to be born, and when you see one going the other way, it's a soul leaving."

"My Dad used to tell me," Jeanette said smiling, "that shooting stars are magic. You should make a wish."

Chris leaned over and kissed her. "I already got my wish."

EPILOGUE

Inauguration Day, 2024

Isabelle Fortune placed her left hand on the Bible held by her husband. She raised her right hand. The Chief Justice of the United States administered the Oath of Office.

"I do solemnly swear," Isabelle declared in a strong, confident voice, "that I will faithfully execute the office of the President of the United States, and will to the best of my ability, preserve, protect and defend the Constitution of the United States."

The crowd, undaunted by the freezing temperatures that blanketed the ancient Capital dome with snow, went wild. The Mall, glistening white in the winter sun, was filled with a sea of faces stretching all the way to the Washington Monument.

Behind the President on the dais sat Isabelle's beaming parents, Jeanette and Christopher Fortune. The old couple looked very sweet and proud. Their eyes shone. The old man held his wife's hand as she rested her head on his shoulder, dabbing at the tears that spilled from her eyes.

Isabelle's son and two daughters were sitting behind her parents. The President's son-in-law held her first grandchild on his lap. Next to him sat her brother and two sisters with their families.

Isabelle's second cousins, Eddie and Olivia Lightly, looked almost as proud as her parents. The movie of Eddie Lightly's Pulitzer prize-winning book about his experiences in the war in Vietnam had been honored with ten Golden Globe nominations, including Eddie's screenplay and best picture of the year.

The Lightlys' son, Lincoln, raised his thumb and mouthed "well done." Isabelle smiled. If not for her cousin Lincoln, she would not be standing here now, making history. She could not have asked for a better campaign manager.

Before she stepped up to the podium to deliver her Inaugural Address to the Nation, Isabelle Fortune, the first woman President in the Nation's history, embraced her family. Then she turned toward the cheering crowd.

Behind Isabelle's left shoulder, unseen by the multitude, stood a magnificent angel with rose-colored wings. The angel positively glowed with pride.